MYSTERY
THE BEST OF 2001

JON L. BREEN
Editor

ibooks
new york
www.ibooks.net

Contents

CONTENTS

MYSTERY
THE BEST OF 2001
AN INTRODUCTION

by Jon L. Breen

Irony is one of the sharpest arrows in the short-story writer's quiver—and the continued good health of the mystery short story is an irony in itself. Fifty to a hundred years ago, novelists used lucrative magazine sales to support book-length works that were more rewarding in prestige but less so in negotiable currency. In more recent decades, with the high-paying slick magazine fiction markets down to a handful, the high-volume pulps gone altogether, and the prestigious digests down to two (*Ellery Queen's Mystery Magazine* and *Alfred Hitchcock's Mystery Magazine*), the real money has increasingly been in novels, longer and longer novels.

Therefore, one might conclude, the short story, surely as the Broadway theatre, must be either dead or dying. But if so, why do most of the major writers of mystery fiction continue to produce at least occasional short stories? Here are some reasons.

- They offer different challenges, engage different authorial muscles.
- They offer more artistic freedom, demanding less obeisance to commerce.
- They don't take as long to write.
- They serve an advertising function, as samples to entice readers to try the longer works.

• Finally, and possibly most important, short stories done really well can have a more powerful impact than a five-hundred-page blockbuster.

Is there an ideal length for the crime or mystery story? Maybe not. But Edgar Allan Poe invented the tale of detection and Arthur Conan Doyle did the most to popularize it in short stories. Even when novels became predominant, writers from Dorothy L. Sayers to Dashiell Hammett continued to produce some of their best work in the shorter form. And few crime novels have made the indelible imprint on their readers' memories of Agatha Christie's "The Witness for the Prosecution" or Stanley Ellin's "The Specialty of the House" or Roald Dahl's "Lamb to the Slaughter."

Every kind of crime or mystery story, from pure puzzle to private eye to police procedural to confidence game to psychological suspense to legal conundrum, can be done as effectively in short story as novel length. For evidence, I offer the stories in this collection. They range in mood from grim and terrifying to light and satirical; in locale from contemporary Alaska to Territorial Arizona, London to Miami, big-city America to an English village. In short, I believe they will give more distilled mysterious pleasure than a stack of novels.

Edward D. Hoch

"The San Agustin Miracle"

In any given year, short-story specialist Edward D. Hoch probably turns out more scrupulously fair detective puzzles than any dozen novelists. A mainstay of *Ellery Queen's Mystery Magazine* since the 1960s, he has appeared in every issue beginning with May 1973. One of his many series characters is Western drifter Ben Snow, who encounters here a Hoch specialty: a seemingly impossible crime.

Yₒᵤ still hear occasional stories about the miracle at the San Agustin Mission on that September afternoon in 1899, and Ben Snow was there to see it happen. He'd spent most of the year in the Arizona Territory, earning money at odd jobs, and had finally drifted south to Tucson. A city of about 7,500 residents, it was located on the often-dry Santa Cruz River. Tucson had begun life as a military garrison under Spanish and Mexican rule, and even with the arrival of the railroad and settlers from the east it remained more than half Mexican as the century was ending.

There was copper mining in the hills, but it was also cotton country, which surprised Ben. Even more surprising was Jud Withers, a leathery-skinned man in his fifties who'd been a Confederate soldier thirty-five years earlier. He was the first man Ben met when he rode into town, and he had a story to tell over a beer at a local saloon with the unlikely name of Custer's Café.

"Bet you never knew that Confederate troops occupied Tucson back in sixty-two, did you?" he asked Ben, obviously launching into a favorite and familiar story. "It was the cotton that brought us, of course. The Union wanted to keep slaves out of the new states and territories, and

2

we rode across the desert from west Texas to seize the area. I do believe this was the furthest west the Confederate Army ever got."

"How long were you here?" Ben asked, sipping his beer. He'd spent half his lifetime listening to stories in bars.

"Well, not long," Jud Withers admitted. "But I wasn't driven out like the rest of 'em. Married me a sweet young Injun gal and settled down here. She's dead now, but I'm still hanging on. I'll see the twentieth century if I'm lucky."

Ben signaled the barkeep for a refill and tossed a silver dollar on the polished wood. "Any jobs around here?"

"In the cotton fields?"

"I was thinking more of ranching. How's the weather been?"

"Well, we just finished our rainy season. Everything's growing nice." Eyeing Ben's gunbelt he asked, "You from around here?"

"I've been up north, riding the circuit with Judge Hark. Sort of a bodyguard job."

"Don't have too much call for bodyguards. Things are pretty peaceful around here."

"I can do cowhand chores. It wouldn't be the first time."

"You don't want to be in one place. You're a traveling man. I can see that. There's a Mexican coming up this way in a few days with a hot-air balloon. He gives exhibitions. He might need somebody to travel with him, handle his gear."

Ben was skeptical. "A balloon?"

"The Mex is really good, I hear tell. Pancho Quizas is his name. He and his wife have been working the border towns, and this time of year they come a bit farther north. They used to have somebody with them, but they're traveling alone now."

Ben Snow had seen fliers, men with wings strapped to their bodies, launching themselves from a cliff or high platform, relying on air currents to carry their wings of cloth some distance before depositing them gently on the ground. He'd watched one of them in Texas a few years back. The man had been killed while flying, but that was another story. A balloon was something else, and it might be worth a look.

A young woman at the back of the room had mounted a small stage and was strumming a guitar. Ben left the bar and walked back in that direction. He expected she might sing something by Stephen Foster, or perhaps one of the Civil War songs still popular in the region, but instead she seemed to be reciting poetry to the guitar accompaniment. Ben listened to one about a cactus flower, and when she ended to a smattering of applause he asked her who wrote it.

"I did," she replied softly, and Ben took a closer look at her. She was maybe in her late twenties, a decade or so younger than him, with long silky hair the color of sand. She was dressed in jeans and a plaid shirt, with a sombrero hanging at the back of her neck.

"Do you write much poetry like that?"

She blushed a bit. "It's meant to be a song, but I'm not too good at blending the words and music yet."

"You have a nice voice. You should put the sombrero out for tips."

"Thank you." She went back to strumming her guitar, making no effort to remove the hat from her neck.

"What's your name?"

"Gert."

"Fellow at the bar was just telling me about a Mexican who flies in a balloon."

"Sure, that's Pancho Quizas. I met him once, down south. He'll be here any day now, maybe tomorrow."

"I'd like to meet him. Could you introduce us?"

"Sure could, if I knew your name."

"It's Ben. Ben Snow."

"Familiar kind of name. You from around these parts?"

"Off and on."

"Where can I find you, when Pancho shows up?"

"I'll be around. Any good card players in this town?"

"You were just talkin' to the best of them. Jud Withers."

Ben glanced around at the old Confederate. "Thanks," he said and moved away.

Withers told him there'd be no card game that night but to come back the next night, which was Saturday. Ben found a room he could rent over the stable where he'd boarded Oats, and decided to sleep there until the Mexican showed up. The following evening after supper he stopped in Custer's Café and found a game already in progress. Jud Withers spotted him at once and waved him over to the table.

"Got a place all saved for you, Ben. Sit right here."

He slid into the wooden armchair and nodded greetings to the other three men at the table. All were younger than Jud Withers and at least one, seated with his back to the wall, had the look of a gunfighter with his black shirt and matching gunbelt. Ben felt like telling him his time had passed, that the West was getting civilized now, but if he said it the kid probably would have drawn on him. His name was Scooter Colt and he didn't offer to shake hands after Withers introduced them.

The other two were a Mexican named Sanchez and a well-dressed cotton farmer named Edgar Blaise. There was a sixth chair at the table and Ben was surprised when the poetic guitar player named Gert appeared from the back of the room to claim it. "I like poker," she told Ben as she sat down.

Withers brought out a new deck of cards and they started a game of stud poker. Gert seemed more at ease with the cards than with her guitar, and before long she was ahead. Scooter Colt's eyes were on her, especially when she dealt. Ben couldn't decide whether he was guarding against cheating or merely admiring her breasts.

They'd been playing for about an hour when the doors of Custer's Café swung open to allow the entry of a tall Mexican with a goatee, carrying a tattered carpetbag. Jud Withers immediately stopped the game with a wave of his hand. "Pancho! We've been expecting you."

In his black suit and string tie Pancho Quizas looked more like a mortician than a flying man. He appeared to carry no weapon, though Ben couldn't be certain a derringer wasn't concealed in his breast pocket. When he smiled, a gold tooth sparkled. "It took longer than expected with the balloon," the Mexican explained in slightly accented English. "Elana is still a few miles out of town with the wagon."

"Want to sit in for a few hands?" the Confederate asked.

"Perhaps later."

Ben dropped out of the hand and followed Pancho over to the bar. After introducing himself, he said, "Withers told me you might be interested in someone to handle your gear."

"*Sí.* It is difficult for my wife. Tonight, handling the wagon, she is tired. But she insists I come ahead to arrange for lodgings."

"If you hire me I'll ride out now and meet her. Did you come from the border?"

Pancho Quizas nodded. "Nogales."

"I know that trail. I'll meet her and help with the wagon."

"I would be grateful, Ben Snow."

"Just Ben is good enough. We'll talk about money when I get back."

He retrieved Oats from the stable, saddled up, and took the road south. About fifteen minutes out of town he spotted the wagon's lanterns and slowed Oats to a trot. The two horses pulling the wagon had run out of energy, leaving the frustrated woman yanking uselessly at the reins. Ben could barely see her in the dim lantern glow, but he quickly identified himself to calm her fears.

"Your husband sent me out to help you. This is quite a load you're hauling."

"It shifted after he rode off. I think one of the ropes broke. I couldn't fix it in the dark."

Ben dismounted and took the nearest lantern, going back to inspect the wagon's cargo. The balloon itself was deflated into a pile of limp fabric, but there was also a large wicker bucket and a heater of some sort, all of which added weight to the wagon. He took a rope from his saddle and pulled the bucket into place, securing it as best he could. Then he tied Oats's reins to the wagon and climbed up next to the woman. "That's a little better. Let me see if I can get these horses moving now."

"Thank you," she said, gladly handing over the reins. "I'm Elana, Pancho's wife."

"Ben Snow. I need a job and I'm hoping your husband will take me on."

"The people pay to see him fly. We lead a precarious existence." She sounded more educated than her husband did and he wondered how they'd ever gotten together. "But I'm sure he'll pay you for helping me tonight, at least."

"Will he fly tomorrow?"

"If the winds are not too strong."

Pancho Quizas was waiting when the wagon pulled up. "You are a good man, Ben Snow," he ventured after Elana told him how their cargo almost came loose. "Help me fly tomorrow and I will pay you ten silver dollars."

"Fair enough."

Ben finished the evening in the poker game, his confidence renewed, and won sixteen dollars.

The hot, calm morning seemed perfect for Pancho's balloon ascent. "I will go up at two this afternoon," he announced, "at the Mission San Agustin."

A crowd of townspeople came out to watch, and Elana dutifully collected a small fee from each one. They stood in front of the mission church, a few miles outside the city, paying little attention to the dust devils—harmless whirlwinds of air made visible by the dust and sand they raised from the ground. Ben had seen them many times before in dry regions, especially when the temperature was high and the wind was calm, and he knew that some superstitious people viewed them as the devil come to collect the souls of the dead.

Ben worked with Pancho, positioning the basket, laying out the balloon, and igniting the brazier of wood and coal used to inflate it. Through the thick cloth fabric Ben noticed a shape approaching them. It proved to be an elderly priest who'd come out of the mission church to observe their progress. "I am Padre Paul," he told them. "Do you plan an ascent this afternoon?"

"I do, Padre," Pancho Quizas told him. "It is a perfect day."

"The Lord's day," the priest replied. "And you have brought dust devils with you."

"Have no fear, Padre," Pancho told him with a grin, and his gold tooth caught the afternoon sun. "We will rise above them."

The old priest turned his weathered face toward the clear blue sky. "Sometimes one cannot go high enough to escape the devil."

As the balloon began to inflate, almost covering the basket, its colorful design became visible to the spectators. Some Indians from a nearby reservation moved forward for a closer look, attracted by the Apache and Navajo symbols that formed a border around a design of Mexican and American flags. In the very center, Ben noticed, was an advertisement for a Mexican beer.

"Did you paint this?" Ben asked. "It's very good."

"No, no! Elana is the artist."

She came forward then, smiling as her work of art grew taller before their eyes. Then Pancho climbed into the wicker basket suspended beneath the air bag and signaled for Ben and Elana to free it from its moorings. As it rose into the afternoon sky another dust devil appeared, seeming to give chase.

"A bad sign," the old priest murmured.

But the crowd let out a cheer, and Ben saw Pancho's balloon rising straight up. "How will he get down?" he asked Elana.

"As the hot air cools the balloon will gradually sink back to earth. He'll only be up for five or ten minutes. If it comes down too fast, he can release one or two of those sandbags on the side to lighten the load."

The colorful balloon went up perhaps a hundred feet, easily clearing the top of the mission's twin bell towers. Ben felt a movement behind him and turned to see Scooter Colt, the gunslinger from last night's poker game, his right hand resting on the butt of his gun. Ben's own weapon had been left in Elana's wagon, and for an instant he wished it were closer at hand.

"He's coming down!" someone from the crowd shouted after a few minutes, and indeed the balloon was starting its descent. It drifted off to the north, beyond the church, and the spectators broke into a run to catch sight of its landing.

Ben was in the midst of the crowd, well behind the leaders, when he rounded the corner of the church and saw at once that something was wrong. His first thought was that Pancho had landed badly, injuring himself, but it was more than that. Old Jud Withers was the first to raise his voice and spread the improbable news. "He's not here!" he shouted. "Pancho Quizas is gone!"

He must have fallen out of the balloon's basket as it descended. There could be no other explanation. And yet, as Ben and the others scanned the landscape, they could detect no sign of him. There were no hiding places on the flat desert terrain, only a few small cactuses incapable of giving shelter to a child, much less a grown man. The balloon had come down about thirty yards from the rear of the mission, and Ben's first thought was that Pancho had made it unseen to the back entrance. It seemed unlikely, given the distance, but he hurried over to try the door. It was firmly locked.

"A man doesn't just disappear," Ben argued.

"Perhaps the dust devils have taken his soul," the priest said.

"Then where is his body?"

The wicker basket had landed on its side, overturning the brazier. Nothing else was there except the ropes used to anchor the balloon to the ground. Ben noticed that none of the sandbags had been cut free to slow the descent. It was as if Pancho had wanted to return to earth as quickly as possible. The multicolored airbag, settled in a heap beside the basket, was still exhaling air as it flattened out.

"You tell me where he is," Jud Withers demanded of Ben. "You were working for him, weren't you?"

"I think we'd better ask his wife," Ben suggested, seeing Elana hurrying toward them.

"What's happened to Pancho?" she asked. "Is he hurt?"

"He's disappeared," Ben told her.

"Disappeared?" She looked around, as if expecting him to pop out of the ground at any moment. "How could that be?"

"We don't know. Did it ever happen before?"

"Of course not!" She ran over to the wicker basket, righting it as she searched beneath and around it for clues. She lifted a corner of the balloon and peered underneath. Finally she just stood and stared at the sky, as if waiting for him to come down.

That was when Scooter Colt walked up to join them. "You think he's still up there, lady? We can find out quick enough!" He drew his six-gun, pointed it at the sky, and started shooting.

11

Ben counted six shots before Scooter toppled over backwards, as if from the recoil of his own weapon. Old Jud Withers was the first to reach the body. "God Almighty! He's been shot! Drilled right through the eye."

And that was how Scooter Colt died, in a gunfight with the sky, or with the spirit of Pancho Quizas, who was still floating around up there. Edgar Blaise, the cotton farmer, was the first to scoff at the idea. "How fast a draw is a dead man?" he wanted to know.

"You haven't found Quizas's body yet," Gert reminded them. "You don't even know that he's dead."

But the area behind the mission, and the church itself, had been carefully searched and there was no trace of the Mexican balloonist. Elana drove the wagon around and started gathering up the deflated balloon. Ben went over to help her load the wicker basket onto the wagon along with the balloon, though he knew there was little chance now of payment for his work. "Perhaps you could sell this equipment," he told her.

"Not yet. He may return. I have faith in the Lord."

They'd roused Tucson's sheriff from somewhere, and he arrived on horseback to look at Scooter Colt's body. "Who shot him?" he asked.

"Don't know," Withers replied. "We were all here but we didn't see who fired the shot."

The sheriff, whose name was Morton, seemed annoyed at being disturbed on a Sunday afternoon. "Can't you handle this, Padre?" he called out to the mission priest. "This is your day, not mine."

"I can bury him," Padre Paul replied. "That is all."

"All right." Sheriff Morton could see some sort of investigation was necessary. "Who all is carrying a gun?"

"No one but the dead man," Withers said.

"I have a gunbelt in the wagon," Ben volunteered, "but I wasn't wearing it."

"Let's see it," the sheriff said, examining the dead man's gun. "There are five shots fired from this one."

"I counted six," Ben told him. "One must have been the shot that killed him." He brought his gun from the wagon to show Sheriff Morton it was fully loaded.

Padre Paul cleared his throat. "There were dust devils in the air at the time, Sheriff. They seemed to rise up with his balloon."

"You're telling me he went up but he didn't come down?"

"That's right," Ben agreed. "When we couldn't find him, Scooter said he must still be up there. He drew his pistol and started firing at the sky."

"And the sky fired back," another voice said. It was young Gert. She had her guitar slung over one shoulder and she plucked at the strings as she sang:

"Scooter was his name, it wasn't Tex,
He came here lookin' for that old Mex.
He fired his gun right at the sky,
The sky fired back 'cause it ain't shy.
Now Scooter is dead and that's a shame,
No one here will remember his name."

She finished the song with the lyrics barely audible. No one applauded because that didn't seem right. When she headed back to her wagon, only Ben followed.

Later, at Custer's Café, he asked her, "What did your song mean?"

"I made it up. Does it need a meaning?" She picked up her guitar and started to strum it.

"The second line: *He came here lookin' for that old Mex.* What does it mean?"

"Just what it says, I guess." Her face was as stony as it had been during the poker game.

"Are you saying that Scooter Colt came to Tucson to kill Pancho Quizas?"

She shrugged. "I guess so. When he came here from Texas a few weeks back he was askin' questions about Pancho. Did any of us know him? Had he been flyin' his balloon around here?"

"What did you tell him?"

"Sure, we'd heard of Pancho and his balloon. Everyone in these parts had heard of him. He usually came through here in September. I guess Scooter decided to wait for him."

"What made you think he wanted to kill Pancho?"

"Well, he kept wearin' that gunbelt in a city where hardly anyone else does. He was expectin' he'd need it."

Ben pondered that. "Where had he been staying, these past few weeks?"

"Out at Edgar Blaise's cotton farm," Gert answered. "He was working there."

In the morning, Ben rode out to the Blaise place and found the farmer weighing bags of freshly picked cotton. He was dressed like one of his workmen, and bore little resemblance to the natty gentleman who'd shared the poker table with Ben Saturday night. "Looking for work?" he asked as Ben dismounted.

14

"I might be, but not today. I wanted to ask you about Scooter Colt. He was working for you, wasn't he?"

"Yeah, for a few weeks. I always need extra people at harvest time."

"I've been in the Arizona territory before but I never knew you grew cotton around here. Did settlers bring the plants from Texas?"

"Could be. More likely it came up from Mexico. They say the Indians there have been raising cotton for centuries." He hoisted the bag off the scale and handed it over to a workman, making some jottings on a pad. "What do you want to know about Scooter?"

"Some say he was looking for Pancho Quizas so he could kill him."

"I guess there was bad blood between them, all right. Did you catch the look on Scooter's face when Pancho walked into Custer's Café the other night?"

"I missed that," Ben admitted.

"Scooter told me one night that Quizas cheated him on a business deal involving some Mexican horses. He'd paid the Mex some money and the horses were never delivered. Quizas claimed the Texas Rangers intercepted the horses at the border, but Scooter suspected he'd sold them to somebody else and kept the money from both transactions."

"I thought Pancho was strictly a showman, traveling around with his balloon."

"He and his wife couldn't live on that, not even by selling advertising space on their balloon."

"Did you ever hear Scooter say he wanted to kill Pancho?"

"He said the next time they met it would be his six-gun did the talking."

Ben nodded, watching Blaise lift another bag of cotton

onto the scale. "What do you think happened to Pancho yesterday?"

The cotton farmer shrugged. "Padre Paul thinks the dust devils got him. I'm more of a practical sort. I don't think Pancho was ever in that balloon. He let it go up and come down without him. He was hiding in the crowd somewhere and when Scooter started shooting he shot back."

"He was in the balloon's basket when it went up," Ben insisted. "I was right there, releasing the moorings."

"Then somebody else shot Scooter, maybe Pancho's wife."

Ben couldn't remember where any of them had been at the moment of Scooter's death, but he was pretty sure no one was facing Scooter when he fired at the sky. *The sky fired back*, Gert had sung. Maybe it had. "Did anyone else have a motive for wanting Scooter dead?"

"He told me last week he pulled Jud Withers's daughter into the stable one night and she told him if he ever tried that again she'd shoot him, but that was just talk."

"Jud has a daughter?"

"Sure. Gert Withers, the one who plays the guitar and sings. Her mother's dead; Jud is her father."

When Ben rode back into town that afternoon, Gert was nowhere in sight. Jud Withers was at the bar in Custer's Café, as usual, describing Sunday's strange shooting to anyone who hadn't yet heard about it. When he took time out to order a beer, Ben slipped in next to him. "You never told me Gert was your daughter."

"Never asked me, did you?"

"If Scooter was bothering her, that might have been reason enough for a father to shoot him."

"Gert fights her own battles. She doesn't need my help."

"Has Pancho's body turned up yet?"

Withers shook his head. "Padre Paul says he went straight to heaven, says it was a miracle."

"It might have been. Has Elana left with the wagon yet?"

"She needs the sheriff to say it's all right. He'll probably let her go soon unless Pancho's body turns up."

There was only one place to go after that. Ben rode out to the San Agustin Mission once more. Padre Paul was talking to some Mexican women out front, enjoying the cooling breeze on a warm day. "It's Ben Snow, isn't it?" he asked as Ben dismounted and led Oats up to the group.

"That's right, Padre. We're still baffled by what happened yesterday."

"You mean the miracle?"

"Well, yes." He glanced skyward. "I was wondering if I might go up in one of your bell towers to get a better view of the land."

"Certainly. I'll take you up there."

Ben followed the priest into the church, which was filled with the glow of votive candles. "This building is one hundred and sixteen years old," he announced proudly, "and the mission itself has been on this location even longer. You can see the grime on the walls from all these candles the faithful have lit over the past century."

He unlocked a small door to the right of the entrance and led the way up a winding stairway to the bell tower. The view was spectacular, with the flat land stretching to the distant mountains, broken only by a few low trees and stately cactuses. But Ben realized at once that from this angle the rear of the church probably would have obscured the spot where the balloon came down.

Padre Paul seemed to read his disappointment. "You were thinking that Scooter Colt might have been shot from this bell tower."

17

"The thought crossed my mind. He was looking toward the sky when he fired his pistol."

"No one was up here, not Pancho Quizas nor anyone else."

"Where were you, Padre?"

"On the ground with the rest of you."

"Then you can't be certain no one was up here."

"The doors to this tower and the other one are kept locked at all times. There were too many instances of children climbing up here."

They went back downstairs and Padre Paul locked the tower door behind them. Ben left the mission and rode away with a wave of his hand.

He went back into Tucson to the sheriff's office and found Elana there, getting ready to leave. Her wagon was already stowed with Pancho's balloon and other gear. Ben offered to accompany her back across the border but she declined. "I have an uncle there who will meet me," she said. "Thank you for your kindness." She gave him the ten dollars he'd been promised.

"Someone told me Scooter Colt was looking for Pancho because of a horse-trading deal that went bad."

"I don't know anything about that. I doubt if my husband even knew the man."

There was little more to say. "I hope we'll meet again under better circumstances," he told her with a tip of his Stetson. Then he went inside to see the sheriff.

"Nice woman," Sheriff Morton said, lighting up a Mexican cigar. "Can't figure out what happened to her husband."

"Or who killed Scooter Colt."

"Or that either," the sheriff admitted.

"Have you examined the body?"

"I guess the undertaker examined him more than I did."

"I was wondering about the angle of the bullet. Could he have been shot from above, while he was looking at the sky?"

"No, the undertaker tells me it looks like he was shot from below. But that doesn't mean anything since they all say he was looking up when the bullet hit him. Somebody in the crowd just got off a lucky shot and nobody saw who did it. We'll probably never know."

"Did he have enemies?"

"Let's put it this way. Scooter Colt made mighty few friends in the short time he was here. Wearing that gun in town turned folks off right away." His eyes flickered on Ben's own holstered revolver. "We're moving into the twentieth century here."

"So I've heard."

"You going to be around long?"

"Not too long. I think I'll be riding on soon."

Ben ate supper at Custer's Café and listened for a time to Gert Withers's songs. Her father was starting another poker game up front and asked Ben to sit in, but he declined. It was getting dark when he mounted Oats and headed south out of Tucson. He knew that if he rode fast he'd be able to overtake Elana's wagon before it reached the border.

He saw the lanterns first, just after sundown along the road to Nogales. Elana seemed surprised to see him and reined up the horses as he drew abreast of her. "What is it?" she asked. "What do you want?"

"I've come for Scooter Colt's killer," Ben told her.

"And you think that I did it?"

"I know you didn't do it. Pancho Quizas is alive and well and hiding in your wagon. He killed Scooter Colt."

* * *

The collapsed balloon rose up then, and there was Pancho beneath it, pointing a deadly little derringer at Ben's head. "If I have to kill you, I will," he said.

"Before you pull that trigger, aren't you curious as to how I knew?"

"Mildly," the balloonist admitted. "What mistake did I make?"

"No mistake. Even Padre Paul thinks you were whisked away by a dust devil. But I was seeking a more natural explanation for your disappearance. You had to be in that basket when the balloon took off because I saw you myself from just a few feet away. You couldn't have jumped or fallen from it without people seeing you. Therefore, barring the supernatural, you had to have been in it when it landed."

"The basket was empty."

"But not the balloon itself," Ben told him: "It hung down almost over that wicker basket when it was inflated. As the air cooled and the balloon began its descent, you must have seen Scooter Colt on the ground waiting for you, his hand on the butt of his gun. There was only one place to hide. Obscured by the balloon's own deflation, you hoisted yourself inside it, until you were completely hidden from view as it landed. It must have been a bumpy landing but you froze there on the ground, letting the fabric of the balloon settle down around you."

"He was going to kill me," Pancho said. "I knew he was. I had to hide somewhere."

"So when he started firing into the air you feared he might shoot at the deflated balloon too. As I noticed earlier, shapes could be seen even through the thick cloth of the air bag. You saw him shooting, and you fired one shot through the balloon with your little derringer."

"You knew I was armed?"

"I didn't see a weapon, but I considered the possibility you might carry a derringer under your coat. The sheriff told me the bullet seemed to come from below, and I figured you were the only one who could have done it. Shooting like that from inside the air bag, no one saw the muzzle flash of your gun. Elana must have known you were hiding there when she went to load the balloon onto her wagon, but once again all that deflated cloth hid your movements until you were on the wagon."

"I didn't mean to kill him. I only wanted to wound him before he shot me."

"It was this business with the horses?"

He nodded. "Scooter wanted me to steal them and run them across the border. When I refused, he said I'd double-crossed him."

Ben realized Pancho was still holding the derringer on him. "Put away that gun," he said. "I'm not going to turn you in."

"Thank you," Elana said. He could see she was relieved.

"Where will you go, now that you no longer exist?"

Pancho Quizas smiled, revealing his gold tooth one more time. "A new identity is easy to find in Mexico."

Ben turned to ride off. "Remember to sew up the bullet hole in your balloon before you fly again."

Some time later he heard there were still songs and legends about the San Agustin miracle, but he never told anyone the true story.

Loren D. Estleman

"Evil Grows"

Loren D. Estleman, a master of many styles, has written dead-on-target Sherlock Holmes pastiches, award-winning Westerns, and the Chandleresque novels about Detroit private eye Amos Walker. The story that follows is a gritty piece of fiction noir as told by a man in a bar.

No, I'm not prejudiced. Well, not any more than the majority of the population. I'm an organic creature, subject to conditioning and environment, and as such I'm entitled to my own personal set of preconceptions. No, I'm not disappointed; relieved is the word. If you'd shown up with cauliflower ears or swastikas tattooed on your biceps, the interview would have been over right then. So let's sit down and jabber. What do you drink? Excuse me? Jack and *Coke?* Don't get defensive, you're young, you'll grow out of it. You grew out of your formula. Miss, my friend will have a Jack and Coke, and you can pour me another Chivas over rocks and don't let it sit too long on the bar this time. Scotch-flavored Kool-Aid is not my drink.

What's that? No, I'm not afraid she'll spit in my glass. She's got miles on her, no wedding ring, she needs this job. People will put up with what they have to, up to a point. Which is the point where my job begins. Or began. See, I'm not sure I'm still employed. It isn't like I go to the office every day and can see if my name's still on the door. I'm talking too much; that's my third Scotch the barmaid's spitting in. You don't mind that I'm a motor-mouth? I forgot, you're one of the new breed. You want to know why. I'm down with that. Thank you, miss. Just keep the tab going.

Let's see. You ever watch the news, read a paper? Don't bother, the question's out of date. You can't avoid the news. The wise man on the mountain in Tibet picks up Dan Rather in his fillings. But that's network; it's the local reports I'm talking about, the police beat. I know what you're thinking. Crime's the last thing I should be interested in when I get home. Truth is, I can't relate to wars in eastern Europe, not since I got too old for the draft, but give me a carjacking two streets over from where I live and you can't pry me away from the screen. Past forty you get selective about what you take in. I'm not just talking about your stomach.

Anyway, have you ever noticed, once or twice a month there's a story about some schnook getting busted trying to hire a hit man? Some woman meets a guy in a bar and offers him like a thousand bucks to knock off her husband or boyfriend or her husband's girlfriend or the mother of the girl who's beating out her daughter for captain of the cheerleading squad? Okay, it's not always a woman, but let's face it, they're still the designated child-bearers, it's unnatural for them to take a life. So they engage a surrogate. The reason they get caught is the surrogate turns out to be an undercover cop. I mean, it happens so often you wonder if there aren't more cops out there posing as hit men than there are hit men. Which may be true, I don't know. Assassins don't answer the census.

That's how it seems, and the department's just as happy to let people think that. Actually there's very little happenstance involved. The woman's so pissed she tells her plans to everyone she knows and a few she doesn't, gets a couple of margaritas in her and tells the bartender. Working up her courage, see, or maybe just talking about it makes her feel better, as if she went ahead and did it. So in a week or so twenty people are in on the secret. Odds are pretty good one of them's a cop. I don't know a bookie who'd bet against at least one of them *telling* a cop. So the next Saturday night she's sitting in a booth getting blasted and a character in a Harley jacket with Pennzoil in his hair slides in, buys her a zombie and a beer for himself, and says I understand you're looking for someone to take care of a little problem. Hey, nothing's subtle in a bar. People want their mechanics to be German and their decorators gay, and when they decide to have someone iced they aren't going to hire someone who looks like Hugh Grant.

You'll be happy to hear, if you're concerned about where civilization is headed, that many of these women, once they realize what's going on, are horrified. Or better yet, they laugh in the guy's face. These are the ones that are just acting out. The only blood they intend to draw will be in a courtroom, if it ever gets that far; a lot of couples who considered murder go on to celebrate their golden anniversaries. A good cop, or I should say a good person who is a cop, will draw away when he realizes it's a dry hole. It's entrapment if he pushes it, and anyway what's the point of removing someone from society who was never a threat to begin with? It just takes time away from investigations that might do some good. Plus he knows the next woman whose table he invites himself to will probably take him up on it.

Hell yes, he's wearing a wire, and I'm here to tell you Sir Laurence Olivier's got nothing on an undercover stiff who manages to appear natural knowing he can't squirm around or even lift his glass at the wrong time because the rustle of his clothing might drown out the one response he needs to make his case. I was kidding about the Harley jacket; leather creaks like a bitch, on tape it sounds like a stand of giant sequoias making love, and you don't want to hear about corduroy or too much starch in a cotton shirt. Even when you wear what's right and take care, you need to find a way to ask the same question two or three times and get the same answer, just for insurance. Try and pull that off without tipping your mitt. I mean, everyone's seen *NYPD Blue*. So you begin to see, as often as these arrests make the news, the opportunity comes up oftener yet. You can blame Hollywood if you like, or maybe violent video games. I'm old enough to remember when it was comic books. My old man had a minister when he was ten who preached that Satan spoke through *Gangbusters* on the radio. My opinion? We've been fucking killers since the grave.

Lest you think I draw my munificent paycheck hanging around gin mills hitting on Lizzie Borden, I should tell you life undercover most of the time is about as exciting as watching your car rust. When the lieutenant told me to meet this Rockover woman I'd been six weeks raking leaves in the front yard of a druglord in Roseville, posing as a gardener. I never saw the man; he's in his bedroom the whole time, flushing out his kidneys and playing euchre. He's got maybe a year to live, so assuming I do gather enough for an indictment, he'll be in hell trumping Tupac's hand by the time they seat the jury. I don't complain when I'm pulled off. Friend, I'd work Stationary Traffic if it meant getting out of those goddamn overalls.

The briefing's a no-brainer. This Nola Rockover has

had it with her boss. He's a lawyer and a sexual harasser besides, it's a wonder the Democrats haven't tapped him for the nomination. It's her word against his, and he's a partner in the firm, so you know who's going to come out on the short end if she reports him. Her career's involved. Admit it, you'd take a crack at him yourself. That's how you know it's worth investigating. The odd thing, one of the odd things about getting a conviction is the motive has to make sense. Some part of you has to agree with the defendant in order to hang him. It's a funny system.

Getting ready for a sting you've got to fight being your own worst enemy. You can't ham it up. I've seen cops punk their hair and pierce their noses—Christ, their tongues and belly buttons too—and get themselves tossed by a nervous bouncer before they even make contact, which is okay because nine times out of ten the suspect will take one look at them and run for the exit. I know what I said about bars and subtlety, but they're no place for a cartoon either. So what I do is I leave my hair shaggy from the gardening job, pile on a little too much mousse, go without shaving one day, put on clean chinos and combat boots and a Dead T-shirt—a little humor there, it puts people at ease—and mostly for my own benefit I clip a teeny gold ring onto my left earlobe. You have to look close to see it doesn't go all the way through. I've spent every day since the academy trying to keep holes out of me and I'm not about to give up for one case. Now I look like an almost-over-the-hill Deadhead who likes to hip it up on weekends, a turtleneck and sportcoat on Casual Friday is as daring as he gets during the week. Point is not so much to look like a hit man as to not look like someone who isn't. Approachability's important.

The tech guy shaves a little path from my belt to my

solar plexus, tapes the mike and wire flat, the transmitter to my back just above the butt-crack. The T's loose and made of soft cotton, washed plenty of times. Only competition I have to worry about is the bar noise. Fortunately, the Rockover woman's Saturday night hangout is a family-type place, you know, where a kid can drink a Coke and munch chips from a little bag while his parents visit with friends over highballs. Loud drunks are rare, there's a juke but no band. The finger's a co-worker in the legal firm. I meet him at the bar, he points her out, I thank him and tell him to blow. First I have to reassure him I'm not going to throw her on the floor and kneel on her back and cuff her like on *Cops*; he's more worried she'll get herself in too deep than about what she might do to the boss. I go along with this bullshit and he leaves. Chances are he's got his eye on her job, but he hasn't got the spine not to feel guilty about it.

The place is crowded and getting noisy, the customers are starting to unwind. I order a Scotch and soda, heavy on the fizz, wait for a stool, and watch her for a while in the mirror. She's sitting facing another woman near the shuffleboard table, smoking a cigarette as long as a Bic pen and nursing a clear drink in a tall glass, vodka and tonic probably. I'm hoping I'll catch her alone sometime during the evening, maybe when the friend goes to the can, which means I don't count on getting any evidence on tape until I convince her to ditch the friend. So I wait and watch.

Which in this case is not unpleasant. Nola Rockover's a fox. Not, I hasten to add, one of those assembly-line beauties on the order of Heather Locklear or some other blond flavor of the month, but the dark, smoldering kind you hardly ever see except in black-and-white movies

29

and old TV shows. She's a brunette, slender—not thin, I've had it with these anorexic bonepiles that make you want to abduct them and tie them down and force-feed them mashed potatoes until they at least cast a decent shadow—I'm talking lithe and sinuous, like a dancer, with big dark eyes and prominent cheekbones. You're too young to remember Mary Tyler Moore on *The Dick Van Dyke Show*. I know you've seen her on Nick at Nite, but your generation's got some fixation on color, so I'm betting you're thinking about that thing she did in the seventies. You had to have seen her in capri pants and a pullover to understand what I'm getting at. If you were a man or a boy, you fell in lust with that innocent female panther, and she was all yours. I mean, you knew she was beautiful, but you thought you were the only one in the world who knew it. Well, that was Nola Rockover.

She was sitting there in this dark sleeveless top and some kind of skirt, no cleavage or jewelry except for a thin gold necklace that called your attention to the long smooth line of throat, and she had a way of holding her chin high, almost aloof but not quite, more like she hadn't forgotten what her mother had told her about the importance of good posture. She's not talking, except maybe to respond to something the other woman is saying, encourage her to go on, except I'm thinking she's not really that interested, just being polite. In any case it's her friend who's flapping her chin and waving her hands around like she's swatting hornets. Probably describing her love life.

Yes, miss, another Chivas, and how's yours? Sure? Now you're making me look like a lush.

Nola's friend? Okay, so I'm a chauvinist pig. Maybe she's talking abut the Red Wings. She's got on this ugly business suit with a floppy bow tie, like she hasn't been to see a movie since *Working Girl*. Jogs, drinks bottled water by the gallon and two percent milk, got enough calcium in her you could snap her like a stick. Takes the *Cosmo* quiz on the G spot. One of those goddamn silly women you see walking in sheer hose and scruffy tennis shoes, poster child for penis envy. I'm giving you a better picture of her than Nola, and I never saw her again or learned her name. I'm thinking Nola tolerates her company to avoid drinking alone in public. Maybe she already suspects she's said too much in that condition. You can see I'm kindly disposed to her before I even make contact. There's no rule saying you can't like 'em and cuff 'em. I get Christmas cards, sincere ones from killers and pushers I sent to Jackson. Meanwhile I don't know a lawyer I'd go out for lunch with, and we're supposed to be on the same side.

I watch twenty minutes, my drink's all melted ice, and I'm starting to think this other woman's got a bladder the size of Toledo when she gets up and goes to wee-wee. I give it a minute so as not to look like a shark swimming in, then I wander on over. Nola's getting out another cigarette and I'm wishing, not for the first time, I didn't give up the weed, or I could offer to light her up from the Zippo I no longer carried. Sure, it's corny, but it works. That's how some things stay around long enough to get corny. So I do the next best thing and say, "I hear the surgeon general frowns on those."

She looks up slowly like she knows I've been standing there the whole time, and you'll like what she says. "I don't follow generals' orders any more. I got my discharge." And she smiles, this cool impersonal number, that in a book would be a page of dialogue about what a load of crap the mating ritual is, and why can't we be more like cats and get right down to the scratching and yowling. Either that or she's saying go fuck yourself. I'm not sure because I'm too busy noticing what nice teeth she has—not perfect, one incisor's slightly crooked, but she keeps them white, which is not easy when you smoke, and it's good to know there's someone with the self-confidence to refuse to send some orthodontist's kid to Harvard just to look like a model in a toothpaste ad. Her eyes don't smile, though. Even if I didn't know her recent history I'd guess this was someone for whom life had not come with greased wheels.

I'm scraping my skull for what to say next when she throws me a life preserver. "You like the Dead?"

Copy that. Not, "You're a Deadhead?" Which is a term they know in Bowling Green by now, it's hip no more, but most people are afraid not to use it for fear of appearing unhip. The way she doesn't say it, though, tells me she's so hip she doesn't even bother to think about it. I admit that's a lot to get out of four words, but that was Nola, a living tip-of-the-iceberg. Thanks, honey; I like my Scotch good and orange.

I lost the thread. Oh, right, the Dead. I take a chance. Remember everything hangs on how I broach the subject, and the conventional wisdom is never, ever jump the gun. If opening it up standing in front of her table with her friend about to come back any second is not jumping it, I don't know what is. I say: "I like the dead."

That was it. Lowercase, no cap. Which you may argue makes no difference when you're talking, but if you do, good day to you, because you're not the person for what I have in mind. No comment? There's hope for you. Then you'll appreciate her reaction. Her face went blank. No expression, it might have been enameled metal with the eyes painted on. She'd heard that lowercase *d*, knew what it meant, and quick as a switch she shut down the system. She wasn't giving me anything. Wherever this went, it was up to me to take it there.

"I know about your problem," I said. "I can help."

She didn't say, "What problem?" That would have disappointed me. Her eyes flick past my shoulder, and I know without looking her friend's coming. "Have you a card?"

This time I smile. "You mean like 'Have gun, will travel'?"

She doesn't smile back. "I'm known here. I'll be at the Hangar in an hour." And then she turns her head and I'm not there.

I confer with the boys in the van, who take off their earphones long enough to agree the Hangar is Smilin' Jack's Hangar, a roadhouse up in Oakland that's been around since before that comic strip folded, a trendy spot once that now survives as a place where the laws of marriage don't apply, which is enough to pay the bills even after it gets around that it's not Stoli in the Stoli bottles but cheap Smirnoff's and that a ten-dollar bill traded for a three-fifty drink will come back as a five-spot more often than not. Every community needs a place to mess around.

So forty minutes later, wearing fresh batteries, I'm groping through the whiskey-sodden dark of a building that was once an actual hangar for a rich flying enthusiast under the New Deal, my feet not touching the floor because the bass is so deep from the juke, looking for a booth that is not currently being used for foreplay. When I find one and order my watered-down Scotch, I'm hoping

Nola's part bat, because the teeny electric lamp on the table is no beacon.

No need to worry. At the end of ten minutes, right on time, I hear heels clicking and then she rustles into the facing seat. She's freshened her makeup, and with that long dark hair in an underflip and the light coming up from below leaving all the shadows where they belong, she looks like someone I wish I had a wife to cheat on with. I notice her scent: Some kind of moon-flowering blossom, dusky. Don't look for it, it wouldn't smell the same on anyone else.

"Who are you?" She doesn't even wait for drinks.

"Call me Ted."

"No good. You know both my names, and if we do this thing you'll know where I work. That's too much on your side."

I grin. "Ted Hazlett." Which is a name I use sometimes. It's close to "hazard," but not so close they won't buy it.

"And what do you do, Ted Hazlett?"

"This and that."

"Where do you live?"

"Here and there. We can do this all night if you like."

My Scotch comes. She asks for vodka tonic—I'm right about that—and when the waiter's gone she settles back and lights up one of those long cigarettes. Determining to enjoy herself.

"We're just two people talking," she says. "No law against that."

"Not according to the ACLU."

" 'This and that.' Which one is you kill people?"

I think this over very carefully. " 'That.' "

She nods, like it's the right answer. She tells her story then, and there's nothing incriminating in the way she tells it, at least not against her. She's a paralegal with a downtown firm whose name I know, having been cross-examined by some of its personnel in the past. Attends law school nights, plans someday to practice family law, except this walking set of genitalia she's assigned to, partner in the firm, is planning even harder to get into her pants. You know the drill: whispered obscenities in her ear when they're alone in an office, anonymous gifts of crotchless panties and front-loading bras sent to her apartment in the mail, midnight phone calls when she's too groggy to think about hitting the *Record* button on the machine. At first she's too scared to file a complaint, knowing there's no evidence that can be traced to him. Then comes the day he tells her she'd better go down on him if she wants a job evaluation that won't get her fired. These evaluations are strictly subjective, there's nobody in the firm you can appeal to, the decks are stacked in management's favor. The firm's as old as habeas; no rec means no legal employment elsewhere. To top it off, this scrotum, this partner, sits on the board of the school she attends and is in a position to expel her and wipe out three years of credits. Any way you look at it he's got her by the smalls.

What's a girl to do? She's no Shirley Temple, lived with a guy for two years, object matrimony, until she caught him in the shower with a neighbor and threw his clothes out a window—I mean every stitch, he had to go out in a towel to fetch them. So she does the deed on the partner, thinking to hand in her two weeks' notice the next day and take her good references to a firm where oral examinations are not required.

Except she's so good at it the slob threatens to with-hold references if she refuses to assign herself to him permanently, so to speak. Sure, I could have told her too, but it's a lot easier from the sidelines. She knew the odds, but she rolled the dice anyway and came up craps.

After stewing over it all weekend, she decides to take it up with the head of the firm, file a complaint. But the senior partner won't sully himself and fobs her off on an assistant, who by the time she finishes her story has pegged her as an immoral bitch who's gone to blackmail when she found out she couldn't advance herself on her knees, if you get what I'm saying; she can see it in his face when he tells her the incident will be investigated. Next day she's assigned to computer filing. It's obvious the investigation stopped with the partner, who is now out to hound her out of the firm, filing being a notorious dead end whether it involves a modem or a bunch of metal cabinets.

But he doesn't stop there. She tries to finance a new car but gets denied for bad credit. Pulls out her card to buy a blouse at Hudson's, the clerk makes a call, then cuts up the card in front of her. Some more stuff like that happens, then late one night she gets another phone call. It's the walking genitalia, telling her he's got friends all over and if she isn't nice to him he'll phony up her employment record, get her fired, evict her, frame her for soliciting, whatever; it's him or a cell at County, followed by a refrigerator carton on Woodward Avenue, choice is hers. He's psycho, no question, but he's a psycho with connections. The refrigerator carton seals the deal. She's his now, and the law is no longer her parachute. What the partner hasn't figured on is that by blocking all the legal exits, he's left her with only one way out.

There's no way I can tell you all this the way Nola told it. She lays it out flat, just the facts, without a choke or a sob. I'm ready for the waterworks; I've seen some doozies, Oscar-quality stuff, they don't call undercover Umbrella Duty for nothing. The only hint Nola's stinging at all is when she breaks a sentence in half to sip her drink, like a runner taking a hit of oxygen before he can go on. Maybe she's just thirsty. What I'm saying is there's nothing to distract from the bare bones of her story. And I know every word's true. I can see this puffed-up fucker in his Armani, ripping up some poor schmoe in court for stepping out on his wife, then rushing back to the office for his daily quickie with the good-looking paralegal. And while I'm seeing this—I can't say even now if I knew I was doing it—I sneak a hand up under my shirt and disconnect the wire.

Nola won't talk business in a bar. She suggests we meet at her place the next night and gives me an address on East Jefferson. I stand up when she does, pay for the drinks—there's no discussion on that, it's an assumption we both make—and I go to the can, mainly to give her a chance to make some distance before I meet with the crew in the van. Only when I leave the roadhouse, I know she's somewhere out there in the dark, watching me. I walk right past the van and get into my car and pull out. I don't even give the earlobe-tug that tells them I'm being watched, because I *know* Nola would recognize it for what it was. And I spend an extra fifteen minutes crazying up the way home, just in case she's following me.

My telephone's ringing when I get in, and I'm not surprised it's Carpenter, from the van. What's the deal, he wants to know, something went wrong with the transmitter and you forgot we were out there freezing off our asses, you get drunk or what? I tell him I'm wiped out, sorry, I must have pulled loose a wire without knowing. Not to worry; the Nola thing didn't pan out, she was just looking for a sympathetic ear, had no intention of following up on her wish-dream of offing the partner. I didn't like the way the bartender was giving me the fish-eye, thought if I was seen climbing in and out of a van in the parking lot I might blow any chance of a future bust involving the high-stakes poker game that went on in the back room Tuesday nights. Which was the only truth I told Carpenter that night.

I don't know if he believed me about Nola, but he didn't question it. Carpenter's not what you call gung ho, would just as soon duck the graveyard shift for whatever reason. It's not for fear of his disapproval I stay awake most of that night wishing I still smoked. I can still smell her cigarettes and that dusky scent on my clothes.

Most of the next day is spent filling out reports on the nonexistent Rockover Case. I log out in time to go home and freshen up and put on a sport shirt and slacks, no sense working on the image now that the hook's in. Understand, I have no intention of whacking the son of a bitch who's bringing Nola grief. In twelve years with the department I've never even fired my piece except on the range, and even if I had I'm not about to turn into Sammy the Bull for anyone. I'm sympathetic to her case, maybe I can help her figure a way out—brace the guy and apply a little strongarm if necessary, see will he pick on someone his own size and gender. Okay, and maybe wrangle myself some pussy while I'm at it. Hey, we're both single, and it's been a stretch for me, what with everyone so scared of AIDS and GHB; I'm telling you, the alphabet's played hell with the mating game. I figure I'm still leagues above the prick in the two-thousand-dollar suit.

She's on the second floor of one of those converted warehouses in what is now called Rivertown, with a view of the water through a plate-glass window the size of a garage door in her living room. Decor's sleek, all chrome and glass and black leather and a spatter of paint in a steel frame on one wall, an Impressionist piece that when you stand back turns out to be of a nude woman reclining, who looks just enough like Nola I'm afraid to ask if she posed for it. I can tell it's good, but the colors are all wrong: bilious green and violent purple and a kind of rusty brown that I can only describe as dried blood, not a natural flesh tone in the batch. It puts me in mind less of a beautiful naked woman than a jungle snake coiled around a tree limb. Just thinking about it makes my skin crawl.

It takes me a while to take all this in, because it's Nola who opens the door for me. She's wearing a dark turtleneck top with ribs over skin-tight stirrup pants with the straps under her bare feet, which are long and narrow, with high arches and clear polish on the toenails. It's as if she knows I'm a connoisseur of women's feet. With plastic surgery getting to be as common as root canals, pretty faces come four-for-a-quarter, and the effect is gone when you look down and see long bony toes with barn paint. Nola's perfect feet are just about the only skin she's showing, but I'm telling you, I'm glad I brought a bottle of wine to hold in front of myself. It's like I'm back in high school.

She takes the bottle with thanks, her eyes flicker down for a split second, and the corners of her lips turn up the barest bit, but she says nothing, standing aside to let me in and closing the door behind me, locking it with a crisp little snick. Bird Parker's playing low on a sound system I never did get to see. She has me open the wine using a wicked-looking corkscrew in the tiny kitchen, and we go to the living room and drink from stemware and munch on crackers she's set out on a tray on the glass coffee table, crumbly things that dissolve into butter on the tongue. I'm sitting on the black leather sofa, legs crossed, her beside me with hers curled under her, as supple as the snakewoman in the picture, giving off that scent. She looks even better by indirect light than she did in the Hangar. I'm thinking the Gobi at noon would be no less flattering.

We start with small talk, music and wine and the superiority of streamlined contemporary over life in a museum full of worm-eaten antiques, then she lifts her glass to her lips and asks me if I approve of the police department's retirement package.

She slides it in so smoothly I almost answer. When it hits, I get the same shuddery chill I got from the picture, only worse, like the time I had my cover blown when I'd been moled into a car theft ring downriver for a month, bunch of mean ridgerunners whose weapon of choice was a welding torch. Don't ask me why. All she's armed with is crystal.

I don't try to run a bluff, the way I did with the car thieves—successfully, I might add. Rivertown is not Downriver, and Nola Rockover is not a gang of homicidal hillbillies, although I know now they'd be a trade-up. I ask her how she doped it out.

"You forget I'm in computer filing. I ran that name you gave me through the system; you shouldn't have used one you'd used before. It came up on the transcript when you testified against one of our clients as arresting officer. Are you getting all this on tape?"

And would you believe it, there's no emotion in her

tone. She might have been talking about some case at work that had nothing to do with either of us. All I see in her eyes is the reflection of the wine glass she's still holding up. I look into them and say no, I'm not wearing a wire; I was before, but I yanked it. I want to help.

"Am I supposed to believe that?"

"Lady, if it's a lie, you'd be in a holding cell right now."

Which has its effect. She drinks a little more wine and then she leans across me to set her glass down on the table. Before I know it she's got her hands inside my sport shirt. She goes on groping long after it's obvious there's nothing under it but me. And in a little while I know there's nothing but Nola under the sweater and pants. It's like wrestling a snake, only a warm one with a quicker tongue that tastes like wine when it's in my mouth and burns like liquid fire when it's working its way down my chest, and down and down while I'm digging holes in the leather upholstery with my fingers trying to hang on.

Understand, I'm not one of these fools that regales his friends with the play-by-play. I want you to see how a fairly good cop brain melted down before Nola's heat. I was married, and I've had my hot-and-heavies, but I've never even *read* about some of the things we did that night. We're on the sofa, we're off the sofa, the table tips over and we're heaving away in spilled wine and bits of broken crystal; I can show you a hundred little healed-over cuts on my back even now and you'd think I got tangled in barbed wire. In a little while we're both slick with wine and sweat and various other bodily fluids, panting like a couple of wolves, and we're still going at it. I'm not sure they'd take a chance showing it on the Playboy Channel.

Miss? Oh, miss? Ice water, please. I'm burning up.

That's better. Whew. When I think about that night—hell, whenever I think about Nola—this song keeps running through my head. It isn't what Bird was playing on the record, he died years before it came out. It wasn't a hit, although it should have been, it was catchy enough. I don't even know who recorded it. *"Evil Grows,"* I think it was called, and it was all about this poor schnook realizing his girl's evil and how every time he sees her, evil grows in him. Whoever wrote it knew what he was talking about, because by the time I crawled out of that apartment just before dawn, I'd made up my mind to kill Nola's boss for her.

His name's Ethan Hollis, and he's living beyond his means in Grosse Pointe, but if they outlaw that they'll have to throw a prison wall around the city. I don't need to park more than two minutes in front of the big Georgian he shares with his wife to know it won't happen in there, inside a spiked fence with the name of his alarm company on a sign on the front gate. Anyway, since I'm not the only one who's heard Nola's threats, we've agreed that apparent accidental death is best. I'm just taking stock. The few seconds I get to see him through binoculars, coming out on the porch to tell the gardener he isn't clipping the hedge with his little finger extended properly—I'm guessing, I can't hear him across four acres of clipped lawn—is enough to make me hate him, having worked that very job under the druglord in Roseville. He's chubbier than I had pictured, a regular teddy bear with curly dark hair on his head and a Rolex on his fat wrist, with a polo shirt, yet. He deserves to die if for no other reason than his lack of fashion sense.

I know his routine thanks to Nola, but I follow him for

a week, just to look. I've taken personal time, of which I've built up about a year, undercover being twenty-four/seven. The guy logs four hours total in the office; rest of the time he's lunching with clients, golfing with the senior partner, putting on deck shoes and dorky white shorts and pushing a speedboat up and down the river, that sort of bullshit. Drowning would be nice, except I'd join him, because I can't swim and am no good with boats.

These are my days. Nights I'm with Nola, working our way through the *Kama Sutra* and adding footnotes of our own.

The only time I can expect Hollis to be alone without a boat involved is when he takes his Jaguar for a spin. It's his toy, he doesn't share it. Trouble is not even Nola knows when he'll get the urge. So every day when he's home I park around the corner and trot back to his north fence, watching for that green convertible. It's a blind spot to the neighbors too, and for the benefit of passersby I'm wearing a jogging suit; just another fatcat following the surgeon general's advice.

Four days in, nothing comes through that gate but Hollis's black Mercedes, either with his wife on the passenger's side or just him taking a crowded route to work or the country club. I'm figuring I can get away with the jogging gig maybe another half a day before someone gets nervous and calls the cops, when out comes the Jag, spitting chunks of limestone off the inside curves of the driveway. I hustle back to my car. Hollis must need unwinding, because he's ten miles over the limit and almost out of sight when I turn into his street.

North is the choice today. In a little while we're up past the lake, with the subdivisions thinning out along a two-lane blacktop. It's a workday—Nola's in the office, good alibi—and for miles we're the only two cars, so I'm hanging back, but I can tell he's not paying attention to his rearview or he'd open it up and leave me in the dust. Arrogant son of a bitch thinks he's invulnerable.

You see how I'm taking every opportunity to work up a good hate? I'm still not committed. I'm thinking when I get him alone I'll work him over, whisper in his ear what's in store if he doesn't lay off Nola. He's such a soft-looking slob I know he'll cave if I just knock out a tooth.

After an hour and a half we've left the blacktop and are towing twin streamers of dust down a dirt road with farms on both sides and here and there a copse of trees left for windbreaks. Now it's time to open the ball. I've got police lights installed inside the grille, and as I press down the accelerator I flip them on. Now he finds his rearview mirror, begins to slow down. But we're short of the next copse of trees, so I close in and encourage him forward, then as we enter the shade I signal him to pull over.

I've shucked the jogging suit by this time, and am wearing my old uniform. I put on my cap and get out and approach the Jag with my hand resting on the sidearm on my right hip. The window on the driver's side purrs down, he flashes his pearlies nervously. "Was I speeding, Officer?"

"Step out of the car, please."

He's got his wallet out. "I have my license and regis-tration."

I tell him again to step out of the car.

He looks surprised, but he puts the wallet away and grasps the door handle. His jaw's set. I can see he thinks it's a case of mistaken identity and he may have a lucrative harassment suit if he can make himself disagreeable enough. Then his face changes again. He's looking at the uniform.

"You're pretty far out of your jurisdiction, aren't you? This area is patrolled by the county sheriff."

I repeat myself a second time, and this time I draw my sidearm.

"Fuck you, fake cop," says he, and floors it.

But it's a gravel road, and the tires spin for a second, spraying gravel, bits of which strike my legs and sting like hornets, which gives me the mad to make that lunge and grab the window post with my free hand. Just then the tread bites and the Jag spurts ahead and I know I'm going to be dragged if I don't let go or stop him.

I don't let go. I stick the barrel of my revolver through the window, cocking the hammer for the effect, and who knows but it might have worked, except my fingers slip off the window post and as I fall away from the car I strike my other wrist against the post and a round punches a hole through the windshield. Hollis screams, thinks he's hit, takes his hands off the wheel, and that's the last I see of him until after the Jag plunges into a tree by the side of the road. The bang's so loud if you even heard my revolver go off you'd forget about it because the second report is still ringing in your ears thirty seconds later, across a whole fucking field of wheat.

I get up off the ground and sprint up to the car, still holding the gun. The hood's folded like a road map, the radiator pouring steam. Hollis's forehead is leaning against the cracked steering wheel. I look up and down the road and across the field opposite the stand of trees. Not a soul in sight, if you don't count a cow looking our way. Just as I'm starting to assimilate the size of my good break, I hear moaning. Hollis is lifting his head. Lawyers are notoriously hard to kill.

His forehead's split, his face is covered with blood. It looks bad enough to finish him even if it wasn't instantaneous, but I'm no doctor. I guess you could say I panicked. I reached through the window and hit him with the butt of the revolver, how many times I don't know, six or seven or maybe as many as a dozen. The bone of his forehead started to make squishing sounds like thin ice that's cracking under your feet, squirting water up through the fissures. Only in this case it wasn't water, of course, and I know I'm going to have to burn the uniform because my gun arm is soaked to the elbow with blood and gray ooze. Finally I stop swinging the gun and feel for a pulse in his carotid. He wasn't using it any more. I holstered the revolver, took his head in both hands, and rested his squishy forehead against the steering wheel where it had struck. The windshield's still intact except for the bullet hole, so I look around and find a fallen tree limb and give it the old Kaline swing, smashing in the rest of the glass from outside. I settle the limb back into the spot where it had lain among the rotted leaves on the ground, take a last look to make sure I didn't drop anything, get into my car, and leave, making sure first to put the jogging suit back on over my gory uniform. And only the cow is there to see me make my getaway.

For the next few days, I stay clear of Nola. I don't even call, knowing she'll hear about it on the news; I can't afford anyone seeing us together. I guess I was being overcautious. Hollis's death was investigated as an accident, and at the end of a week the sheriff tells the press the driver lost control on loose gravel. I guess the cow didn't want to get involved.

I was feeling good about myself. I didn't see any need to wrestle with my conscience over the death of a sexual predator, and a high-price lawyer to boot. As is the way of human nature I patted my own back for a set of fortunate circumstances over which I'd had no control. I was starting to feel God was on my side.

But Nola isn't. When I finally do visit, after the cops have paid their routine call and gone away satisfied her beef with her employer was unconnected with an accident upstate, she gives me hell for staying away, accuses me of cowardly leaving her to face the police alone. I settle her down finally, but I can see my explanation doesn't satisfy. As I'm taking off my coat to get comfortable she tells me she has an early morning, everyone at the firm is working harder in Hollis's absence and she needs her sleep. This is crap because Hollis was absent almost as often when he was alive, but I leave.

She doesn't answer her phone for two days after that. When I go to the apartment her bell doesn't answer and her car isn't in the port. I come back another night, same thing. I lean against the building groping in my pockets, forgetting I don't smoke any more, then Nola's old yellow Camaro swings in off Jefferson and I step back into the shadows, because there are two people in the front seat. I watch as the lights go off and they get out.

"If you're that afraid of him, why don't you call the police?" A young male voice, belonging to a slender figure in a green tank top and torn jeans.

"Because he *is* the police. Oh, Chris, I'm terrified. He won't stop hounding me this side of the grave." And saying this Nola huddles next to him and hands him her keys to open the front door, which he does one-handed, his other arm being curled around her waist.

They go inside, and the latch clicking behind them sounds like the coffin lid shutting in my face. Nola's got a new shark in her school. I'm the chum she's feeding him. And I know without having to think about it that I've killed this schnook Ethan Hollis for the same reason Chris is going to kill me; I've run out of uses. So for Chris, *I'm* now the sexual predator.

That's why we're talking now. It's Nola or me, and I need to be somewhere else when she has her accident. I've got a feeling I'm not in the clear over Hollis. Call it cop's sense, but I've been part of the community so long I know when I've been excluded. Even Carpenter won't look me in the eye when we're talking about the fucking Pistons. I've been tagged.

Except you're not going to kill Nola, sweetie. No, not because you're a woman; you girls have moved into every other job, why not this? You're not going to do it because you're a cop.

Forget how I know. Say a shitter knows a shitter and leave it there. What? Sure, I noticed when you reached up under your blouse. I thought at the time you were adjusting your bra, but—well, that was before I said I'd decided to kill Hollis, wasn't it? I hope your crew buys it, two wires coming loose in the same cop's presence within a couple of weeks. I'll leave first so you can go out to the van and tell them the bad news. I live over on Howard. Well, you know the address. You bring the wine—no Jack and Coke—I'll cook the steaks. I think I can finish convincing you about Nola. Like killing a snake.

Carolyn Wheat

"The Only Good Judge"

One of the most talented of the many lawyers-turned-crime-writers is Carolyn Wheat, whose Brooklyn advocate Cass Jameson appears in several novels and only a few short stories. In 2001, Wheat edited an original anthology of legal mysteries. They're a distinguished group, but her own contribution may be the best of the lot.

W hat do you say to a naked judge?

I said yes. Averting my eyes from the too, too solid judicial flesh.

I mean, the steam room is a place for relaxation, a place where you close your eyes and inhale the scent of eucalyptus and let go the frustrations of the day—most of which were caused by judges in the first place, so the last thing you want to do while taking a *schvitz* is accept a case on appeal, for God's sake, but there was the Dragon Lady, looking not a whit less authoritative for the absence of black robes, or indeed, the absence of any other clothing including a towel.

She'd been a formidable opponent as a trial judge, and we at the defense bar breathed a sigh of relief when she went upstairs to the appellate bench. The Dragon Lady was one of the great plea-coercers of her time; she could strike fear and terror into the hearts of the most hardened criminals and have them begging for that seventeen-to-life she'd offered only yesterday.

Yes, I said she "offered." I know, you think it's the district attorney who makes plea offers while the judge sits passively on the bench. You think judges are neutral parties with no stake in the outcome, no interest in whether the defendant pleads out or goes to trial.

You've been watching too much *Law & Order*. The Dragon Lady made Jack McCoy look like a soft-on-crime liberal. She routinely rejected plea bargains on the ground that the DA wasn't being tough enough. She demanded and got a bureau chief in her courtroom to justify any reduction in the maximum sentence.

So what was she doing asking me, as a personal favor, to handle a case on appeal? I almost fell off the steam room bench. I was limp as a noodle well past *al dente*, and I'd been hoping to slide out the door without having to acknowledge the presence of my naked nemesis parked on the opposite bench like a leather-tanned Buddha. It seemed the health club equivalent of subway manners: you don't notice them, they won't notice you, and the city functions on the lubrication of mutual indifference.

But she broke the invisible wall between us. She named my name and asked a favor, and I was so nonplussed I said yes and I said "Your Honor" and three other women in the steam room shot me startled open-eyed glances as if to say, who are you to shatter our illusion of invisibility? If you two know one another and talk to one another, then you must be able to see us in all our nakedness and that Changes Everything in this steam room.

They left, abruptly and without finishing the sweating process that was beginning to reduce me to dehydrated delirium. I murmured something and groped my way to the door. I left the Dragon Lady, who'd been there twice as long as I had, yet showed no signs of needing a respite; like a giant iguana, she sat in heavy-lidded torpor, basking in the glow of the coals in the corner of the room. She lifted a wooden ladle and poured water on the hot rocks to raise more steam.

I stumbled to the shower and put it on cold, visualizing myself rolling in Swedish snow, pure and cold and crystalline.

The frigid water shocked me into realizing what I'd just done.

A favor for the Dragon Lady.

Since when did she solicit representation for convicted felons?

Four days later, she was dead.

My old Legal Aid buddy Pat Flaherty told me, in his characteristic way. He always said the only good judge was a dead judge, so when he greeted me in Part 32 with the words, "The Dragon Lady just became a good judge," I knew what he meant.

"Wow. I was talking to her the other day." I shook my head and lowered my voice to a whisper. "Heart attack?"

A sense of mortality swept over me. The woman had looked healthy enough in a reptilian way. I'd noticed her sagging breasts and compared them to my own, which, while no longer as perky as they'd once been, didn't actually reach my navel.

But give me ten years.

"No," Flaherty said, an uneasy grin crossing his freckled face. "She was killed by a burglar."

"Shot?"

"Yeah. Died instantly, they said on the radio."

"Jesus." At a loss for words—and believe it or not, considering how much I'd resented the old boot when she was alive, annoyed at Flaherty for making light of the murder.

Good judge. It's one thing to say that about a ninety-year-old pill who dies in his sleep, but a woman like the DL, cut down in what would be considered the prime of her life if she were a man and her tits didn't sag—that verged on the obscene.

The big question among the Brooklyn defense bar: should we or should we not go to the funeral?

We'd all hated her. We'd all admired her, in a way. I loved the fact that she used to wear a Wonder Woman T-shirt under her black robe. She was tough and smart and sarcastic and powerful and she'd been all that when I was still in high school.

But she'd also been one hell of an asset to the prosecution, a judge who thought her duty was to fill as many jail cells as possible and to move her calendar with a speed that gave short shrift to due process of law.

In the end, I opted to skip the actual funeral, held in accordance with Jewish custom the day after the medical examiner released the body, but I slipped into the back row of Part 49 for the courthouse memorial service two weeks later.

What the hell, I was in the building anyway.

I was in the building to meet Darnell Patterson, the client she'd stuck me with. It had taken me two weeks to get him down from Dannemora, where he was serving twenty years for selling crack.

Twenty years. The mind boggled, especially since he wasn't really convicted of the actual sale, just possession of a sale-weight quantity, meaning that someone in the DA's office thought the amount he had in his pocket was too much to be for his personal use. Since he'd been convicted before, he was nailed as a three-time loser and given a persistent felony jacket.

"It's like they punishing me for thinking ahead," he

said in a plaintive voice. "I mean, I ain't no dealer. I don't be selling no shit, on account if I do, the dudes on the corner gonna bust my head wide open. I just like to buy a goodly amount so's I don't have to go out there in the street and buy no more anytime soon. I likes a hefty stash; I likes to save a little for a rainy day, you hear what I'm saying?"

"Yeah," I said. "You're the industrious ant and all the other users are grasshoppers. The law rewards the grasshoppers because they bought a two-day supply, whereas you, the frugal one, stocked up."

"You got that right," he said with a broad smile. "I think you and me's gonna get along fine, counselor. You just tell that to the pelican court and they'll knock down my sentence."

It was conservative economics applied to narcotics addiction. Maybe I could get an affidavit from Alan Greenspan on the economic consequences of punishing people for saving instead of spending. I could hear my argument before the appellate court:

"Your Honors, all my client did was to invest in commodities. He wanted a hedge against inflation, so he bought in quantity, not for resale, but to insure himself against higher prices and to minimize the number of street buys he had to make, thus reducing his chances of being caught. Punishing him with additional time for his prudence is like punishing someone for saving instead of running up bills and declaring bankruptcy."

The more I thought about it, the more I liked it. The appellate judges—"pelicans" in defendantese—had heard it all. They were unlikely to buy the "mandatory sentences suck" argument and they had no interest in hearing the drug laws attacked as draconian, and they sure as hell didn't give a damn about my client's lousy childhood. Supply-side economics had the advantage of novelty.

When I walked out of the ninth-floor pens, I still had no idea why I'd been asked to take Darnell's case. The sentence was a travesty, of course, far outweighing whatever harm to society this man had done, but what was new or unusual about that? And why had the Dragon Lady, of all people, taken such an interest in a low-level crack case?

With her dead, I'd probably never know.

I had no inkling of a connection between the case and her untimely death.

It took the second murder for the connection to become apparent.

The deceased was a district attorney we called the Terminator; that quality of mercy that droppeth as a gentle rain from heaven was completely absent from his makeup. So once again, there were few tears shed among us defense types, and, in truth, a lot of really bad jokes made the rounds, considering how Paul French died.

He fell out a window in the tall office building behind Borough Hall, the same building that housed the Brooklyn DA's office, but not the actual floor the trial bureau was on. Which, in retrospect, should have told us something. What was he doing there? Had he fallen, or was he pushed? And had the Dragon Lady really died at the hands of a clumsy burglar who picked her house at random, or was somebody out to eliminate the harshest prosecutors and judges in the borough of Brooklyn?

His own office called it suicide. Word went around that he was upset when someone else was promoted to bureau chief over him.

Bullshit, was what I thought. I knew Paul French, tried

cases against him and was proud to say we were even—three wins for him, three for me, which in the prosecution-stacked arithmetic of the criminal courts put me way ahead as far as lawyering was concerned. And I knew that while he might have enjoyed cracking the whip for a while as bureau chief, it was the courtroom he loved. It was beating the opponent, rubbing her nose in his victory, tussling in front of the judge and selling his case to the jury that got his heart started in the morning. He might have gotten pissed off if someone else got a job he thought should have been his, but no way would that have pushed him out a tenth-story window.

The suicide story was bogus, a fact that was confirmed for me when two cops rang the bell of my Court Street office and said they wanted to discuss Paul French. I invited them in, poured them coffee—Estate Java, wasted on cops used to drinking crankcase oil at the station-house—and congratulated them on not buying the cover story. The man was murdered; the only question was which of the fifty thousand or so defendants he'd sent up the river could legitimately take the credit.

The larger and older of the cops opened his notebook and said, "You represented a Jorge Aguilar in September of 1956, is that right, counselor?"

It took a minute to translate his fractured pronunciation. It took another minute to recall the case; 1995 might as well have been twenty years ago, I'd represented so many other clients in so many other cases.

"Jorge, yeah," I said, conjuring up a vision of a cocky, swaggering kid in gang colors who'd boasted he could "do twenty years standing on his head." Despite his complete lack of remorse and absence of redeeming qualities, I'd felt sorry for him. In twenty years, he'd be broken and almost docile, still illiterate and unemployable, and he'd probably commit another crime within a year just so he could get back to his nice, safe prison. He could do twenty years, all right. He just couldn't do anything else.

It took all of thirty seconds for me to disabuse them of the notion that Jorge's case killed Paul French. "Look," I pointed out, "the whole family rejoiced when the kid went upstate. It meant they could keep a television set for more than a week. And he was no gang leader; the real gang-bangers barely tolerated him. So I don't think—"

"What about Richie Toricelli, then?" The older cop leaned forward in my visitor's chair and I had the feeling he was getting to the real point of his interrogation.

"Now we're talking. Toricelli I could see killing Paul French. I'm not sure I see him pushing anyone out a window, though. I'd have expected Richie to use his sawed-off shotgun instead. He liked to see people bleed."

The younger cop gave me one of those "how can you defend those people" looks.

"I was appointed," I said in reply to the unspoken criticism. Which was no answer at all. I wouldn't have been appointed if I hadn't put myself on a list of available attorneys, and I wouldn't have done that if I hadn't been committed with every fiber of my being to criminal defense work.

I'd long since stopped asking myself why I did it. I did it, and I did it the best way I knew how, and I let others work up a philosophy of the job.

Some cases were easier to justify than others. Richie Toricelli's was one of the tough ones.

And if you thought he was a dead loss to society, you ought to meet his mother.

"Tell you the truth," I said, only half-kidding, "I'd sure

like to know where Rose Toricelli was when French took his dive."

"She was in the drunk tank over on Gold Street," the younger cop said, a look of grim amusement on his brown face. "Nice alibi, only about fifty people and ten pieces of official paperwork put her there."

"Pretty convenient," I said, hearing the echo of the Church Lady in my head.

"Counselor, you know something you're not telling us?"

I dropped my eyes. A slight blush crept into my cheeks. I hated admitting this.

"I changed my phone number after Richie went in," I said. "For a year, I lived in fear that Rose Toricelli would find some way to get to me. She didn't just blame Paul French for Richie's conviction, she blamed me too."

The older cop cut me a look. Skeptical Irish blue eyes under bushy white eyebrows over a red-tinged nose. I got the message: *You're gonna do a man's job, you need a man's balls. Afraid of an old lady doesn't cut it.*

It pissed me off. This guy didn't know Richie's ma. "You look at her, you see a pathetic old woman who thinks her scurvy son is some kind of saint; I look at her and I see someone who wants me dead and who could very easily convince herself that shooting me is the best way to tell the world her boy is innocent."

"Did she ever make threats? And did you report any of this?"

"Only in the courthouse the day they took Richie away. And, no," I said, anger creeping into my voice, "I didn't report it. I know what cops think about defense lawyers who get threats. You think we ask for it. And I didn't want to look like a wimp who couldn't handle a little old lady with a grudge."

What really chilled me weren't Rose Toricelli's threats to do damage to the sentencing judge, to Paul French, to me—that was standard stuff in the criminal courts. What really had my blood frozen were the words she said to her son as they shuffled him, cuffed and stunned like a cow on his way to becoming beefsteak:

"You show them, Richie. You show them you're innocent. It would serve them right if you hung yourself in there."

For a year after that, I waited for the news that Richie's body had been discovered hanging from the bars. Doing what Mamma wanted, like he always did.

But as far as I knew, he was still alive, still serving his time, which gave him an iron-bar-clad alibi for French's death, so why were the cops even bringing it up?

The question nagged at me even after the cops left. I turned to my computer, supplementing the information I pulled up with a few phone calls and discovered something very interesting indeed.

Once upon a time, Richie Toricelli's cellmate had been Hector Dominguez.

You remember the case. It made all the papers and even gave birth to a joke or two on Letterman. Funny guy, that Hector.

He'd kidnapped his son, claiming the boy's mother was making him sick. A devout believer in Santeria, he accused his ex of working roots, casting spells, that sapped the boy's strength. He said God told him to save his little boy from a mother who had turned witch.

You can imagine how well that went over in the

Dragon Lady's courtroom. She gaveled him quiet, had him bound and gagged because he wouldn't stop screaming at his sobbing wife. He hurled curses and threats throughout the trial, bringing down the wrath of his gods on the heads of everyone connected to the proceeding.

The day he was to be sentenced, they found the doll in his cell. Carved out of soap, it wore a crude robe of black nylon and sported a doll's wig the exact shade of the Dragon Lady's pageboy. Out of its heart, a hypodermic syringe protruded like a dagger.

Like I said, a lot of criminal defendants threaten the judge who sends them upstate, but a voodoo doll was unique, even in the annals of Brooklyn justice. The *Post* put it on the front page; the *News* thundered editorially about laxness in the Brooklyn House of Detention; *Newsday* did a very clever cartoon I'd taped to my office bulletin board; and the *Times* ignored the whole thing because it didn't happen in Bosnia.

I really wasn't in the courtroom when Dominguez was sentenced because I wanted to see the show. Unlike the two rows of reporters and most of the other lawyers present that day, I had business before the court. But I had to admit a certain curiosity about how the Dragon Lady was going to handle this one.

The lawyer asked her to recuse herself, saying she could hardly be objective under the circumstances. I could have told him to save his breath; the DL was never, under any circumstances, going to admit she couldn't do her job. She dismissed out of hand the notion that she'd taken the voodoo doll personally; it would play no part, she announced in ringing tones, in her sentencing.

Hector Dominguez was oddly compelling when he began to address the court. His English was so poor that an interpreter stood next to him in case he lapsed into his Dominican Spanish, but Hector waved away the help, determined to reach the judge in her own language.

"You Honor, I know it looking bad against me," he said in his halting way. "I just want to say I love my son with my whole heart. *Mi corazon* is hurt when my son get sick. I want her to stop making him sick. Please, You Honor, don't let that woman hurt my boy. He so little, he so pale, he so sick all the time and it all her fault, You Honor, all her doing with her spells and her evil ways."

The child's mother dabbed at her eyes with a tissue, shaking her head mournfully.

The DL gave Dominguez two years more than the District Attorney's office asked for, which was already two years more than the probation report recommended.

This, she insisted, had nothing to do with the doll, but was the appropriate sentence for a man who tried to convince a child that his loving mother was a witch.

Dominguez's last words to the DL consisted of a curse to the effect that she should someday know the pain he felt now, the pain of losing a child to evil.

The papers all commented on the irony of a man like Hector calling someone else evil. And Letterman milked his audience for laughs by holding up a voodoo doll in the image of a certain Washington lady.

But three years later, when the boy's mother was charged with attempted murder and the court shrinks talked about Munchausen's syndrome by proxy, the attitudes changed a bit. Now Hector was seen, not as a nut case who thought his wife was possessed, but as a father

trying to protect his son and interpreting events he
couldn't understand in the only context he knew, that of
his spirit-based religion.

He was up for parole, and it was granted without
much ado. He was free—but his little boy, six years old by
now, lay in a coma, irreparably brain-damaged as a result
of his mother's twisted ministrations.

By not listening to him, by treating him like a criminal
instead of a concerned father, the Dragon Lady had prevented authorities from looking closely at the mother's
conduct.

He had shared a jail cell with Richie Toricelli. That had
to mean something—but what?

The theory hit me with the full force of a brainstorm:
defendants on a train. Patricia Highsmith by way of Alfred Hitchcock.

What if Ma Toricelli, instead of killing the prosecutor
who sent her precious Richie upstate, shot the Dragon
Lady—who had no connection whatsoever to her or her
son? And what if Dominguez, who had no reason to want
Paul French dead, returned the favor by pushing French
out of the window? Each has an alibi for the murder they
had a motive to commit, and no apparent reason to kill
the person they actually murdered.

The more I thought about it, the more I liked it. I liked it
so much I actually asked a cop for a favor. Which was how
I ended up sifting through DD5s in the Eight-Four precinct
as the winter sun turned the overcast clouds a dull pewter.

I learned nothing that hadn't been reported in the papers, and I was ready to pack it in, ready to admit that
even if Ma Toricelli had done the deed, she'd covered her
tracks pretty well, when one item caught my attention.

62

The neighbor across the street had seen a Jehovah's Witness ringing doorbells about twenty minutes prior to the crime. He knew the woman was a Witness because she carried a copy of the *Watchtower* in front of her like a shield.

This was a common enough sight in Brooklyn Heights, where the Witnesses owned a good bit of prime real estate, except for one little thing.

Jehovah's Witnesses traveled in pairs. Always.

One Jehovah's Witness just wasn't possible.

My heart pounded as I read the brief description of the bogus Witness: female, middle-aged, gray hair, gray coat, stout boots. Five feet nothing.

Ma Toricelli to a T.

I wasn't as lucky with the second set of detectives. I was told in no uncertain terms that nothing I had to say would get me a peek at the Paul French reports, so I left the precinct without any evidence that Hector Dominguez could have been in the municipal building when French took his dive.

Still, the idea had promise. I had no problem picturing Rose Toricelli firing a gun point-blank into the judge's midsection and I was equally convinced that in return for the Dragon Lady's death, Hector Dominguez would have pushed five district attorneys out a window. But proving it was another matter.

I pondered these truths as I trudged down Court Street toward home. The sidewalks wore a new coat of powder, temporarily brightening the slush of melting gray snow. Dusk had arrived with winter suddenness, and only the snow-fogged streetlights lit the way. I was picking my way carefully in spite of well-treaded snow boots, my attention fixed on the depth of the chill puddle at the corner of Court and Atlantic Avenue, when the first shot zipped past my ear.

I didn't know it was a shot until the guy in the cigar store yelled at me to get down.

Get down where?

Get down why?

I honestly didn't hear it.

I couldn't even say it sounded like a car backfiring or a firecracker. And I didn't hear the second shot either, although this one I felt.

A sting, like a wasp or a hornet, and blood coursing down my cheek. A burning sensation and a really strong need to use a bathroom. I was ankle-deep in very cold water and couldn't decide whether to keep making my way across the street or run to the shelter of the cigar store. While I considered my options, a black SUV swerved around the corner, straight into the icy puddle, drenching me in dirty, frigid water.

That did it. I turned quickly, wrenching my knee, and hoisted myself onto the curb. I slid at once back into the puddle, landing hard on my backside. A couple of teenagers stopped to laugh, and I suppose it would have been funny if I hadn't been scared out of my mind. Limping and holding my bleeding cheek, I slipped and slid on my way to the amber-lighted cigar store on the corner.

Tobacco-hater that I am, I'd never been inside the cigar emporium before. The scent was overwhelming, but so was the warmth from the space heater on the floor.

The counterman met me at the door, a solicitous expression on his moon face. He was short, with a big bristling mustache and two chins. He reeked of cigar smoke, but I didn't mind at all when he put an arm around me and led me into the sanctuary of his store. He seated me on a folding chair and offered the only comfort he possessed. "Want a cigarillo, lady? On the house."

I started to laugh, but the laughter ended in tears of frustration and relief.

I was alive.

I was bleeding.

I'd been shot at.

The cops were on their way, the cigar man told me, and then he proudly added that he'd seen the shooter's car and had written down the license plate.

The cops, predictably enough, talked drive-by shooting and surmised that a gang member might have been walking nearby when the shots rang out. Since my attention was fully absorbed in not falling into the puddle, King Kong could have been behind me on the street and I wouldn't have noticed.

The second theory was the Atlantic Avenue hotbed-of-terrorism garbage that gets dragged out whenever anything happens on that ethnically charged thoroughfare. Just because Arab spice stores and Middle Eastern restaurants front the street, everything from a trash fire to littering gets blamed either on Arab extremists or anti-Arab extremists.

I have to admit, I was slow. Even I didn't think the shooting had anything to do with my visit to the Eight-Four precinct.

That didn't happen until the next day, when I learned that the car whose license plate the cigar man wrote down belonged to one Marcus Mitchell.

Marcus Mitchell had been royally screwed by Paul French in one of those monster drug prosecutions where everyone turned state's evidence except the lowest-level dealers. People who'd made millions cut deals that had the little guys serving major time for minor felonies, and Mitchell was a guy who had nothing with which to deal.

My own client gave up the guys above him and walked away with a bullet—that's one year and not even a year upstate, a year at Riker's, which meant his family could visit him and—let's be honest here—he could still run a good bit of his drug business from his cell. I know, that sucks, but French was only too happy to get the goods on the higher-ups and made the deal with open eyes. All I did was say yes.

All Marcus Mitchell did was keep his mouth shut, and he did that not out of stubbornness but out of sheer ignorance. He'd been the poor sap caught with a nice big bag of heroin, but the only thing he knew was that a guy named Willie handed it to him at the corner of Fulton and Franklin and told him not to come back until it was all sold.

For this, he got twenty to life. Released after three years on a technicality, but by that time his wife had left him, he'd lost his job, and his parents had died in shame. He had plenty of reason to want Paul French dead.

But why had he taken a potshot at me?

I had taken the day off work, called in shot. It was in the papers, so the judges bought it and told me to take all the time I needed to recuperate, then put my cases over a week. I sipped Tanzanian Peaberry while I felt the blood ooze into the gauze bandage on my cheek and reconsidered my theory.

It was still sound, except for two little things.

One: there were three, not two, defendants on a train.

Two: Ma Toricelli's chosen victim wasn't Paul French—

it was the defense lawyer she blamed for her son's conviction. Me.

It went like this:

Ma Toricelli kills the Dragon Lady for Hector Dominguez.

Dominguez kills Paul French for Marcus Mitchell.

Marcus Mitchell tries to kill me for Ma Toricelli.

This time the cops listened. This time they questioned everyone in the building where Paul French died and found several witnesses who described Hector Dominguez to a T. Add that to the description of the bogus Witness, squeeze all three defendants until someone cracked, and the whole house of cards would tumble down.

I went to the arraignment. I was the victim, so I had a right to be there, and besides, I wanted to see firsthand the people who'd tried to end my life in an icy puddle.

When the time came for Ma Toricelli to plead for bail, she thrust her chin forward and said, "She was supposed to be my boy's lawyer, but all she did was look down on him. She never did her job, Your Honor, not from the first day. She thought Richie was trash and she didn't care what happened to him."

I opened my mouth to respond, then realized it made no difference what I said. Even if I'd been the worst lawyer in the world, that didn't give Rose Toricelli the right to order my death. And I'd done a good job for Richie, a better job than the little sociopath deserved.

Perhaps my mental choice of words was what caught my attention.

If I really thought Richie was a sociopath, had I done my best for him? Or had I slacked off, let the prosecution get away with things I'd have fought harder if I'd truly believed my client innocent? It was a hard question.

There were cases I'd handled better, but I honestly didn't see Richie getting off if Johnnie Cochran had been his lawyer. Still, my cellside manner could have been improved; I could have at least gone through the motions enough to convince Richie's mother that I was doing my best.

The letter came in due course, as we say in the trade. It was enclosed in a manila envelope with the name of a prominent Brooklyn law firm embossed in the left corner. I had no clue what was inside; I had no business pending with the firm and no reason to expect correspondence from them. I slit the thing open with my elegant black Frank Lloyd Wright letter opener, the one my dad gave me for Christmas two years ago.

Another letter with my name handwritten on the front, no address, no stamp, fell into my hands.

This one's return address was the Appellate Division, Second Department.

It was a message from beyond the grave.

Ms. Jameson:

I'm sure you have had reason to wonder why I asked you in particular to handle the case of Darnell Patterson on remand from this court.

Let us just say that I have had reason to regret the current fashion for mandatory minimum sentences and maximum jail time for defendants who commit nonviolent offenses. While I am not one to condone lawbreaking, I firmly believe in distinctions between those who are truly dangerous to society and those who are merely inconvenient.

Mr. Patterson would appear to fall into the latter category. I trust you will agree with me on this point and use your best efforts on his behalf.

You and I, Ms. Jameson, have seldom seen eye to eye, but those traits of yours that I most deplore, your tendency toward overzealousness and your refusal to "go through the motions" on even the most hopeless case, will prove to be just what Mr. Patterson needs in a lawyer.

I expect you will wonder what brought about my change of heart with respect to low-level narcotics cases.

I also expect you to live with your curiosity and make no effort to trace my change of heart to its roots. Suffice to say that it is a private family matter and therefore is nobody's business but my own.

Once again, I thank you for your attention to this matter.

There was no signature. The Dragon Lady had died before she could scrawl her name in her characteristic bold hand.

The compliments brought a traitorous tear to my eyes—especially since the words weren't true.

Mostly true. I was well-known in the Brooklyn court system as a fighter who didn't give up easily, who didn't back down in the face of threats from prosecutors or judges. The DL had been right to rely on me.

But Richie Toricelli hadn't been. I'd been so disgusted by his crimes, so turned off by his attitude, that I'd given less than my best to his defense. Ma Toricelli, for all her craziness, had a point. I'd phoned it in, done a half-baked job of presenting his alibi witnesses, given the jurors little reason to believe his story over that of the prosecution.

The irony was huge. The DL, of all people, sending me compliments on my fighting spirit while Ma Toricelli planned to kill me for rolling over and playing dead on her son's case. Me bailing on Richie and the Dragon Lady getting religion over a three-time loser who hoarded drugs like a squirrel saving up for winter.

The image of Hector Dominguez's voodoo doll swam before my eyes—the weapon protruding from its soap heart wasn't a knife, but a hypodermic. "May you lose a child to evil," he'd cursed, and perhaps she had. Perhaps reaching out to help Darnell Patterson was a way of atoning for that child. Perhaps she'd finally seen that justice needed a dose of mercy, like a drop of bitters in a cocktail.

I sat like a stone while the letter fluttered to the hardwood floor of my office.

Pat Flaherty had been right after all.

The Dragon Lady *had* become a good judge.

Ruth Rendell

"The Wink"

Under her own name and the pseudonym Barbara Vine, Ruth Rendell has become one of the most celebrated contemporary writers of crime fiction. Her books range from formal whodunits about Inspector Wexford to non-series studies of criminal psychology. The brief story that follows illustrates beautifully her insight into character.

The woman in reception gave her directions. Go through the day room, then the double doors at the back, turn left, and Elsie's in the third room on the right. Unless she's in the day room.

Elsie wasn't, but the Beast was. Jean always called him that, she had never known his name. He was sitting with the others watching television. A semicircle of chairs was arranged in front of the television, mostly armchairs but some wheelchairs, and some of the old people had fallen asleep. He was in a wheelchair and he was awake, staring at the screen where celebrities were taking part in a game show.

Ten years had passed since she had last seen him, but she knew him, changed and aged though he was. He must be well over eighty. Seeing him was always a shock, but seeing him in here was a surprise. A not unpleasant surprise. He must be in that chair because he couldn't walk. He had been brought low, his life was coming to an end.

She knew what he would do when he saw her. He always did. But possibly he wouldn't see her, he wouldn't turn round. The game show would continue to hold his attention. She walked as softly as she could, short of tiptoeing, round the edge of the semicircle. Her mistake was to look back just before she reached the double doors. His eyes were on her and he did what he always did. He winked.

Jean turned sharply away. She went down the corridor and found Elsie's room, the third on the right. Elsie, too, was asleep, sitting in an armchair by the window. Jean put the flowers she had brought on the bed and sat down on the only other chair, an upright one without arms. Then she got up again and drew the curtain a little way across to keep the sunshine off Elsie's face.

Elsie had been at Sweetling Manor for two weeks, and Jean knew she would never come out again. She would die here—and why not? It was clean and comfortable and everything was done for you and probably it was ridiculous to feel as Jean did, that she would prefer anything to being here, including being helpless and old and starving and finally dying alone.

They were the same age, she and Elsie, but she felt younger and thought she looked it. They had always known each other, had been at school together, had been each other's bridesmaids. Well, Elsie had been her matron of honour, having been married a year by then. It was Elsie she had gone to the pictures with that evening, Elsie and another girl whose name she couldn't remember. She remembered the film, though. It had been Deanna Durbin in *Three Smart Girls*. Sixty years ago.

When Elsie woke up she would ask her what the other girl was called. Christine? Kathleen? Never mind. Did Elsie know the Beast was in here? Jean remembered then that Elsie didn't know the Beast, had never heard what happened that night, no one had, she had told no one. It was different in those days, you couldn't tell because you would get the blame. Somehow, ignorant though she was, she had known that even then.

Ignorant. They all were, she and Elsie and the girl called Christine or Kathleen. Or perhaps they were just afraid. Afraid of what people would say, would think of them. Those were the days of blame, of good behaviour expected from everyone, of taking responsibility, and often punishment, for one's own actions. You put up with things and you got on with things. Complaining got you nowhere.

Over the years there had been extraordinary changes. You were no longer blamed or punished, you got something called empathy. In the old days, what the Beast did would have been her fault. She must have led him on, encouraged him. Now it was a crime, *his* crime. She read about it in the papers, saw about things called helplines on television, and counselling and specially trained women police officers. This was to avoid your being marked for life, traumatised, though you could never forget.

That was true, that last part, though she had forgotten for weeks on end, months. And then, always, she had seen him again. It came of living in the country, in a small town; it came of her living there and his going on living there. Once she saw him in a shop, once out in the street, another time he got on a bus as she was getting off it. He always winked. He didn't say anything, just looked at her and winked.

Elsie had looked like Deanna Durbin. The resemblance was quite marked. They were about the same age, born in the same year. Jean remembered how they had talked about it, she and Elsie and Christine-Kathleen, as they left the cinema and the others walked with her to the bus

74

stop. Elsie wanted to know what you had to do to get a screen test and the other girl said it would help to be in Hollywood, not Yorkshire. Both of them lived in the town, five minutes' walk away, and Elsie said she could stay the night if she wanted. But there was no way of letting her parents know. Elsie's parents had a phone, but hers didn't.

Deanna Durbin was still alive, Jean had read somewhere. She wondered if she still looked like Elsie or if she had had her face lifted and her hair dyed and gone on diets. Elsie's face was plump and soft, very wrinkled about the eyes, and her hair was white and thin. She smiled faintly in her sleep and gave a little snore. Jean moved her chair closer and took hold of Elsie's hand. That made the smile come back, but Elsie didn't wake.

The Beast had come along in his car about ten minutes after the girls had gone and Jean was certain the bus wasn't coming. It was the last bus and she hadn't known what to do. This had happened before, the driver just hadn't turned up and had got the sack for it, but that hadn't made the bus come. On that occasion she had gone to Elsie's and Elsie's mother had phoned her parents' next-door neighbours. She thought that if she did that a second time and put Mr. and Mrs. Rawlings to all that trouble, her dad would probably stop her going to the pictures ever again.

It wasn't dark. At midsummer it wouldn't get dark till after ten. If it had been, she mightn't have gone with the Beast. Of course, he didn't seem like a Beast then, but young, a boy really, and handsome and quite nice. And it was only five miles. Mr. Rawlings was always saying five miles was nothing, he used to walk five miles to school every day and five miles back. But she couldn't face the walk and, besides, she wanted a ride in a car. It would only be the third time she had ever been in one. Still, she would have refused his offer if he hadn't said what he had when she told him where she lived.

"You'll know the Rawlings, then. Mrs. Rawlings is my sister."

It wasn't true, but it sounded true. She got in beside him. The car wasn't really his, it belonged to the man he worked for; he was a chauffeur, but she found that out a lot later.

"Lovely evening," he said. "You been gallivanting?"

"I've been to the pictures," she said.

After a couple of miles he turned a little way down a lane and stopped the car outside a derelict cottage. It looked as if no one could possibly live there, but he said he had to see someone, it would only take a minute and she could come, too. By now it was dusk, but there were no lights on in the cottage. She remembered he was Mrs. Rawlings's brother. There must have been a good ten years between them, but that hadn't bothered her. Her own sister was ten years older than she was.

She followed him up the path, which was overgrown with weeds and brambles. Instead of going to the front door, he led her round the back where old apple trees grew among waist-high grass. The back of the house was a ruin, half its rear wall tumbled down.

"There's no one here," she said.

He didn't say anything. He took hold of her and pulled her down in the long grass, one hand pressed hard over her mouth. She hadn't known anyone could be so strong. He took his hand away to pull her clothes off and she screamed, but the screaming was just a reflex, a release of fear, and otherwise useless. There was no one to hear.

What he did was rape. She knew that now—well, had known it soon after it happened, only no one called it that then. Nobody spoke of it. Nowadays the word was on everyone's lips. Nine out of ten television series were about it. Rape, the crime against women. Rape that these days you went into court and talked about. You went to self-defense classes to stop it happening to you. You attended groups and shared your experience with other victims.

At first, she had been most concerned to find out if he had injured her. Torn her, broken bones. But there was nothing like that. Because she was all right and he was gone, she stopped crying. She heard the car start up and then move away. Walking home wasn't exactly painful, more a stiff, achey business, rather the way she had felt the day after she and Elsie had been learning to do the splits. She had to walk anyway, she had no choice. As it was, her father was in a rage, wanting to know what time she thought this was.

"Anything could have happened to you," her mother said.

Something had. She had been raped. She went up to bed so they wouldn't see she couldn't stop shivering. She didn't sleep at all that night. In the morning she told herself it could have been worse, at least she wasn't dead. It never crossed her mind to say anything to anyone about what had happened; she was too ashamed, too afraid of what they would think. It was past, she kept telling herself, it was all over.

One thing worried her most. A baby. Suppose she had a baby. Never in all her life was she so relieved about anything, so happy, as when she saw that first drop of blood run down the inside of her leg a day early. She shouted for joy. She was all right! The blood cleansed her and now no one need ever know.

Trauma? That was the word they used nowadays. It meant a scar. There was no scar that you could see and no scar she could feel in her body, but it was years before she would let a man come near her. Afterwards she was glad about that, glad she had waited, that she hadn't met someone else before Kenneth. But at the time, she thought about what had happened every day; she relived what had happened, the shock and the pain and the dreadful fear, and in her mind she called the man who had done that to her the Beast.

Eight years went by and she saw him again. She was out with Kenneth, he had just been demobbed from the Air Force and they were walking down the High Street arm-in-arm. Kenneth had asked her to marry him and they were going to buy the engagement ring. It was a big jewellers they went to, with several aisles. The Beast was in a different aisle, quite a long way away, on some errand for his employer, she supposed, but she saw him and he saw her. He winked.

He winked, just as he had ten minutes ago in the day room. Jean shut her eyes.

When she opened them again, Elsie was awake.

"How long have you been there, dear?"

"Not long," Jean said.

"Are those flowers for me? You know how I love freesias. We'll get someone to put them in water. I don't have to do a thing in here, don't lift a finger. I'm a lady of leisure."

"Elsie," said Jean, "what was the name of that girl we went to the pictures with when we saw *Three Smart Girls?*"

"What?"

"It was nineteen thirty-eight. In the summer."

"I don't know, I shall have to think. My memory's not what it was. Bob used to say I looked like Deanna Durbin."

"We all said you did."

"Constance, her name was. We called her Connie."

"So we did," said Jean.

Elsie began talking of the girls they had been at school with. She could remember all their Christian names and most of their surnames. Jean found a vase, filled it with water, and put the freesias into it because they showed signs of wilting. Her engagement ring still fitted on her finger, though it was a shade tighter. How worried she had been that Kenneth would be able to tell she wasn't a virgin! They said men could always tell. But of course, when the time came, he couldn't. It was just another old wives' tale.

Elsie, who already had her first baby, had worn rose-colored taffeta at their wedding. And her husband had been Kenneth's best man. John was born nine months later and the twins eighteen months after that. There was a longer gap before Anne arrived, but still she had had her hands full. That was the time, when the children were little, that she thought less about the Beast and what had happened than at any other time in her life. She forgot him for months on end. Anne was just four when she saw him again.

She was meeting the other children from school. They hadn't got a car then, it was years before they got a car. On the way to the school, they were going to the shop to buy Anne a new pair of shoes. The Red Lion was just closing for the afternoon. The Beast came out of the public bar, not too steady on his feet, and he almost bumped into her. She said, "Do you mind?" before she saw who it was. He stepped back, looked into her face, and winked. She was outraged. For two pins she'd have told Kenneth the whole tale that evening. But of course she couldn't. Not now.

"I don't know what you mean about your memory," she said to Elsie: "You've got a wonderful memory."

Elsie smiled. It was the same pretty teenager's smile, only they didn't use that word teenager then. You were just a person between twelve and twenty. "What do you think of this place, then?"

"It's lovely," said Jean. "I'm sure you've done the right thing."

Elsie talked some more about the old days and the people they'd known and then Jean kissed her goodbye and said she'd come back next week.

"Use the shortcut next time," said Elsie. "Through the garden and in by the French windows next door."

"I'll remember."

She wasn't going to leave that way, though. She went back down the corridor and hesitated outside the day-room door. The last time she'd seen the Beast, before *this* time, they were both growing old. Kenneth was dead. John was a grandfather himself, though a young one, the twins were joint directors of a prosperous business in Australia, and Anne was a surgeon in London. Jean had never learned to drive, and the car was given up when Kenneth died. She was waiting at that very bus stop, the one where he had picked her up all those years before. The bus came and he got off it, an old man with white hair, his face yellowish and wrinkled. But she knew him, she would have known him anywhere. He gave her one of his rude stares and he winked. That time it was an exaggerated, calculated wink, the whole side of his face screwed up and his eye squeezed shut.

She pushed open the day-room door. The television was still on but he wasn't there. His wheelchair was empty. Then she saw him. He was being brought back from the bathroom, she supposed. A nurse held him tightly by one arm. The other rested heavily on the padded top of a crutch. His legs, in pyjama trousers, were half-buckled and on his face was an expression of agony as, wincing with pain, he took small tottering steps.

Jean looked at him. She stared into his tormented face and his eyes met hers. Then she winked. She winked at him as he had winked at her that last time, and she saw what she had never thought to see happen to an old person. A rich dark blush spread across his withered face. He turned away his eyes. Jean tripped lightly across the room towards the exit, like a sixteen-year-old.

Dorothy Cannell

"Bridal Flowers"

The old actor who said on his deathbed, "Dying is easy; comedy is hard," might have added, "because comedy has to look easy." One of the best at combining crime and detection with humor is Dorothy Cannell. The following tale of spinster private eyes achieves Wodehousian drollness despite a very serious underlying theme.

T hat obnoxious woman!" Hyacinth Tramwell set down her cup and saucer with a bang on the coffee table. "I ran into her last year at the church bazaar, and she bored me for an entire hour. What on earth can she want?"

"Probably come collecting for one of her pet projects." Her sister Primrose gave a fluttering sigh. "And the bother of it is that I'll probably agree to make a donation to a group I despise simply because she intimidates me so."

"Nonsense, Prim. You will square your shoulders and remember that you are a woman in your sixties and a private detective to boot, not a child to be ordered to hand over a bag of sweets."

"Yes, dear."

Before either woman could say more, the sitting room door opened and their butler, a man of uncertain age and nondescript appearance, entered. "Mrs. Smith-Hoggles," he intoned, as if informing them of an outbreak of bubonic plague in the village. Behind him loomed a shadow, which took on form and substance when he bowed and retreated.

"Does he always do that?" The woman in the brown

84

felt hat and camel coat was slimly built but she had a large voice.

"Always do what?" Hyacinth raised an eyebrow.

"Pad about the place in his socks."

"Certainly. He is an ex-burglar, excellent training for his present job. We could not ask for a more unobtrusive butler."

"But aren't you afraid he'll pinch the silver?"

"Dear me, no," twittered Primrose. "His passion is eighteenth-century clocks, quite single-minded about it. His brother specialized in sundials before his retirement. And there is a sister who I believe still deals in pocket watches. Quite the family business one might say. But I must not rattle on, pray do sit down, Mrs. Smith-Hoggles, and tell us what brings you here on such an inclement morning."

Their visitor hesitated before taking a seat. She had met the Misses Tramwell on several occasions at village functions but had not previously been to Cloisters, their ancestral home. She had passed it numerous times in the car and occasionally on foot, and although she preferred modern dwellings, she had conceded that its mellow brick and pigeon gray roof were charming. The same, she now admitted, must be said of the interior. The hall had been imposing with its walnut paneling and family portraits, and this room, whilst small, whispered of old money. The sisters sat on chintz sofas facing each other on either side of a fireplace whose mantel displayed brass candlesticks and several pieces of Minton china. A grandfather clock stood in one corner, two floor-to-ceiling bookcases housed leather-bound volumes, and Mrs. Smith-Hoggles was herself seated on a striped Regency chair. Indeed, nothing could be faulted, from the silver tea service on the rent table under the window to the time-muted colors of the needlepoint rug. Even so, she winced as she settled her handbag, a recent purchase from Harrods, on her knees.

Hyacinth Tramwell had not, in Mrs. Smith-Hoggles's opinion, aged gracefully. Indeed, she looked as though she had battled the process every inch of the way. Her improbably black hair was plaited into a coronet on top of her head, which in itself might not have been so outré if it had not been poked around with stick pins that flashed with a variety of colored stones. Mrs. Smith-Hoggles suspected that there might be genuine emeralds and rubies among them. But that only compounded the absurdity, when offset by a pair of dangling, dagger-shaped earrings and the ankle-length dress of some gauzy red material topped by a black lace shawl. With her sallow complexion and dark eyes, the woman could have been a gypsy come in from hawking clothes pegs and bunches of wax flowers door to door. Mrs. Smith-Hoggles had a well-bred distaste for gypsies along with a great many other things that she did not consider to be top drawer. And for all her bizarre appearance, Hyacinth Tramwell was from among the country's leading families.

The sister Primrose was definitely more what one might hope to expect. Her silver curls, periwinkle-blue eyes, and crumpled petal complexion reminded one of a sweet little aunt whose days were mainly spent knitting or writing beautifully penned letters to beloved nieces and nephews. The only perceivable oddity was that she wore a long Mickey Mouse watch and—Mrs. Smith-Hoggles noted, looking down—a pair of frilly socks instead of stockings. But eccentricities, even in Hyacinth Tramwell's case, should perhaps be overlooked, given what was rumored to be their vast wealth and the cousin several times removed who was either a duke or an earl. Besides, if they weren't the least bit untraditional, they wouldn't have entered the private detection business, and she wouldn't be sitting here.

"May we offer you some tea? We can ring for Butler," Hyacinth indicated a tasseled bell rope, "and have him bring you a cup."

"No, thank you, I had one just before leaving home." Mrs. Smith-Hoggles replied in her oversized voice. "How curious that he should be called that!"

"Butler?" Hyacinth picked up her own teacup. "It's an alias. As with all self-respecting criminals, he had dozens when we first met him hiding in the wardrobe in Primrose's room."

"After all those years spent looking for a man under my bed." Her sister's eyes twinkled at the folly of it. "Life never turns out the way we expect it to, does it? I had the idea that you had come collecting for some charity, but I have a presentiment that an unexpected turn of events in your life is what has brought you to us. In other words, you seek the services of Flowers Detection."

"That is the case," said Mrs. Smith-Hoggles.

"You have a daughter." The dagger earrings sliced against Hyacinth's neck as she leaned forward. "Could this be a matter touching upon her? Has she disappeared?"

"No, it's not that."

"Then you fear some danger threatens her."

"How astute of you." Mrs. Smith-Hoggles drew a deep breath. "To think immediately of Emily."

"You are sadly a widow." Primrose adjusted the cuffs of her lavender cardigan. "Therefore there is no husband to be a cause of distress. Also, you have no other children. And if it were anything other than a personal matter, you would presumably have contacted the police."

Mrs. Smith-Hoggles eyed her thoughtfully. She was clearly more astute than those guileless blue eyes would indicate. "It is so difficult when one is in the position of being both mother and father to an impressionable young girl. And one feels the burden most astutely at a time when one's darling child is about to make the greatest mistake of her life." She reached into her handbag for a monogrammed handkerchief and dabbed at her eyes.

"What sort of mistake?" asked Hyacinth.

"She wants to get married."

"And how old is Emily?"

"Twenty-five."

"Hardly a child; unless." Primrose paused delicately, "the poor dear is simpleminded."

"Certainly not!" Mrs. Smith-Hoggles balled up the handkerchief and returned it to her handbag. "Emily is an intelligent girl. She went to the very best schools and has had every possible advantage. I sacrificed my own social life to be there for her every possible minute. I still tuck her into bed at night. Still cut her bread and butter into soldiers for her when she has a boiled egg. And now this!"

"You have something against the young man. Dear me!" Primrose patted her silvery curls. "I remember how grieved my parents were when I expressed an interest in an insurance salesman. My father did not approve of insurance. He considered it a form of gambling."

"If only it were that simple! Not that I think much of James Watson's means of making a living. He writes articles for a small newspaper. Worse, Emily says he wants to write books. So thoroughly irresponsible. But that is nothing against the fact"—Mrs. Smith-Hoggles shuddered—"that he is the grandson of a man suspected of poisoning his young wife in 1947. Surely you remember the case, seeing that it was a local one?"

"Here in Flaxby Meade?"

"No, in Longbourton, but that is only twenty miles away. The trial was widely reported at the time."

"I do seem to remember." Hyacinth sat ramrod stiff on her sofa. The dagger earrings hung still against her neck. "It was referred to as the Black Hearted Murder because that was the name of the accused: Black. And wasn't his Christian name also James?"

Mrs. Smith-Hoggles nodded. "He and his poor murdered wife had a daughter who is James Watson's mother. That surely tells you what sort of a woman she is, to have named her son after her villain of a father. And this is the family into which Emily is intent on marrying! When there is that perfectly delightful George Hubbard, who is so fond of her and has an irreproachable background and a house with a granny flat already in place."

"But if I recall correctly," said Hyacinth, "James Black was acquitted of his wife's murder."

"Because he'd been clever enough to have her body cremated."

"Before people started fanning the flames of suspicion." Primrose looked pained.

"They didn't take much fanning." Mrs. Smith-Hoggles gave a snort that hadn't been taught at her finishing school. "The poor woman was barely disposed of before James Black married his pretty blond secretary. But from what I've heard, there was talk even before that of the first wife, whose name was Elizabeth, being violently sick after meals and being afraid to eat until she languished away to skin and bone. The housekeeper gave evidence that she once saw James Black pry her mouth open when she refused to touch her soup and force her to swallow a spoonful. There were days—weeks—when she never left her bedroom and would see no one, or more likely was not permitted to receive visitors." Mrs. Smith-Hoggles looked as though she, too, had been given a dose of poison. "And my poor, foolish Emily wants to marry into that family. I have told her it will be over my dead body, but you know how young people are." She stared mournfully at the sisters. "They don't look ahead."

"What of the grandson's character? Is he a reprehensible person?" Hyacinth roused herself from several moments of reflection.

"Not on the surface, although I can't say I appreciate the way he encourages Emily to 'be her own person,' as he calls it. The other day she came home with her ears pierced—something she would never have done without talking to me about it first. Knowing, as she must, how upset her dear father would have been. And of course it led to a row with Emily in tears and Jim, as she calls him, making a great big fuss of her. But I don't see that he needs to have robbed a bank or hit an old lady over the head for me to oppose this marriage. The stigma is bad enough, but bad blood will out. And I have not only Emily to think about but also my future grandchildren." Mrs. Smith-Hoggles reached again for her handkerchief. "Who knows what horrible criminal tendencies they will display as they mature! But I have endeavored, in the midst of my heartbreak, to be fair. As you said"—addressing Hyacinth—"James Black was acquitted of murder, and

I suppose there is the remote chance that he was indeed innocent, which is why I have come to ask you to investigate the case."

"One that is more than fifty years old?"

"Oh, but only think, Hy." Primrose pressed her hands together. "What a delightful challenge. One can hardly wait to begin. It is to be hoped"—she eyed Mrs. Smith-Hoggles—"that some of those on the scene are still alive."

"James Black has been dead for more than thirty years."

"That would make him unavailable for questioning." Primrose's face crumpled. "What about the doctor who attended his first wife?"

"Deceased."

"And the housekeeper."

"Succumbed to old age."

"Let us not forget the blond secretary who became the second Mrs. Black," said Hyacinth.

"Died at a health spa," replied Mrs. Smith-Hoggles with another of her less-than-refined snorts. "There was a maid, Kathleen somebody, who lived-in, and gave evidence at the trial, but she left the area immediately afterward. She was young, only seventeen or eighteen years old, so she very likely married. I think she may have immigrated to Australia. So I am afraid that really only leaves the daughter—Jim's mother—as a candidate for questioning. He's very fond of her, I will say that." She returned the handkerchief to the handbag for what the Tramwell sisters hoped was the final time and snapped it shut. "Quite devoted in fact. But, as I said to Emily, that's not always such a good thing. She could end up living with both of them. Unlike dear George Hubbard with his pots of money and impeccable pedigree, I can't see Jim ever having the financial wherewithal to spring for a granny flat."

"Does Emily know you have come to see us?" Hyacinth's eyes were on her teacup, which she had picked up.

"Of course. I wouldn't have dreamed of acting behind her back. She was upset, just as I expected, but I stressed my hope—faint as it is—that you will bring something to light that will set my maternal fears at rest. You will then agree to take on the case?" Mrs. Smith-Hoggles rose to her feet and pulled on a pair of gloves that matched her handbag.

"If you are sure this is what you want," said Hyacinth to the teacup.

"I have thought the matter over carefully and see no alternative course of action."

"Some of our clients are not pleased by what we uncover."

"I have already told you that I don't hold out high hopes of a reassuring outcome."

"Precisely." Hyacinth jangled the bell rope and the sitting room door opened instantly. "Ah, Butler," she said, "our guest is leaving; kindly attend her outdoors with an umbrella. I see"—her black eyes turned to the window—"that it is raining."

"Very good, madam."

"We have not yet discussed the matter of your fee," Mrs. Smith-Hoggles pointed out.

"Oh, I am sure you will not find it unreasonable, but should you do so," responded Primrose at her most fluttery, "we will be only too happy to adjust it. And do not worry; we will be in touch with you the moment we have something to report. Timeliness is the byword of Flowers Detection. Which is not to say that any stone will be left uncovered. That maid you mentioned . . . it may be possible to trace her. We have our ways. And James Black's daughter, of course . . . no, do not bother to delay yourself giving us her address. Those clouds look quite menacing. Was that not thunder I just heard?"

Mrs. Smith-Hoggles found herself out in the hall with an ex-burglar, and when he withdrew the umbrella from its stand, she wished for a moment that she had not come. But when he did not cosh her over the head and make off up the stairs with her handbag, she left the house feeling that she had made a good morning's work of it.

"So," said Hyacinth to Primrose, "we await a visit from Emily."

"And in all likelihood her young man."

"Possibly on their lunch hours."

"Yes, I don't think they will allow us much time in which to set about our inquiries." Primrose looked at the clock. "Time for a little something, as Pooh would say. But I can't say I fancy either condensed milk or honey. That Dundee cake Butler made yesterday would, I think, do very nicely with a fresh pot of tea."

"My thoughts precisely." Hyacinth smiled at her, but her black eyes held a glitter that did not bode well for whoever occupied her thoughts. Before she could again pull the bell rope, Butler slipped silently back into the room with a loaded tray.

"Wonderful man. You anticipate our every whim," she informed him.

"Certainly, madam. I made sure that I took the umbrella that leaked." He appeared about to say more when the doorbell rang, and he vanished back into the hall to return a few moments later with a fair-haired young woman of a pleasantly plump build and a dark, handsome man in his early thirties.

"Miss Emily Smith-Hoggles and Mr. James Watson," he announced before again disappearing.

"Mother's been here already, hasn't she?" The girl's lips quivered. "I can always tell when she's been in a room. She takes something out of it, leaving it somehow horribly blank. No matter who's left in it or how much furniture there is."

"Em, darling, don't do this to yourself." The man was helping her off with her damp raincoat. He was, Primrose noted with a maidenly flutter, extremely handsome. Dangerously so, some might have said, but she liked the way his eyes lingered on Emily Smith-Hoggles's flushed face, and she thought his mouth kind.

"Yes, do get out of those wet coats, that's right—I'll take them." Hyacinth did so and tossed them on the settle in front of the fireplace. "And now sit yourself down on that sofa and unburden yourselves to my sister Primrose and me."

"But you've already talked to Mother," Emily protested, "which means you're bound to be on her side. She'll have told you the whole lurid story about Jim's grandparents. Only I don't see it that way any more than Jim does. He told me all about it, soon after we first met at a party—neither one of us realizing at first that we came from the same part of the country. Well, Jim hadn't ever lived around here, but it's where his roots were, and I wasn't horrified to think that his grandfather had been tried for murder. Not in a grisly sort of way. The whole thing seemed to me so very sad. A terrible tragedy, but not something that alters who Jim is. It was Mother who went and put her dreadful spin on it. Scolding and nagging day in and day out that I was putting my head in a noose by wanting to marry him. Such rubbish"—her eyes filled with tears—"because he is the dearest man in the entire world."

"I wouldn't go that far." Jim stroked back a lock of her hair.

"Your only fault is that you're too modest." Emily gave him a watery smile. Her hand reached out to the plate filled with the slices of Dundee cake, but she immediately drew it back.

"Please have some," urged Hyacinth.

"No, thank you, I mustn't really. I'm not the sort who can get away with eating between meals."

"Go on, Em," said Jim. "Your mother's not here to pull that face at you. And it looks like excellent cake."

"Oh, indeed it is." Primrose beamed as she handed them each a plate. "I intend to have at least three slices myself."

"You can afford to," replied Emily dolefully, "you're so dainty: I don't suppose you ever gain an ounce."

"And you, my dear, are so young and pretty it won't matter if you do. Now, eat up while I pour you and Mr. Watson each a cup of tea and then we will discuss your side of things. Sugar?"

"No—"

"She likes two spoonfuls and plenty of milk," Jim told Primrose while looking tenderly at Emily.

When the cups and saucers and cake plates had been handed out, Hyacinth rearranged the black lace shawl around her shoulders and leaned forward so that her dagger earrings swung in a wide arc. Her face might have been an engraved invitation, and the couple seated on the sofa across from her and Primrose began talking, adding to each other's sentences as they went along.

"Mother has involved you ladies for one reason only. To cause pain to Jim by injuring his widowed mother. And Lizzie has been through enough already." Emily bit into a slice of Dundee cake.

"Em's not just talking about my father's death," Jim explained. "She suffered terribly growing up, as you might imagine, from being branded the daughter of a murderer. And she doesn't deserve to have the business raked up after all these years.

"She's such a darling." Emily swallowed a second mouthful of cake. "One of the most loving, caring people in the whole world, just as you would expect Jim's mother to be. But she's emotionally fragile."

"Under a strong exterior."

"That's exactly it. Lizzie—she was named after her mother, Elizabeth—has shouldered so much through the years that most people who know her think she's invincible, but she isn't. I realized that as soon as I met her. She deserves cosseting. Breakfast in bed and flowers and lots of hugs."

"And the thing is"—Jim put another piece of cake on Emily's plate—"my mother loved her father. If she hadn't, she wouldn't have named me after him, would she?"

"Lizzie never believed he was a murderer."

"Or that anything was going on between him and his secretary before his wife's death. It developed afterward, when he was going through the grief and the ugly rumors being spread around. She was the one person who stood by him through it all. My mother grew very fond of her over the years."

"Surely you can see what Mother's doing?" Emily appealed to Hyacinth and Primrose. "She doesn't for one moment think you will uncover anything of significance either way. What she's counting on is that I love Jim too much to put him through this and will break it off with him. That's why she told me she was coming to see you. Playing fair with me had nothing to do with it. She can be diabolical."

"Not a nice thing to say about one's mother." Primrose replenished their teacups. "But one does tend to agree with you, my dear."

"Then you did see through her?"

"That surprises you?" Hyacinth raised a black-painted eyebrow.

"Well, yes, it does in a way because . . ." Emily resorted to more cake.

"What Em is trying to say," Jim grinned engagingly, "is that we're convinced Mrs. Smith-Hoggles made you her first choice for the job at hand because she had you pegged as a pair of well-to-do women playing at being private detectives. The Sam Spades of this world would very likely have ushered her out the door before she was five minutes into her nonsense."

"Whilst a pair of eccentric elderly ladies would leap at the chance to interrogate your poor mother." Primrose nodded her silvery head. "But you young people put your faith in the possibility that we might also be kind. There is a fly in the ointment, however, my dears. If we get back in touch with Mrs. Smith-Hoggles to say we have rethought the matter and will not be taking on the case, I very much fear that she will find someone else willing to take her money. As in all professions, there are those in the private detection business who will do pretty much anything for the money."

"Despicable, but there it is," agreed Hyacinth.

"So Mother gets what she wants." Emily set down her

plate as if the sight of the cake crumbs on it revolted her. "Oh, darling." She turned to Jim and caught up his hands. "You do see we can't take our happiness at the expense of Lizzie's pain. But I do promise you that I'll never marry George Hubbard. That's one thing about which Mother won't get her way."

"We'll find a way out of this mess, Em."

"That goes without saying when Flowers Detection is on the job." Primrose looked genteelly smug.

"Don't worry your heads about it." Hyacinth readjusted the black lace shawl, setting the earrings in motion. "It is as well that my sister and I did not show your mother the door within five minutes of getting into her old murder story because that was all it took to make the case entirely clear to myself and—"

"Absolutely, Hy," Primrose concurred. "Nothing could have been more obvious than who caused the first Mrs. Black's death, and it was not, let me reassure you two nice young people, her husband. Of course it must needs be said that he made things hard on himself by having her cremated, but men don't always think ahead. A woman would have been far more alert to the possibilities that doing so would stoke the fire . . . if you will forgive the unfortunate pun."

Jim looked astounded. "Do you mean to say that you sorted out what really happened just sitting here, using your little gray cells like Hercule Poirot?"

"Oh, we wouldn't dream of putting ourselves in his elevated category," remonstrated Primrose. "The man was sheer genius. God rest his soul."

"But I thought he was a fictional character." Emily looked confused.

"Correct." Hyacinth inclined her head. "But my sister

believes that if one lives and breathes on the printed page, one is entitled to go to one's heavenly reward when the time comes. She has not discussed the matter with our vicar, who holds to more conventional views."

Jim looked suddenly less cheerful. "The trouble is, I don't see that your knowing will be enough for Mrs. Smith-Hoggles. She will want proof."

"Very little in life comes stamped with a seal of authenticity." Hyacinth got to her feet and plied the bell robe. "The best we can offer is compelling evidence of the sort that it will be difficult for her to refute. There is one question I have for you. Did your mother ever mention the maid who worked for her parents? Mrs. Smith-Hoggles said that her Christian name was Kathleen."

"Yes." Jim's brow furrowed. "But what was her surname? I could ask Mum, but she would wonder why I wanted to know. Give me a moment . . . I've got it! It was Rose. I remember because Kathleen Rose sounded like two first names, but Mum said it wasn't that way."

"That should be helpful," said Hyacinth.

"Jim has a marvelous memory." Emily looked adoringly at him. "It's what makes him such a wonderful writer. One day he could be famous, but even if he isn't, we're going to be blissfully happy. If all goes as you promise." The two young people were on their feet when Butler appeared in the room.

"We'll be in touch in a couple of days," Hyacinth assured them. When she and Primrose again had the room to themselves, she said, "Having but a few minutes ago maligned other members of our profession, I fear we must take an unethical step in this proceeding."

"No need to say more!" Primrose beamed at her. "Our minds work as one, although I prefer to regard our methods as creative rather than as a breach of the code. Ah, Butler!" she said as he padded toward them, his expression at once deferential and inquiring.

"I sensed that I might be needed."

"You are in tune as always." Hyacinth regarded him fondly. "As a reward you may take the Louis VI clock up to bed with you tonight. Meanwhile, Miss Primrose and I wish you to locate a maid."

"My services aren't up to snuff?"

"Dear me, your grammar does go out the window when visitors go out the door." Primrose fluttered back to the sofa. "We're not looking for a maid to work for us. Sometimes I wonder why we need the services of Mrs. Brown three times a week when you leave so little for her to do. But sit yourself down, and we will explain exactly what we require of you. I am sure it will present you with very few difficulties."

"I should 'ope not." Butler settled himself on a chair and flipped open the cigar box on the side table. "Go on ladies, fill me in. What's it you want me to wangle for you this time?"

Even Primrose could be succinct when she set her mind to it, and Hyacinth rarely waffled.

"So them's me orders." Butler tapped ash into a saucer. "A piece of cake. I'd say you can have your meeting with that nasty Mrs. Smith-Hoggles the day after next. I could get things done sooner, but I've got eight dozen pots of jam promised to the Women's Institute for tomorrow. And they'll have me underpants for garters if I lets them down."

"No need for that," replied Hyacinth crisply. "We don't want to make this look too easy. We'll set up the meeting for three days from now. That will be Thursday." Hyacinth went over to the secretary desk in the alcove by the window and made a notation on the calendar she took from one of its drawers. You're sure that will give you enough time to produce Kathleen Rose?"

"H'ample."

He was not a man to make a promise he couldn't keep, and Hyacinth and Primrose went about the business of the day unruffled by qualms. On the following day, he delivered the jam to the church hall. The day after, he went up to London on the early train. And on Thursday evening, he ushered Mrs. Smith-Hoggles into the sitting room where she met with the unwelcome sight of her daughter and James Watson seated hand in hand on a sofa. She had been told that they would be present. It was the coziness to which she objected.

"Good evening, Mrs. Smith-Hoggles." Jim got to his feet.

"Hello, Mother," said Emily.

"Why don't we all sit down." Hyacinth entered the room just as Butler exited it.

"Yes, do let's." Primrose came in behind her, appearing more fluttery than ever as she moved toward a chair. "We do believe, Mrs. Smith-Hoggles, that we have information for you that will lay to rest all your worries on your daughter's behalf and encourage you to embrace her fiancé with open arms."

"They are not yet engaged," came the icy reply.

"Oh, yes we are." Emily held up her left hand on which a diamond ring sparkled.

"I'm afraid you're going to have to get used to the idea," said Jim.

"Nothing will induce me to do anything of the sort." Mrs. Smith-Hoggles remained standing.

"Not even the news that James Black did not murder his wife?" Primrose responded in a soothing voice. "I thought you said . . . but never mind, we don't expect you to take our words at face value. We have a witness for you. Someone who was in the house during Elizabeth Black's final months. It is the maid, Kathleen Rose."

"And I suppose she is going to say it was the house-keeper who did the poisoning, now that the woman isn't alive to defend herself." Mrs. Smith-Hoggles gave one of her inelegant snorts. "All I can say is that this Kathleen person must have been in on the murder. Perhaps she hoped to marry that wicked man, but he dumped her for his secretary, when he no longer needed her."

"Why don't you hear what she has to say?" Hyacinth opened the sitting room door to a pleasant-faced woman in a shabby coat and a hat that looked as though it had been sat on more times than it had been worn.

"Oh, Mr. Jim!" She clutched at her black plastic hand-bag as he stood. "How very like your grandfather you are! I'd have known you anywhere, and that's no lie! Such a nice man he was, always so kind and thoughtful to me, and him with all his troubles. And I'm speaking about when his wife was sick, not that awful business after she died. The worst was over for him then, poor Mr. Black. It was watching her suffer that was so hard for him to bear."

"I thought you went out to Australia," Mrs. Smith-Hoggles interrupted in her oversized voice.

"It was a nice place to visit, but when it came to it, I didn't want to live there," said Kathleen. "I'd had all these fantasies, you see, about kangaroos hopping around in the back garden and handsome young men lying out there on beach towels. But it was just like Brighton, if you ask me. Only hotter. And I perspire something awful at the best of times."

"But weren't you supposed to get married?"

"My fellow let me down at the church gate, so to speak. And I never did meet anyone else that seemed worth the bother."

"This is the right Kathleen Rose." Hyacinth eyed Mrs. Smith-Hoggles austerely.

"I'm not saying it isn't."

"Well, I can't see why I'd come pretending to be someone I'm not." Kathleen looked hurt. "It was a shock when my employer told me there was a firm of private detectives looking for me. It's not the sort of thing a decent woman expects. But when it was all explained to me, I was glad of the chance to have my say. The police and those lawyers in their silly wigs only wanted me to say what they wanted to hear. About Mrs. Black being sick so often after she'd eat. And her losing all that weight till she looked like a skeleton, poor soul. Of course, I didn't understand at the time. Such things weren't talked about in them days. I don't think anyone even knew what it was."

"What *what* was?" asked Emily.

"This anorexia business. And that's what was wrong with Mrs. Black. I can see that now plain as day. When I said I'd hear her making herself sick in the toilet, no one wanted to listen. And most of the time she wouldn't eat at all. I remember her husband getting so upset once he tried to force some broth down her. Course, he didn't understand, either. It's a sickness in the mind, isn't it?"

"That explains it." Jim gripped Emily's hand.

"Explains what, darling?"

"Mum said that when her mother was hours away

from dying, she made her promise to eat—not just her vegetables to make her hair curl, but everything. Including lots of cake."

Mrs. Smith-Hoggles sat down heavily. "So perhaps your grandfather didn't murder your grandmother. But there's still instability in your family. And I refuse to allow Emily to . . ."

Hyacinth cut her off. "I think you might do better to concern yourself with the fact that your daughter could end up with an eating disorder, given the fact that you nag her about what she eats."

"You said that?" Mrs. Smith-Hoggles glowered at Emily.

"No, I did," said Jim. "And it's going to stop."

"Don't worry, I don't intend to visit if she marries you." The outraged mother rose to her feet in a swirl of camel coat. "Don't even think about building a granny flat!"

"It never crossed our minds," replied Emily serenely. "Lizzy is going to live with us, under the very same roof. She's earned herself lots of love, and she is going to get it. And if you try to hurt her or Jim ever again, you'll have to answer to me."

She was talking to an empty space. Her mother had stalked from the room. A few moments later, after gratitude had been expressed, Kathleen Rose said she would go and have a cup of tea in the kitchen with that nice Mr. Butler before leaving to catch her train.

"So," Hyacinth said when she and Primrose had Emily and Jim to themselves. "I hope you are satisfied with the results of our investigation."

"Lizzie will be so relieved." Emily gave each sister a hug. "It's awfully sad about her mother, of course, but at least she no longer has to live with questions about what really happened. I do hope you will get to meet her."

"Of course they will." Jim took her hand. "They'll do so at the wedding. You will come, won't you?" The smile he gave them was enough to turn their spinster heads.

"Oh, you must," exclaimed Emily. "You'll be our bridal flowers."

"What a lovely thing to say." Hyacinth's black eyes sparkled suspiciously. "And please don't spoil it by mentioning our fee. There is none. To have allowed you two fine young people to be kept apart would have been a crime of the heart."

"Very true," Primrose assured her after they left, "but don't you feel the least bit guilty. Hy, about having Butler produce that shoplifting acquaintance of his to pose as Kathleen Rose?"

"Not a petal!" came the crisp response.

Marianne Wilski Strong

"The Honored Guest"

Past crimes that cast shadows in the present have been a frequent element of recent crime fiction, usually at novel length. They can be successful in shorter form as well, as shown by Marianne Wilski Strong's evocative memory piece describing the Christmas customs of a Polish immigrant family in Pennsylvania mining country.

I was six years old when I first saw the honored guest. He slipped quietly and with bowed head into the empty chair at the family dinner table. I didn't know, then, that he would haunt me into my adult life.

I went to our local Catholic school, rode my red bike to the local playground on Saturdays, played hopscotch with my friends, excelled in history in high school, went to the senior prom with the boy of my dreams, went to college in Washington D.C., finished Georgetown Law School, and landed a position with a high-powered firm.

In the course of all those years, I saw him only a very few times, always a soft-spoken guest who came, sat in his chair at the dinner table, and then went away as quietly as he had entered, leaving me with an ache of love and sadness as palpable as an open wound.

By the time I was fifteen, he'd come for our holiday meal four times, exactly once every three years. I knew that he was Mr. Porchek, my parents having told me to address him as such. I knew he was my father's brother, but I knew little else. After that Christmas Eve when I was fifteen, I didn't see him again until the day of my Aunt Catherine's wake, thirteen years later.

By that time, I thought that I had forgotten all about

Mr. Porchek, but he was always there, a shadow somewhere in my soul, or in my imagination. He wasn't a visible ghost, trailing chains like old Marley in Dickens. He
was a feeling rather than a presence, like an uprising of
mist from some subterranean stream that ebbed and
flowed inside me, a mist that rose unbidden and then was
forced back into the depths by law books, exams, briefs,
boyfriends, new suits, new furniture, all the flotsam and
jetsom of life that clogs the waters underneath.

No, he wasn't like Marley, but he was a Christmas
ghost all right, a ghost of Christmases past.

Christmas Eve twenty-two years ago began, as Christmas Eves always did, with my waking to wonderful
smells. Mother had made the cookies and cakes days ago,
but on the day before Christmas, by ten in the morning,
she had begun the preparations for our traditional Polish
Christmas Eve dinner, the *Wigilia*, more important to
Poles than Christmas itself.

Unlike Dad, Mom had been born in the United States
rather than in Poland, so our *Wigilia* wasn't strictly traditional. We'd have the usual fish, potatoes, and cabbage,
but Mom also made a piquant cranberry sauce, and an
apple-and-sweet-potato casserole whose sweet-smelling
brown sugar and orange juice bubbled in its baking dish.

I spent that morning helping Mom with the mundane
tasks of wiping washed pots and pans, bringing up jars of
red beets from the cellar, and squealing on Ray, my eight-
year-old brother, whenever he tried sneaking out of the
kitchen to head for the back door. I generally don't like
squealing, but if I had to work, so did he.

By three o'clock, I had pestered Mom enough to fraz-
zle her into allowing me to get out the *oplatek* to lay on
the table, and that's when I found out about our honored

guest. You see, just before dinner starts, Poles share *oplatek*, rectangular wafers of unleavened bread, with each other. You offer the wafer to someone who breaks off a small piece and eats it. At the same time, you make a wish for the person: good health, happiness for their upcoming wedding, etc. Of course, Ray and I always wished each other things like, "Hope you get bit by an anaconda," "Hope all your ugly hair falls out," "Hope your nose gets even bigger," all under our breath to avoid censorship from Mom or Dad.

I liked to set the wafers at each person's place, because that way I got to choose what color and picture I wanted. The wafers were generally white, pink, or blue, with pictures of the nativity, a choir of angels, etc. I always chose the three kings.

I usually set the least desirable wafer at the place set for the guest. We always kept the tradition of inviting an honored guest, because if you had an odd number at dinner, it was bad luck. Mom, Dad, Ray, me, and the baby, Annie, made five. Aunt Mary and Uncle Joe and their two children made nine altogether, so Mom always invited another guest, often somebody from the church who lived alone.

That Christmas Eve, I put the white wafer with its rather sketchy picture of the town of Bethlehem on the guest's plate. "Who's the guest this year, Mom?" I asked.

Mom, opening the jar of red beets, didn't answer.

I assumed that she was concentrating so hard on getting off the top of the jar that she hadn't heard me. So I repeated the question.

Still no answer.

"Mom," I yelled in my most annoyingly squeaky pitch, "who's the guest?"

"A new guest."

"From the church?"

"No."

This terseness was a mistake on Mom's part, because it only set off my determination to have my question answered. "From where, then?"

"From nowhere."

I thought about that. "Everybody's from somewhere," I announced.

"Yeah," Ray piped in, "even you. From the moon."

I stuck out my tongue at him, then turned back to Mom. "Mom!" I screeched.

Mother turned on me. "You don't need to know. Go upstairs and get the good napkins."

I was hurt, incensed, and amazed at such insensitivity on Christmas Eve, especially from Mom. It didn't help that Ray was chuckling evilly behind me.

"I have to know what to call him," I sulked.

To my surprise, Mom turned to me again and nodded. "Yes," she said, "you do. He is Mr. Porchek."

I was confused. That was our name. "You mean Grandpa?" I said.

Ray guffawed. "Grandpa's dead."

"Ray," Mother said, in her Mother, not Mom, voice.

Ray stopped.

"Not Grandpa," Mom said to me. "Just Mr. Porchek, Helen. You must be polite to him and don't ask questions. He is the honored guest and he comes from a very long way away."

I swallowed the "where" that sat on my tongue and began imagining what this Mr. Porchek would look like. I imagined a portly man with puffs of long gray hair. He wore black trousers and a red jacket. Then, I dismissed that image, which even at the tender age of six I recognized as a version of Santa Claus. I went through the repertoire of men I knew, mostly uncles, rejected them all, and settled on Mr. Porchek as a tall stately man with a solemn expression and carefully groomed thick black hair, a version of Monsignor Losciki, who ran our parish church.

As the day wore on, I became more and more curious about our honored guest and began to bother Ray about him, assuming Ray's knowledge to be superior to mine, an assumption I dropped at age fifteen.

In this case, Ray did know more. "He's Dad's brother, dunce," Ray said. Ray never missed an opportunity to reinforce my belief in his superior knowledge.

I felt vaguely disappointed. Dad had three other brothers that I knew of and another uncle hardly seemed to warrant the solemnity with which my mother had told me about Mr. Porchek.

Since Poles begin Christmas Eve dinner at the sight of the first star, or at dusk if snow or rain clouds block the stars, Aunt Catherine and Uncle Dick arrived at about four-thirty with our two cousins in tow. The four of us, Ray, Carol, Carl, and myself, sat in the parlor by the tree, guessing what was in the packages we would open after dinner. Poles traditionally open gifts on Christmas Eve, though Mom always hid a few gifts to be opened on Christmas Day. Ray and Carl scoffed and made gestures of oncoming violent stomach pains at Carol's and my own expressions of desire for dolls. Aunt Catherine and Uncle Dick, who had come into the parlor with us as guards to foil any attempt to open packages, laughed.

At ten to five, the doorbell rang. I tensed, then relaxed, remembering that Mr. Porchek was only another uncle.

But then I caught the look that passed between Aunt Catherine and Uncle Dick. Aunt Catherine looked frightened and Uncle Dick looked grim and angry.

We waited in the parlor, and each of us kids stiffened with the tension we had caught from Aunt Catherine and Uncle Dick.

I heard Dad, who'd just come up from the cellar where he'd been tending the coal furnace, open the door. I heard Mr. Porchek deliver the formal greeting that Poles give when entering each other's homes.

From behind the frame of the parlor archway, I peeked at the kitchen entrance. I was astonished. Dad was holding Mr. Porchek in a bear hug, an unusual display of emotion for my loving but always reserved and polite father.

I turned to check with Ray on how to receive this display, but Ray had his mouth open in surprise, my very first inkling in a gradual process of realizing that Ray did not know all there was to know.

Even more disconcerting, Aunt Catherine had her head bowed and her hands clasped. Uncle Dick stood stiffly, staring straight ahead as if he were guarding some castle keep about to be invaded by the enemy.

I turned again toward the kitchen to watch Mr. Porchek hand Mother some rather wilted flowers. I wondered where, at the end of December, Mr. Porchek had found flowers.

I did not have time to ask the oracle, and anyway, Ray was still looking a bit unsettled. I saw him glance at Carl, who was staring at Mr. Porchek. Carl was two years older than Ray and, as I was very soon to learn, possessed even more knowledge than Ray of the world and its inhabitants.

Dad led Mr. Porchek into the parlor. We all stood

silently for a moment, like frozen actors at the end of a climactic scene just before the curtain goes down.

Then Mr. Porchek bowed to Uncle Dick. Uncle Dick tipped his head down once. When he raised his head, he kept his eyes looking downward.

Aunt Catherine did not move.

I stood still, too, afraid to move, lest I blunder in some unforgivable way that would bring Mr. Porchek's wrath down upon me. For at that moment, I believed that he held some unassailably high position in the family. He did, but in a way I could not have imagined then.

In the silence, I could hear Mother running water. I thought I could also hear the snowflakes thudding against the ground outside, but I now believe that the noise came from my own tense and excited heart.

Finally, Mr. Porchek went forward to Aunt Catherine. He reached for her hand and lifted it to his lips in the formal hand kiss Polish men give to women. They stood like that for a moment, then Aunt Catherine began to cry softly. Uncle Dick mumbled something about helping Mother and led Aunt Catherine from the room.

Dad led Mr. Porchek over to Carl and Ray and introduced him as Uncle Martin Porchek.

For the first time since Mr. Porchek had entered, I had enough wits about me to register what he looked like. I had not been far wrong when I imagined him to look like our tall, stately Monsignor. He had the same high cheekbones and firm strong jaw, only Mr. Porchek had curly hair, a soft white mixed in with the black that reminded me of the wool on the Christmas lamb that was always led into the church and up to the manger that the nuns had set up in the front of the apse. Usually the lamb sat quietly during Mass, but occasionally a lamb, for reasons best known to itself, got a little rambunctious, began to kick the straw about, and had to be led out.

Mr. Porchek did not look rambunctious. He looked sad and happy at the same time. His eyes glistened with tears, but he was smiling and nodding his head at Ray and Carl as if they looked just as he thought they should look. He reached into one of the deep pockets of his heavy gray coat, took out two packages, and handed one to Ray and one to Carl. He said something to Father, and Father turned to Ray and nodded.

Then Father, taking Mr. Porchek's arm, turned to Carol and myself. I looked at Ray for moral support, but he was busy opening his package, which shocked me since gifts were never to be opened before dinner. For a moment, I considered running into the kitchen to cling to Mother's skirts, but I rejected so undignified a move for which Ray would have teased me unmercifully.

Before I could even so much as back up a step, Mr. Porchek was standing in front of me, Dad having brought him first to me rather than Carol because I was the older child. Dad introduced me formally as Helena, not just Helen, Porchek. For a moment, I didn't know he was talking about me. I bowed my head, as Aunt Catherine had done.

Then, Mr. Porchek took my hand. I almost fainted, but Dad's smile gave me strength. Mr. Porchek lifted my hand to his lips and kissed it. I fell in love.

Mr. Porchek reached into another pocket and handed me a small package. I managed to squeak out a "Thank you."

"Thank you, Mr. Porchek," Dad said, and I remembered that Dad had told me that it was polite to acknowledge by name the person who had given you a gift.

I repeated my thank you, adding Mr. Porchek's name,

and watched with some degree of jealousy as he lifted and kissed Carol's hand. I felt pretty sure that he had not kissed her hand quite as softly as he had kissed mine, and I was sure that he had not smiled as broadly as he had at me. I thought, too, that her package looked a tad smaller than mine. I had no doubt that I was Mr. Porchek's favorite.

"It's all right to open the gift now," Dad said.

I began to remove the blue paper, barely restraining myself from ripping it off, a practice Mother considered very impolite to the person who had taken the time and trouble to wrap the gift. When I had finally unwrapped all the paper, I stared at the wooden king that lay in my palm. It was the most beautiful thing I'd ever seen. The king had his arms outstretched, holding up an intricately carved open box, containing the gold, his gift to the Christ child. He had a silver crown atop his flowing black hair and, just below his neck, a star held together the ends of his blue cape.

I decided then that I would marry Mr. Porchek and remained determined to do so even after, a few months later, Ray, to whom I subsequently refused to speak for three days, told me I could not marry one of my uncles.

Having finished baking the fish, Mother called us all in for dinner. Clutching my king, I entered the room walking beside Mr. Porchek.

Not before or since did the dinner table look so romantically, glitteringly beautiful to me as it did that evening. Nothing could spoil that dinner, not even the frown that lowered the heavy eyebrows over Uncle Dick's eyes or the trembling of Aunt Catherine's hand when she held out her *oplatek* to Mr. Porchek and wished him peace. Uncle Dick offered his *oplatek*, too, muttering a standard wish for good health.

Then, Mr. Porchek slipped into the chair for the honored guest and sat looking at us all in turn, a smile hovering on his lips. He was an elegant guest in his blue suit with its striped vest. It was the beginning of my love of vests.

Mother handed the platter of fish, as was fitting, to the honored guest first. He took two pieces of fish slowly and carefully, as if he wanted to stretch out the dinner as long as he could. He handed the fish to Mother with a "Thank you" and a little bow of his head.

He said little during the dinner, only complimenting Mother's cooking and listening to Father's talk of the new church the parish hoped to build.

No one asked him any questions about himself.

One more incident happened at that dinner that convinced me of Mr. Porchek's worth, though, of course, I didn't realize until years later the significance of the incident.

Father picked up the white horseradish and handed it to Mother. She took a little and passed it to Uncle Dick. "Take a good deal, Dick," she said. "I've made some extra for you to take home." Mother knew how fond of horseradish Uncle Dick was.

I shook my head vigorously when Uncle Dick offered me some of the horseradish, as he did every year, teasing me because he knew how I hated the devil's dish, as I thought of it then, and still do.

Father laughed. "Helen has not yet acquired a taste for horseradish."

Mr. Porchek looked at me. "Perhaps little Helcia," he

said, using the Polish version of my name, "is like me. Perhaps she, too, feels that horseradish is from the devil's own kitchen."

I began to plan my wedding.

When dinner was over, Aunt Catherine and Uncle Dick left earlier than usual. Aunt Catherine kissed Mr. Porchek, and though I hated to see Carol and Carl leave early, I was not unhappy to see Uncle Dick go. He seemed to dislike Mr. Porchek, and so was born in me an antipathy for Uncle Dick that I carried for many years.

Father and Mr. Porchek sat at the table enjoying their coffee and talking while Mother came in to watch Ray and me open our gifts.

Afterwards, Ray and I went in to say goodbye to Mr. Porchek before we had to take an evening's nap so as not to fall asleep at Midnight Mass.

I thanked him again for the king, then, panicking at the idea that he would leave, screwed up my courage. "Wouldn't you like to come to Midnight Mass with us?" I asked.

"Yes, indeed, Helcia," he said, bending toward me, "but I cannot. I must return to my home."

"But there will be plenty of room," I protested. "Mother and Father always go very early. And everyone will sing carols. In Polish. And in English, too. Won't you come?"

"Helen," Mother said.

"Perhaps another year," Mr. Porchek said.

"But when will I see you again?" I said. Ray stared at me.

Mr. Porchek tilted his head. "Perhaps God will allow it to be soon."

But He didn't. I did not see Mr. Porchek again for three

years. By that time, I'd decided that, boys being so clumsy and dumb, I would not marry at all. But then I would pick up my king and remember how gentle and kind Mr. Porchek had been.

When I was nine, Mother told me at Thanksgiving that Aunt Catherine and Uncle Dick would be over on Christmas, but not on Christmas Eve. She said that Mr. Porchek would come to *Wigilia* that year. All my young love welled up again. But a week before Christmas, a dark cloud moved over my memories of Mr. Porchek.

Ray and Carl considered themselves much too worldly to hang around with the likes of Carol and me, but one cool evening the four of us were hanging around Larry's store, eating chips and candy and reading comic books, with a promise to Larry that we would indeed buy a few, when I mentioned that the drawing of Silas Marner in the comic classics version I was reading reminded me of Mr. Porchek.

"He looks lonely and sad, just like Mr. Porchek," I said.

"Well, if he's lonely, it's his fault," Carl said.

I challenged Carl immediately. "How could it be his fault?" I said.

Carl gave me his best look of pity. "You mean you don't know?"

"Don't know what?"

Carl glanced round the store for spies, then leaned forward into our little circle. "I heard Mom and Dad talking. They didn't know I was there," he added proudly.

"So what did you hear?" I shouted.

Ray shushed me, looked at Larry and a customer over by the meat counter, and smiled reassuringly. "Almost got the comics picked out," he said.

Carl scooted a bit closer into the circle. "You have to promise not to tell anybody."

"Okay, okay," I said. I was getting sick of Carl's histrionics.

"Well," he said, puffing up his chest, "Porchek's a murderer."

We all stared at him. Even Ray looked shocked. Carol's mouth was open. I think mine was too.

Ray recovered first. "Who'd he murder?"

"Don't know, exactly," Carl admitted reluctantly, "but I heard Dad say that Porchek was taking a real risk coming back for Christmas. Dad said somebody would see him and recognize him. Then all that stuff about the murder would get stirred up and be in the papers again." Carl sat back, looking very satisfied. "I heard him say that."

"Well, who'd he murder?" Ray repeated.

"I don't know," Carl said. "But I bet it was somebody important, like the mayor, or somebody."

I recovered. "That's stupid. It's all stupid. If he was a murderer, he wouldn't come to visit on Christmas."

"Well, Dad said he shouldn't come," Carl said. "And Mom said . . ." He paused. "Mom said that we couldn't stop him. She said we shouldn't have let him go in the first place."

Carol piped up. "What's that mean?"

"Well," Carl said, leaning forward again, "I think Porchek's a mafia guy and . . ."

"What's a mafia guy?" Carol said.

"A gangster, stupid," Carl said. "I'll bet Porchek did a hit and then left town."

"Why would he leave town?" Ray asked.

"Because he hit the mayor or somebody big like that.

He couldn't stay in town after that. The whole family would have been in trouble."

I'd heard enough. "You're crazy," I said.

"I am not. You're just moony over a murderer," Carl said.

I dropped Silas Marner, jumped up, and leapt on Carl, banging his chest with my fists. He was so shocked he fell over.

Ray pulled me off him. "You're the crazy one," he said, glancing over toward Larry who, thankfully, was busy slicing some luncheon meat.

I struggled to get at Carl again. I hadn't finished with him.

"Stop it," Ray said, holding me by the arms. "Or I'll tell Mom."

That stopped me, but I could see that Ray was looking at me with newfound respect. "All right," I said. "But you," looking at Carl, "better not say anything about Mr. Porchek again."

Carl hadn't yet recovered from his shock.

"C'mon, Carol," I said, looking scornfully at Carl, "we've got better things to do."

Carol rose.

I looked down at Silas Marner lying at my feet. A big bubble rose from my stomach into my throat. I remembered Mom saying that we weren't to talk about Mr. Porchek to anybody.

When I got home, I threw up the potato chips and jujubees.

I brooded about Carl's story for weeks before Christmas. I considered talking to Ray about it, but I was afraid that Ray would just agree with Carl. So Ray and I avoided each other.

Finally, a week before Christmas, helping Mom bake cookies, I couldn't stand it any longer.

"Mom," I asked, "how come Aunt Catherine and Uncle Dick aren't coming over for dinner this Christmas?"

"Aunt Catherine isn't feeling well."

It sounded a bit too pat for me. "Are they not coming because Mr. Porchek is?"

Mother turned and looked at me. "What makes you think that, child?"

I didn't reply.

Mother repeated her question, and I knew I wouldn't get out of that kitchen until I gave her an answer. I debated various lies and evasions, but settled on the truth. "Something Carl said."

Mom put down the cookie cutter. This was serious. "What did he say?"

I was in it now and there was no backing out. "He said Mr. Porchek . . ." I couldn't get it out.

"What?"

"He said Mr. Porchek was a murderer."

Mother pulled in a deep breath. She went over to the dining table and gestured for me to join her.

I expected her to tell me that Carl was a silly boy and that I shouldn't pay any attention to him. She would vindicate Mr. Porchek.

"Where did he hear that?" she said.

I despaired. I felt like I'd been sent to the principal's office. My teacher had told us that you would never mix up principle and principal if you remembered that the principal was your pal. But he wasn't, not when you got sent to his office. I didn't think Mother was a pal at that moment either.

"He heard Aunt Catherine and Uncle Dick talking about it."

Mother nodded, as if she'd expected that would happen.

"Is it true?" I asked.

Mother put her fingers over her lips as if she were preventing something from slipping out. "You needn't be afraid of Mr. Porchek," she said finally. "Helen, sometimes people have to do certain things. It can't be helped."

"Then he *is* a murderer," I wailed.

"Helen, do you know the difference between killing and murdering?"

I shook my head. "Aren't they the same?"

"Do you remember when Father set the mouse traps in October and caught the mice?"

I remembered it well. I'd named the little one "Tiny" and cried for an hour when Tiny got executed. Ray had scoffed. "Yes," I said.

"Well, Father didn't want to kill the mice, but he had to. He had to protect us."

"From Tiny?" I said.

Mother smiled. "Even Tiny could carry diseases. So Father had to do it, to protect you."

"So who was Mr. Porchek protecting?"

Mother hesitated. "All of us," she said finally.

I thought about that. "Did he kill the mayor?"

Mother's eyes widened. "What in the world gave you that idea?"

"Carl said so."

Mother smiled. "You mustn't believe everything you hear from Carl. Remember, Carl does not know what happened. What happened happened years ago when Carl was small. Nor is there any reason for all of this to be

123

raked up. Mr. Porchek is our honored guest. We must treat him as such, for he deserves to be honored."

That was enough for me. I figured Carl to be a jerk, but I didn't tell Mother that. She would have objected.

So Mr. Porchek came as our honored guest for another Christmas and he brought me a second king, this one Caspar, carrying his golden urn of frankincense for the child. I put Caspar on my dresser, wondering if there would be a third.

Mr. Porchek was as gracious as he had been three years ago. He talked and laughed more this time, telling us all about the train ride from Chicago, where he was living, and all about the waves that battered the shore when winter winds roiled up Lake Michigan.

But he still had an air of sadness and loneliness about him, and my heart still beat faster when he kissed my hand.

Two winters later, I did a report on Silas Marner and got an A.

There was a third king when I was twelve and Mr. Porchek was our honored guest again. He had aged; his hair was whiter and he put on glasses when he read the Christmas message I had written for him. But he seemed happier that Christmas, and I, having fallen in love with the neighbor's son, who owned a spiffy new Mustang convertible, did not feel too betrayed when I learned that he was going to marry a widow with two children. Mother said he deserved happiness more than anyone she knew.

Mr. Porchek did not come our to *Wigilia* again. Aunt Catherine, looking more and more frail, returned with Uncle Dick, who grew more and more terse. Each Christmas I sat across from him, watching him eat more and more horseradish, and liking him less and less. He, after all, was the one who had first revealed, however inadvertently, that Mr. Porchek was a murderer.

Each year Mr. Porchek sent a little wooden card, like a thin piece of veneer, on which he had carved a scene: Lake Michigan with snow on its edge and the bright light of a star shining on its waters; a tall building with a Christmas tree in front of it; a lonely peasant gathering wood from a snowy field.

I wondered if he was happy with his wife and adopted children. I asked Mother, and she said she thought he was. I never asked her again about his tragedy and we never spoke of it.

The years passed. I didn't think much about Mr. Porchek anymore, except at Christmas when, faithfully, a little wooden scene would arrive. I would always write a thank-you note to the Chicago address. When I was older I thought of going to Chicago to visit Mr. Porchek, but somehow time escaped me, and I never went. I was busy with my life and the events of my childhood seemed insignificant and the old customs quaint but irrelevant. I did not see him again until the day of my Aunt Catherine's wake.

She had succumbed to congestive heart failure. As she had grown more and more ill, Uncle Dick had grown more and more withdrawn, devoting himself to taking care of her. At the wake, he looked small and lost. I didn't dislike him anymore.

Father had helped him with the funeral arrangements and the day of the wake, Mother and I were baking some dishes for Carl, Carol, and Uncle Dick so they would not have to worry about food after the funeral.

"Mr. Porchek is coming," Mother announced in the same solemn voice she had used twenty-two years ago.

"I wondered if he would," I said. "Aunt Catherine is his sister, after all."

"Indeed she is."

"Mother," I asked, thinking about those Christmases with Mr. Porchek. "Why has he stayed away all these years?"

"I suspect," Mother answered, "that he found some happiness at last. He didn't want to return to a place where . . ."

She paused.

"Where he had known tragedy?"

Mother looked at me. "You never asked again." It was a question.

"No," I said. "I guess I'd imagined and believed my own story about what happened."

Mother waited.

"I imagined that he'd killed a real villain, someone who'd cheated poor widows or stole money from immigrants. Something from romantic literature."

Mother was silent for a moment. "You're not far from right, Helen."

I put down the potato peeler and looked at Mother. It was my turn to wait silently.

Mother was about to tell me the story when the back door opened and Father came in, shaking the rain from his hat. Mother fussed over him a bit for getting her clean floor, as well as his feet, wet.

Father came over to sniff at our pot of stuffed cabbage. "For supper?" he asked.

"For Dick and the kids," Mother said, then relented before Father's hangdog look. "But there'll be plenty for you."

Father looked satisfied. He took a chair at the dining table and watched us.

"Did you tell Dick that Martin was coming?" Mother asked.

"I did," Father said. "Dick said that it was too late."

"Too late for Aunt Catherine?" I asked.

Father said nothing.

I went to the dining room and took a seat across from Father. "Don't you think it's about time you told me the story of your brother?"

Father looked at Mother, who nodded.

"Perhaps it is, Helcia," Father said, using the name Mr. Porchek had used and the name Father used when he wanted to express his love for me as his little girl. "Martin . . ." He stopped and looked at Mother.

Mother came over and sat down. "I'll tell her," she said, "though she knows the heart of it. Martin killed a foreman in the mines," she said. "You were not even a year old, and Carol had just been born. He was a terrible man. The foreman, I mean. He sent the men into dangerous parts of the mines. He made them mine much closer to the river than they should have. He fired men if they refused or complained. And he started fights with men. He was a big man, and they say he killed a man himself once."

"But Mr. Porchek is not a big man," I protested. "How could he have killed this foreman? And why? Did the foreman attack him?"

"That's what the police believed happened," Mother said. "You see, the men worked in teams in the mines, and Chester Maliak, that's the foreman, complained that Martin and your Uncle Dick were afraid to begin loading the coal cars until all the dust settled from the explosive devices they used to blast out the coal."

"They were right to wait," Father said. "That's how the men got black lung. Lungs full of coal dust."

"And so this foreman attacked Mar . . . Mr. Porchek?" I said, incredulous.

"This was the coal mines," Father said quietly. "Even in the fifties things were bad in the mines."

"I know, I know," I said. I'd had plenty of friends whose fathers sat in chairs coughing up black phlegm. I'd always been thankful that Father had not worked in the mines. "But why did the police think Mr. Porchek killed the foreman? Did anybody see the attack?"

"No," Mother said. "But the police suspected Martin because he admitted that while Uncle Dick had been preparing more explosives in the upper tunnel, he himself had been working in a part of the tunnel where Mr. Maliak was found."

"But," I protested, "just because . . ."

Father interrupted, putting his hand on mine. "The police found a lunch bucket in the tunnel not far from the body. Martin admitted that it was his. Of course, it was only normal to have his lunch bucket where he was working. But, then, in another tunnel, the police found the coal shovel Maliak had been struck with. It was one of Martin and Dick's." Father paused.

"Was Mr. Porchek arrested?" I asked.

"No," Father said. "You see, no one could prove that Martin had been using that shovel. Anyone could have taken it in the morning. So there was no arrest."

"But then, why did he go away?" I asked, almost crying, twenty years of sensing injustice welling up from me.

"For the family," Father said. "He felt that everyone would forget sooner if he left."

"But why did you let him go?" I said to Father.

Father flushed. He looked at me squarely. "He would not hear otherwise than to go. He had honor and pride. He did not want the children of the family to grow up under a shadow."

I nodded. "I'm sorry. I should have known that. I did know it. I mean . . ." I felt overwhelmed.

Mother put a hand on my shoulder. "We must get ready for the wake," she said. "We should be there when he comes to the funeral parlor."

I didn't know if she meant Uncle Dick or Mr. Porchek. But I wanted to be there for Mr. Porchek. He was important to me again, more important than the lawsuits and negotiations.

An hour later, we sat before Aunt Catherine's coffin at Jendreski's Funeral Home. Uncle Dick, sitting between Carol and Carl, was pale and forlorn. I felt sorry for him, but my deepest compassion went to Carl and Carol, and my fullest concern was for Mr. Porchek. Every time the door to the funeral parlor opened, I turned, anticipating his entry. I wanted to go to him, to tell him that I still had all his wondrous gifts.

At seven, he entered.

He shook hands with the funeral director and gave that slight bow of the head that always made him seem so much to belong to an older world and an older and more courteous time. He walked into the viewing room, and I stood up.

He smiled and mouthed my name, "Helcia." He had on

a blue pin-striped suit with his usual vest and a light blue shirt that made his blue eyes even bluer. His hair was a thick silver-gray. He was stooped, but steady when he walked.

I couldn't move. I just stood there, as struck by the whole Old World romance of his being as I had been twenty-two years ago.

He came over, lifted my hand, and kissed it.

"Hello, Mr. Porchek," I said.

Mother heard and turned. He kissed her hand, then tilted his head, looking at the coffin. "Catherine," he said, "Catherine."

Dad heard, came over, took Mr. Porchek by the arm, and guided him to the coffin. I followed and stood behind Dad and Mr. Porchek.

Mr. Porchek blessed himself at the coffin, knelt, and prayed. Then, he rose and touched Aunt Catherine's hand lightly. "Rest in peace," I heard him say. Then he turned to Uncle Dick. He held out his hand. "It is all past now," he said.

Uncle Dick looked up and nodded. He took Mr. Porchek's hand, held it for a moment, then released it.

Dad led Mr. Porchek to a chair.

I followed and sat on his right, letting Dad talk with his brother. But I was impatient and tense. I wanted my Mr. Porchek to myself. Finally, I cleared my throat several times. Mother, sitting in front of us, turned, looked at me, then told Dad that she wanted to talk to him in the outer room. I made a mental note to take her out to her favorite restaurant.

Mr. Porchek and I talked for forty-five minutes. I told him that I still had his gifts. He told me how he had carved them. We talked about my career and my travels and his stepchildren and wife.

Then I asked if I could come to visit. He urged it, smiling and nodding and, in a slanted script, wrote down his telephone number and his address.

Someone put a hand on my shoulder. I looked up to see Dad. Concerned that his brother looked tired, Dad urged him to come home and rest from his journey, as the funeral the next day would probably prove taxing. Mr. Porchek agreed. He went up to the coffin again, talked to Carl and Carol, under my watchful eye, then gave something to Carol. I learned later that it was a picture of himself and Aunt Catherine as children. In the picture, he had an arm round his little sister and she was looking up at him with an unconditional worship I recognized immediately.

The funeral went by in a blur of candles, prayers, hymns, and relatives, few of whom I paid any attention. I hovered over Mr. Porchek, seeing to it that he sat with the family, ate properly, and wore his coat at the windy gravesite.

I did not wait many days after the funeral before I went to the library. I didn't think that I would find anything, but I had to look. The librarian helped me dig out the yellowed issues of the *Times Dispatch* from twenty-eight years ago.

I piled them on the table, pulled up my chair, and picked up the first one. FOREMAN KILLED. The first article gave a straightforward rendering of the events, with somewhat more colorful language than a newspaper would use today: Foreman Maliak succumbed at Mercy Hospital at six. His family had gathered round his deathbed for their final sorrowful goodbyes. Chester Maliak never regained consciousness from the dastardly and deadly blow that had been delivered to his head. His attacker remained unknown.

A subsequent article focused on his career in the mines, spanning some fifty years from his days as a breaker boy, separating the valuable coal from the ore, to his promotion to foreman.

The next article focused on his presumed attacker: Martin Porchek. "It was known that animosity existed," the article said, "between Martin Porchek and Chester Maliak." The reporter had interviewed some miners who had talked of the animosity. Only at the end of the article did the reporter note that animosity existed between Maliak and most of the miners.

Then I came to some articles that dealt with the questioning of Martin Porchek. The police had focused on him because he admitted that it was his lunch bucket that had been found near the scene of the crime. According to the article, the lunchbox, one of the old black kind with the rounded tops to hold a thermos, had apparently been kicked, probably accidentally in the scuffle between Martin and Maliak, about ten feet away. In his haste to leave the scene of the crime, the reporter speculated, Martin had neglected to retrieve his bucket.

Martin, the article went on, never admitted to or denied killing Chester Maliak. No evidence to prove unequivocally his guilt or innocence had ever surfaced.

I put down the paper. The articles had told me nothing.

I rifled disconsolately through the remaining four papers, but only one had anything further on the incident.

The reporter had interviewed a few more miners, two of whom had placed Martin, Uncle Dick, and two other miners near the scene of the killing. The reporter reviewed the evidence concerning the head wound, inflicted by a coal shovel belonging to Martin and Uncle Dick, and described again the one item found not far from the body and claimed by Martin: the lunch bucket. The reporter dutifully listed the contents of the bucket, standard lunch fare for the miners except for one item.

I looked round the library, slipped the paper into my purse, gathered the rest together, delivered them to the librarian with only a tinge of guilt at my theft, and raced out to my car.

I wanted to go to the public square with my news, but I knew Father and Mother would have to know first.

Mother was repairing a tear in one of Father's sweaters when I came racing in. She looked up at me with disapproval when I let the door slam.

"Helen," she said, shaking her head, "you know that we do not slam . . ."

"Mother," I said, "where's Father?"

"What's wrong?" Mother said, rising.

"Nothing's wrong. Or everything's wrong. I need to tell the both of you."

Mother peered at me over her glasses, then went to the stairs to summon Father.

I sat them both down at the table and told them where I had spent the afternoon. They looked at each other.

They remained quiet while I told them what I had read. Finally, I came to my climactic discovery. "The reporter described what was in the lunchbox," I said, triumph increasing the volume of my voice. "From his description, I know that Martin never killed that foreman. And I know who did."

Mother and Father looked at each other again.

"One of the items in the lunch bucket," I said, anger rising in me, "was a jar of horseradish. Uncle Martin and I hate horseradish," I almost shouted.

Mother and Father sat quietly.

"But," I said, almost accusingly, "Uncle Dick loves it." I addressed Mother. "You and Aunt Catherine always made jars of it for Uncle Dick. It was his bucket. He killed the foreman."

I was joyous. I had exonerated my beloved Uncle Martin.

Father nodded his head.

Only then did I realize what their silence meant. "You knew," I said, standing up in my indignation. "You knew, and you let him take the blame, all these years. And you didn't tell me the truth."

"Helcia," Mother said, "we did not know at first. And Father could not tell you. You are unfair to your father."

Father put a hand on her arm. "Yes, I knew," he said, turning his head to me. "Not immediately, but a few days after it happened. I guessed. And I told Martin I knew. He refused to let me tell anyone. He made me promise not to tell anyone. Except Mother. He knew that I would tell Mother. But he also knew that Mother would honor his wish. He took the blame, and Uncle Dick let him. But he never held it against Dick. And you mustn't either."

"Not hold it against him?" I sputtered. "How not? Why not?"

"Because you have come to love Martin for his kindness and his generosity. Just as he loved his sister Catherine and her children. He did not want them to suffer, to be without a father. He had no wife, no children. So he went away, letting Carl and Carol grow up without the shadow that he took on himself."

I sat back down. I wanted to shout to the world that Uncle Martin was innocent, that he was a man who had sacrificed himself for others. But I knew Father was right. I would *not* tell Carl *or* Carol or anyone. There were more important values than justice. I would not make Martin's sacrifice empty by revealing his secret, and I wouldn't hurt Uncle Dick needlessly, though I couldn't promise not to hold it against him.

"Uncle Martin will come with his family to be with us on Christmas this year," Father said. "It would be best, Helcia, if you said nothing of this to him. It is past, as he said. He has moved on. To bring this up now would only hurt him."

I sighed and took Father's hand. "Of course. I will not disturb him. He is our honored guest."

Benjamin M. Schutz

"Open and Shut"

Clinical and forensic psychologist Benjamin M. Schutz, author of six novels about Washington D.C. private eye Leo Haggerty, offers an unusual police story. The contemporary procedural addresses not only the ways criminals are brought to justice but the politics, bureaucracy, and (sometimes) internal scandals that afflict big-city departments.

J ust how deep did they bury Kincaid?"

"Across the river. Permanent midnights. He's a clerk at the jail infirmary."

The chief shook his head. That was as far away from the action as you could get and still be a police officer. You sat alone at a desk with a silent phone waiting to push papers around three times a month. You slept in the day. That would have cut Kincaid off from contact with just about everyone in the department.

"How long has he been out there?"

"Two years, Chief." Assistant Chief Morlock was reading from Max Kincaid's personnel file.

"Did he ever apply for a transfer?"

"The first year. He was rejected. He didn't try again."

"Why didn't he resign?"

"Too close to retirement would be my guess. Besides, who else would take him after the stunts he pulled?"

"That's true. Well, wake him up and tell him to get down here. His exile is about to end."

In the dark, Max Kincaid felt for the phone as if it were a hooker with time left on her meter. "Yeah?"

"Sergeant Kincaid. This is Chief Stalling's office. The chief wants you in his office in an hour."

"You've got the wrong number." Kincaid unplugged his phone and went back to sleep.

Twenty minutes later, a battering ram was testing his front door. Kincaid rolled out of bed, walked across his efficiency apartment, and viewed the proceedings through his peephole. *My, my,* he thought. *They've got my old lieutenant down here.* Avery Bitterman was one of the few officers Kincaid would listen to, or at least he once was. Bitterman was leaning against the far wall, massaging his scalp. Two uniforms were banging on the front door in tandem.

Kincaid thought about reporting a disorderly-in-public to the station house and giving everyone a shitload of paperwork to do but decided against it. The pleasure would be pale and brief, and Bitterman was one of his last friends.

"Good morning, Officers," he said, swinging the door wide open. "Anything I can do for you this fine summer day? Sorry if I was a little slow getting to the door. I've only been asleep for . . ." He checked his watch. "Fifty minutes."

"That's enough. I'll talk to Sergeant Kincaid." Bitterman pushed off from the wall. The two officers turned and walked down the hall. Bitterman moved past Kincaid, into the apartment. He sat at the card table next to the kitchenette. "Sit down, Max. You might be interested in what I have to say."

Kincaid pulled out a folding chair and stared at Bitterman. They had worked Homicide together for ten years, until everything came apart. He hadn't seen him in over a year, but Bitterman still looked the same.

"Been awhile, Avery. How've you been?"

"Don't ask. Chief Stalling asked me to come over and roust you as a personal favor. He's pissed about the phone call but he's willing to cut you a little slack. That's because he thinks he needs you. That's a real fragile thought, Max. Listen carefully. This is a onetime offer. You know there's been a directive to retrain and requalify all officers in firearms procedures. To do that, they either have to hire new instructors at the academy or reassign officers. Reassignment is cheaper. He wants you to be one of the instructors. That's the offer. Max, it's day work, you can use your skills, and it's a chance to practice what you preached."

Kincaid walked around the proposal, looking for its tripwire.

"Why me? I'm the last person on earth they'd want over there."

"I'll let the chief explain it to you, Max. Just get dressed, I'm supposed to deliver you personally."

Kincaid arrived at headquarters within the hour he'd been originally allotted. The chief's secretary announced his arrival as soon as he walked in.

Chief Stalling looked up briefly and said, "Take a seat, Sergeant." Kincaid did and stared at the top of the chief's head while he read the file on Max Kincaid. When he looked up, Kincaid marveled at how much he looked like a fruit bat. Jug ears, pug nose, all those uneven teeth in that brown face. Kincaid realized he hadn't been listening.

"Excuse me, Chief, could you repeat that?"

"Am I boring you, Kincaid?"

"No sir, it's just that I'm still a little fuzzy. I'd just come off duty when Lieutenant Bitterman showed up."

"What I asked you is whether you wanted a transfer to the academy. You'd be senior firearms examiner and sit on the weapons-use review team."

"Sir, why am I being offered this position? I can't imagine that you'd want me anywhere near the academy. You've got my file there, you know the history."

"That's exactly why I'm offering you the transfer. You made a lot of enemies when you were doing deadly-force investigations. Your memos pissed off a lot of people. Turns out you were right about a lot of things. You know the mayor has mandated complete retraining and requalification of all officers—I repeat, *all* officers—in proper firearms procedure. I read all your memos, Kincaid. I'd think that you'd jump at this opportunity. You'd be able to train officers so they wouldn't be a danger to themselves, their partners, or the citizens. It's what you said was needed."

"So I'm the poster boy for the department's new get-tough policy. If you read those memos, you know I was especially critical of management. You hired hundreds of officers without background checks just so the budget allocations wouldn't get lost. Many of them were never properly trained on firearms. Hell, the shooting range wasn't open for how long, a year? Most officers have never been requalified. You know that a number of women officers were qualifying on their backs. Yeah, we've got people out there with guns and the authority to use them but no skill or judgment, and I'm all for getting them off the streets, but I won't whitewash the department. They were sent out into a combat zone without the tools to do the job. That's management's fault. Was then, is now."

"Are you through? In case you hadn't noticed, I was not part of that 'you' you so eloquently denounced. I was brought in to change the way things are done. I'm asking you if you want to be part of that change. You take care of your end of this and I'll take care of mine. You look old enough to remember this line, Sergeant: 'If you aren't part of the solution, you're part of the problem.' So, what'll it be?"

Kincaid was silent for a while. "When do I start?" He'd been saying yes inside ever since Bitterman told him of the offer, but he didn't want anyone to know how hungry he was.

"Effective immediately. You have a weapons-use review scheduled for one o'clock. It's a homicide. You can move into your office as soon as you like. Cherise will handle the paperwork. The case file on the shooting is on her desk. Take it on your way out. Dismissed."

"Yes, sir." Kincaid stood up and left the office. He picked up the file and began to read it in the elevator. Out on the street, he blinked at the sunlight, at all the people on the streets. He'd slept through all of this for two years. The solitude, the darkness, hadn't been all bad.

He crossed the street, entered the support-services building, and took the elevator to the top floor. Weapons-Use Review was a secured section. He showed his badge, signed the book, and deposited his weapon in the safe. The receptionist told him that his office was 704 and the door buzzed open. He walked back, following the numbers on the doors. 704 had a window on the back wall that offered a view into another office across the alley. The furniture was strictly functional: gray steel desk, gray steel shelves, gray steel file, a chalkboard for crime-scene diagrams. There was a microphone sticking out of the desk, like an antenna on a bug's head. The tape recorder would be in the upper right drawer. He'd move it over as he was left-handed. One chair for the officer, one for counsel or union rep. He sat behind the desk, moved the phone to the left side, and checked the drawers. His predecessor had cleared out everything but the dust. Fortunately, Max asked little of his surroundings and put little into them. He'd be functional by one o'clock. He called the academy.

"Director Hansen, please. This is Sergeant Kincaid."

"Max. Bruce Hansen. I hear you're coming over here. Is that so?"

"God's truth, Bruce. I need to schedule a time on the range. Get myself requalified."

"What for? Christ, you've forgotten more about procedure than most officers ever learn."

"Maybe, but the word from on high is *everybody* retrains. I need to *show* that I'm qualified, not just say so. And I need to be more than qualified. I need to be better than anyone else. When I tell some A.C. that he's failed and he has to turn in his piece, I want to be able to show him there and then how you do it. I've been off the street for two years, Bruce. That's a lot of rust."

"Okay. How about four o'clock today? I'll have Hapgood be your examiner."

"Thanks, Bruce." Max figured he'd wait a week or so before he suggested to his new boss that all examiners should be on the course at least once a week to work on their own shortcomings.

The next phone call would be much harder. He punched in Vicki's number.

"Hello," he heard.

"Hi, Vicki. It's Dad. I'm glad I caught you. Are you in-between classes?"

"Yeah. Where are you calling from?" She hadn't recognized the number on her screen, which increased the likelihood that she'd answer the call.

"My new job. I'm at the academy. It's day work, like normal people. Monday through Friday. I wanted to let you know right away. Maybe we could do something this weekend. It's been quite awhile, you know."

"Yeah, it has, Dad. Quite awhile. Only thing is, I've got some plans for this weekend. I'm going to the beach with a bunch of friends. They're counting on me and I've already paid for the room, so I'd be out the money if I didn't go."

Kincaid picked up right on cue. He wouldn't want such a reasonable excuse to fall flat between them. "Of course, honey. I understand. It's late notice. I just wanted you to know what my schedule is. We could go out to dinner some night when you don't have a lot of homework, or a weekend—do something together. Are you still playing soccer?"

"Yes, Dad. I still play soccer. Every weekend. Have since I was nine years old."

"Well, I'd like to come see you play. When is your next game?"

"We've got a State Cup game next week. It's down in Roanoke. Why don't you wait until there's one nearby. I'll send you a schedule."

"Thanks. That's great. You have my address, don't you?"

"I have your address, Dad. Look, I've got to go. I'm going to be late for my next class."

"Sure, honey. Have fun at the beach." He almost said "I love you," but no one was listening.

Officer Delbert Tillis entered Kincaid's office at one o'clock. He was tall and thin, with a flattop and a pencil-thin moustache. His features were soft and blunt, and his ears flared out at the bottom like Michael Jordan's.

"Sit down, Officer Tillis. My name is Sergeant Max Kincaid. I'm interviewing you as part of the weapons-use review team. This team will collect evidence and make a finding as to whether the shooting was justified or not and whether you will be subject to any disciplinary action. Because a person died as the result of you discharging your weapon, Homicide is also investigating this and will present their evidence to a district attorney, who may indict you criminally. The information from our investigation may be turned over to the district attorney. You have the right to have an attorney present for this interview, or a member of the police-officers' union. Do you waive that right?"

"Yeah. I've got nothing to hide." Tillis stared straight at Kincaid.

"For the record, state your name, badge number, and present assignment."

"Officer Delbert P. Tillis, Junior. Badge number four-one-oh-nine, assigned to the second district." Crisp, confident.

"This interview is being tape-recorded. You or your attorney is entitled to a copy of the transcript of this interview. Why don't you tell me everything that happened."

"Where do you want me to start?"

"It's your story. Start at the start, go to the end. I'm not going to interrupt you or ask any questions." Too often, questioning improved the quality of the story. Kincaid wanted it to be all Tillis.

"Fine, whatever." Tillis looked annoyed.

Kincaid set a pad in front of himself and adjusted the volume on the recorder. His notes would mostly be diagrams, converting the officer's words to actions. He'd note inconsistencies between approved procedures and the report with brief questions. Later, he'd read the transcript and compare his thought processes as he moved through the story with what Tillis had to say, looking first for plausible differences and then for the lies.

"I saw the guy sitting in the car. He looked like he could have been sleeping, or hurt, or dead. I didn't know what. The place was deserted, man. I didn't have no backup. I didn't know what I was walking into, so I pulled out my piece and I came up alongside the car, and, you know, I tapped on the window with the barrel, just, like, to startle him, to see if he woke up, and, *bam*, the thing went off. You know how the piece is, man, it went off. I didn't even pull the trigger. Shit, man, you gotta believe me, I did not mean to kill that guy. It was an accident."

Tillis was leaning forward in his chair, palms open as a sign of his transparency. His eyes had been fixed on Kincaid's blank face the whole time he spoke.

"How long have you been on the force, Officer?"

"Four years."

"All in the second?"

"Yes."

"When was the last time you were qualified in weapons procedure?"

Tillis looked away. "I don't remember."

"Were you notified, were you scheduled?"

"Yes."

"Did you shoot?"

"Yes."

"How many times?"

"Two."

"Did you qualify?"

"No."

"Do you remember what the proper procedure is for the use of a firearm as a door knocker?"

"No."

"No? There is none. It's a gun. How many times have you done this, Officer? Knock, knock, open up—whoops, guess I shot you. Didn't mean to. Sorry."

"None. It's never happened before."

"Lucky you. Where's your piece, Officer?"

"Homicide took it at the scene."

"Let's go back to the start. I'm a little fuzzy there. You said the place was deserted. What were you doing there?"

"I saw this guy's car there, by itself, so I went down to check it out. You know, maybe it was kids doing the nasty. I'd roust 'em, move 'em out of there. It ain't a good neighborhood."

"Where was the car again?"

"Parked at the end of the road."

"Right. So you went down there." Kincaid looked at his notes. "From where?"

"From the street, man. I was driving by. I just picked up some food at Mickey D's."

"Were you on duty, Officer?"

"No."

"A little bit slower this time. You see the car from the street. Then what?"

"I pulled down the road till I got to the car."

"You see anything in the car?"

"No, it was dark. So I pulled up alongside. I got out and walked towards it. That's when I see the guy."

"And the gun goes off. Then what?"

"Then what? I freak out, man. I reach in the door, the window's all gone, open it up, and he falls out into my arms. I mean, he's dead. I know that right away. Half of his head is gone. I just lost it, man." Tillis looked down and shook his head.

"Lost it how?"

He shrugged. Kincaid leaned forward. "I need your words, Officer Tillis; you lost it how?"

Kincaid turned up the volume on the recorder to catch Tillis's whispered reply. "I just dropped him, right there in the dirt. I jumped back, my heart was pounding. His head had flopped over and all I saw was this big hole, and blood, and bones, and all this soft gooey shit, so I dropped him and he fell in the dirt. And I'm thinking, I shot this guy, I killed him, and I can't even pick him up out of the dirt. He shouldn't be lying there like that. It wasn't right, but I just couldn't pick him up. I couldn't. I just went around the car and got my radio and called it in."

"You ever shot anyone before, Officer Tillis?"

"No. I've never discharged my weapon in the line of duty."

"Has the department psychologist spoken to you yet?"

"No. I'm supposed to see him tomorrow."

"How do you feel about that?"

"I don't know. What good is talking about it? It's done. I did it. Nothing's gonna change that."

"You'd be surprised. Talking about things can make a big difference. Killing a man, that's a heavy load to carry alone. Especially an accident. I think that's even tougher than murder. Murder, you get what you want. An accident, jeez, what a waste. But, hey, I'm no psychologist."

Kincaid reviewed his notes and leaned back in his chair. "Listen, why don't we wrap it up right now. I'll get this typed up and the team will review it. If I have any more questions, you'll be at home, right?"

"Yeah."

"This is Sergeant Max Kincaid. Interview terminated at one fifty-one P.M."

Tillis pushed away from the desk. He stood up and shook his head with sadness as he said, "You gotta believe me. I'm telling the truth. I didn't mean to kill that guy."

Kincaid nodded. "I believe you, Officer Tillis."

Alone, he buzzed the front desk. "I have an interview tape that needs to be transcribed. How do I get that done?"

"That's part of my job, Sergeant. Is there anything else you need?"

"Yeah, get me Officer Tillis's personnel file—and who's handling this investigation out of Homicide?"

"Uh, that would be Detective Seymour."

"Seymour? Don't think I know him."

"Probably not, sir."

"When will the report be sent over?"

"Detective Seymour will be bringing it over this afternoon."

Kincaid left the building and walked around the corner to a sandwich shop and ate a "U-Boat" for lunch: bratwurst, sauerkraut, and mustard on a roll; side of German potato salad. Tillis's file was on his desk when he returned. Pulling the window shade up, he rested his heels on the window ledge while he read. A knock on his door turned him around and upright.

"Come in."

A tall, broad-shouldered woman with short, spiky blond hair opened the door. She wore a camel pantsuit over a black turtleneck. Her eyes were a pale blue-gray. Like ice water.

"Sergeant Kincaid? I'm Detective Seymour. Angela Seymour."

They shook hands and Seymour slipped into a chair.

"How much of your investigation have you completed?" Kincaid asked.

"Crime scene and forensics. We're doing a background on the victim and we took a statement from Tillis at the scene. How about you?"

"Formal statement. I've been reading his personnel file. How do you see it?"

"Forensics and crime scene match his story. There was residue on the window fragments. That's where the shot came from. The clerk at Mickey D's said he'd just picked up some food. His tire tracks and footprints match the story. He pulled up alongside the car, walked around, shot him, opened the door, the body fell out, he walked back and called it in, that sort of thing. The tape of the call seems consistent. You know, 'I shot him. I shot him. It was a mistake. I didn't mean it.' He was real shook up. The timing was right. The guy was still warm when we got there."

"How about the gun? Street-ready?"

"Yeah. The magazine was full, so there was one in the chamber."

"This guy is a field manual for screw-ups. You couldn't handle this situation in a more incompetent fashion. He sees this car at the end of the road. Off-duty, he goes down without calling anyone; parks alongside, not in the rear; doesn't ask the guy to step out of the vehicle; uses his gun as a door knocker. I've been looking at his record. No history of use-of-force complaints, no history of improper discharge, no distinctions of any kind. Officer Tillis is a very thin, very pale blue line. I'm going to check his record at the academy. See what kind of training they were doing when he went through. He's never requalified since he got out. I don't know if his negligence is more his fault or ours."

"He learned the right way. We were in the same class. But if they didn't require him to requalify, he wouldn't do it. Delbert did enough to get by, nothing more. On one hand this surprises me, and on the other it doesn't. I don't see Delbert letting his Big Mac get cold to check out a stack of corpses, much less a parked car. That reminds me, what did he say about seeing the car?"

Kincaid flipped back through his notes. "He saw the car from the street. He was driving by after he picked up the food."

"Never happened." Seymour grew animated. Kincaid knew that feeling when the first lie raised its head above the smooth surface of a case. Something to chase, to hunt back to its lair, see if it had family. Seymour began to talk with her hands, and Kincaid noted that she had rings on all of her fingers.

"I drove by the alley and missed it when we responded to the call. You can't see anything from the street."

"How very curious. Then what brought Officer Tillis to that dark and lonely place? What was the victim's name?"

"Ronnie Lewis."

"What do we know about him?"

"Nothing yet, but we're working on it."

Kincaid checked his watch. He had to be at the range by four. "Listen, I've got to go, uh, let me give you my card." He pulled out his wallet, took out a card, flipped it over, and wrote on the back. "This is my home number and my number here. Call me if you find out anything. I'll do the same." He handed her the card.

She reached into her jacket and pulled out a card case

and gave him hers. As she was leaving, she turned back. "I've just got to ask. How did you ever manage to write that on the watch commander's forehead?" She was referring to the final incident that sent him across the river. He had written "750," the code for dereliction of duty, on the watch commander's forehead. Something he didn't notice until, perplexed by the stares and snickers from everyone he met at the station house, he went into the locker room and saw it in the mirror.

"I'll never tell. Who knows, I may be called on to do it again."

"Well, it was appreciated by some of us. The guy was a complete asshole. The rumors of how you did it got pretty extreme."

"Well, maybe you'll tell me about them someday."

"Only if you tell me the truth."

Kincaid drank two large cups of coffee before heading over to the range. He was crashing. One hour of sleep and his biological clock was busted. He hoped that the coffee would just keep him alert, not shaky, when he shot. The drive over reminded him of one benefit of midnights. Empty streets. At three A.M. you were fifteen minutes from anywhere. At three P.M. you were fifteen minutes from the next intersection. Rust and caffeine notwithstanding, Kincaid qualified easily. At his best, he had shot a rapid-fire perfect with his weak hand and unmarked targets.

Kincaid made it back to his apartment by six, knocked down a couple of gin and tonics as sedatives, reheated a pizza, and wondered how long it would take to train his body to sleep at night. After dinner he took out his Ruger .44 magnum and worked on one of his teaching exercises:

field-stripping and reassembling a sidearm with his eyes closed. He could do it with a dozen different weapons. He could do it with one model while lecturing about another. If he'd known his way around his wife's body like that, he might still be married. Or at least on speaking terms.

Morning came and Kincaid went to his office. He wasn't expected to start his examiner's duties until the following Monday. In the meantime, he wanted to get as far into this case as he could. Tillis's file revealed that he was a native son. This had been one of the biggest problems with the recruitment push of five years ago. Local roots and no background checks meant that a lot of thugs got guns and badges, and those thugs had long histories with many of the local drug crews. Far too often, it was those loyalties that ruled—not the oath, the paycheck, the brotherhood of blue. No officer had, as yet, murdered another to further a criminal enterprise, but police had served as security for drug couriers, killing rivals and warning of raids.

Kincaid read on. Tillis lived nowhere near the scene of the shooting, nor was it in his district. God knows there were other Mickey D's in this town. What brought him to that location? Kincaid knew that things would get much more interesting if Tillis and Lewis knew each other. From that fact you could breed a motive, and negligence would be murder.

At ten, his phone rang. It was Seymour.

"You wanted to know about Lewis. Three priors. Nothing heavy."

"Tillis arrest him?"

"No. I looked at Lewis's entire jacket. Tillis isn't mentioned anywhere. He wasn't second officer, or station clerk. He didn't handle crime scene, forensics, property, or records. Nothing."

"What are the dates on those arrests?"

"Ten February this year, six July ninety-six, and twenty-three October ninety-one."

"What were the home addresses for Lewis on those arrests?"

"Same as now: Sixty-one East Markham Terrace."

"Nowhere near where he was shot. Anything from the M.E.? Drugs in his system? Recent sexual activity?"

"Nothing. You think Tillis was cruising and Lewis threatened to out him? Or Lewis propositioned him and he panicked?"

"No idea. I'm just curious about what brought those two guys to that place at that time. I'll settle for God's will if I have to, but it's never my first choice."

"I'll keep looking into Lewis. Maybe Tillis gave him a ticket. We're pulling his driving record. What are you doing?"

"I'll check into Tillis's background a little more, see if I can put them together, even if it's a fifth-grade study hall. Listen, could you fax over a copy of Tillis's statement at the crime scene and his call in to dispatch."

"Sure. Let me know what you find out."

"Will do. Oh, by the way, he was strapped to a seat."

"Who was?"

"The watch commander."

"No." Seymour was both puzzled and impressed.

"Yes."

There was a knock at his door. Kincaid said, "Come in."

The receptionist came in, a squat black woman with short, tightly curled hair, parted on one side.

"Here's that transcript you wanted, sir." She handed him a stack of papers and the tape.

Reaching out, he said, "Thank you. I should have introduced myself earlier. I'm Sergeant Kincaid, and you are . . . ?"

"Shondell Witherspoon." Deep dimples split her cheeks each time she spoke.

"Pleased to meet you, Ms. Witherspoon. When Detective Seymour's fax arrives, I want to see it right away, and I need the department psychologist's phone number."

"That would be Dr. Rice. He's at extension two-one-oh-one at headquarters."

"Thank you."

Kincaid dialed the number as Witherspoon pulled the door closed.

"Support Services."

"Dr. Rice, please."

"Dr. Rice is on vacation. Can anyone else help you?"

"This is Sergeant Kincaid at Weapons-Use Review. Who's handling post-incident debriefings while Rice is away?"

"No one, Sergeant. The other staff positions haven't been filled. Dr. Rice will be back next week. Is there anyone in particular you're interested in?"

"Officer Tillis. When is he scheduled to be seen?"

"I don't know. He hasn't called this office and didn't respond to my calls. I was just typing up an A71 notice for him to appear. He has ten days, then he's put on leave."

"Ask Dr. Rice to call me when he's returned."

"Will do."

Kincaid opened Tillis's personnel folder and looked at his assignments over the last four years—especially the dates of Lewis's arrests in '96 and '01. He called Tillis's station house. While he was waiting to get through, he opened the desk drawers to see if he had a lockbox for his interview tapes.

"This is Sergeant Kincaid. Get me the duty clerk, please."

"This is Binyon, what can I do for you?"

"I'm checking assignments. How far back do your records go?"

"Not very far, Sergeant. We used to keep them here before the computer center opened downtown. They were kept up in the attic, but we had the pipes burst last fall, you know, that record cold spell back in October. Anyway, everything got soaked and it all kind of turned into big bricks of paper mâché. All the pages got glued together so we sent them to the incinerator."

"Thanks." Kincaid was switched over to procurement. Tillis had never requested money for a confidential informant, so he hadn't been using Lewis that way.

There were no paper records connecting them or ruling out a connection. Kincaid was still wondering where he was going to store his tapes when he saw a possible solution to his problem.

It took Kincaid the rest of the afternoon to put Lewis and Tillis together, and it was late in the day when he returned to the office to get Detective Seymour's fax. Kincaid read Tillis's statement and the transcript of his radio call. They were a match with what he'd said in the interview. Kincaid was glad he hadn't relied on Seymour's memory. Two lies and a damaging truth. A motive was gestating. Buoyed by that thought, he called the morgue.

"Medical Examiner's office."

"This is Sergeant Kincaid. You've got a body there, Ronnie Lewis, shot by an officer. Anyone come by to look at his belongings?"

"No. Homicide's in no hurry. They know who did this one."

"I'm coming by to check them out now."

"Whatever."

Kincaid was now unquestionably poaching on Seymour's turf. His job was procedures and personnel—Tillis. She could also investigate Tillis for criminal purposes, but Lewis, the victim, was exclusively hers.

The morgue was down by the river, cut into the slopes so that much of the building was underground. This reduced the energy required to keep the building and its occupants cool. Hot, muggy summer days would send half a dozen citizens over with lead passports and no luggage.

Outside, Kincaid slipped on his new pair of sunglasses. He'd had to buy sunblock also as he adjusted to being out during the day. Thirty cursing minutes later, he walked into the cool, dark entrance hall to the morgue. The visitors' entrance was a ramp with railings. There were benches at both ends. Too many grief-stricken family members had fallen on the stairs at the old morgue. He pushed through the double doors and was refreshed by the chill air. Property was at the end of the hall. He signed in and had the clerk get Ronnie Lewis's belongings. Kincaid felt the clothing to see if anything was sewn into a seam or pocket. Nothing. He felt the length of the belt for bulges, pried off the heel of a shoe. More nothing. All the victim had had in his pockets was fifty-three cents in coins, a wallet, and a ring of keys: one to a Ford; one, probably, to his house; the third to a deadbolt, perhaps, or a storage unit or any of a dozen other possibilities. Kincaid opened the wallet. It contained thirty-six dollars in cash, a driver's license, a social security card, a receipt for a money order, and a picture of a young woman with verandah-sized breasts and an inviting smile. He turned it over. There was no name or phone number. A subway pass. A video-store card, an ATM card, and some business cards stuck behind the cash. Kincaid wrote down the names and numbers, returned the cards to their place, and left.

Back at the office, he called the impound lot to see what was in Lewis's car. Nothing of any use—an ice scraper, a couple of flares, jumper cables, tire-pressure gauge, some change in the ashtray, the owner's manual and some local maps in the glove compartment. Kincaid asked if the maps had any locations circled or routes highlighted. The clerk said yes but none of them were to the crime scene or Tillis's residence and he'd already told that to Detective Seymour, don't you people ever talk to each other?

Kincaid dialed the numbers on each of the cards he'd taken from Lewis's wallet. The first was to an out-call exotic dancer agency. They weren't sending anybody to visit Mr. Lewis until he paid up for the last visit. Kincaid told them to close the account and kiss the hundred bucks goodbye. They had no account for Officer Tillis. The second card was for a bail bondsman who hadn't heard from Lewis since his last arrest. That bond had been paid for by his mother, who'd invoked her own three-strikes-you're-out rule and told Ronnie he was on his own.

Next up was a disconnected line for Novelties Unlimited. The last card was for a lawyer, Malcolm Prevost. Kincaid asked the secretary to get Mr. Prevost and tell him it was a police matter.

"This is Malcom Prevost, what can I do for you?"

"It's about Ronnie Lewis. Is he a client of yours?"

"I doubt it. I don't do criminal defense work. I'm a personal-injury lawyer and the name doesn't ring a bell."

"Could you check, please. We found your card in his wallet."

"Hold on a second."

Prevost returned and said, "He called this office last week, Friday. I was in court—it's motions day. Anyway, my secretary set up an appointment for him for this Thursday."

"Did he say what he wanted?"

"I'm sorry. That's confidential, Sergeant."

"Let me help you with that. Ronnie Lewis won't be able to complain. Other than meeting his maker, he's not available for anything. We're investigating a conspiracy here. Right now I like you for co-conspirator, or accessory before the fact, at the least. Tell me why he called and I'll downgrade you to helpful citizen."

"Fine, fine. All he said was that he wanted me to represent him. He said that he'd been shot by a police officer."

"Did he say anything else?"

"No, that's all."

"Well, here's a hot tip, Counselor. Don't take any calls from his next-of-kin."

Kincaid was walking past the receptionist's desk when her phone rang. He thought about letting it ring but decided that if it was Seymour he'd just as soon get it over with.

"What the hell were you doing over at the M.E.'s office?"

"Stepping on your toes, Detective." Mea culpa as judo, an old bad habit.

"You don't think I can do my job?"

"Not at all. Homicide's a busy unit these days. I've got time to make this case a priority, so I pushed on it."

"Thanks for nothing, Kincaid. I'm Homicide, you

aren't, and this shit won't help you get back here. This is why no one missed you when you got sent across the river."

"I'd say I'm sorry but it wouldn't be true. I can't remember if I'm impulsive or compulsive. Either way, I'd rather piss you off than stop myself. It's nothing personal, ask my wife." Change was a hard turn of the wheel on a lifetime of momentum, his therapist had said. He'd blown straight through another intersection again.

"Maybe not to you, but it is to me. I've shared my last piece of information with you, Kincaid, and it is personal."

"Let me make it up to you. I'm going to interview Tillis again tomorrow. He knew Lewis and I can prove it. Why don't you watch it behind the glass. Run with whatever I get."

"Oh, I will. After I nail your feet to the floor. What time?"

"Nine o'clock."

Seymour hung up and Kincaid called Tillis and set up the appointment. He went to the range and shot five hundred rounds' worth of tranquilizers and then went home. At home, he watched a first-round game of the women's World Cup. It used to be that the women's play was mercifully free of the ludicrous dives, cynical fouls, and feigned injuries of the men. When a woman went down, she was fouled. If she stayed down she was hurt, period. But big money had changed all that. Maybe Vicki'd like to watch a game with him, was the thought he drifted off to sleep on.

Tillis sat down in the interview room. Kincaid was not obliged to tell him that he was being observed but he had to tell him that the session was being taped. Angela

Seymour pulled her chair closer to the glass, turned the volume up slightly, and flipped open her notebook. If she got anything out of this interview she wouldn't have to wait for a transcript.

"Officer Tillis, who was the man you shot?"

"Don't know. His ID said he was Ronnie Lewis."

"You ever met him before?"

"No. He was a stranger to me."

"That so? This interview is conducted just like any internal-affairs investigation. If you lie to me, you can be dismissed. Did you ever meet Ronnie Lewis before?"

"No. I never met the guy, that's the truth." Delbert's voice rose with righteous conviction.

"No, Delbert. That's not the truth. Let me tell you what the truth is. You knew Ronnie Lewis. You met him at least twice. You were on transport the last two times he was arrested. Transporters don't have to sign anything as long as there's no injury to the prisoner. Reasonable that you'd think there was no way to connect you two, but I matched up the arrest times on the paperwork with the dispatch calls on the runs. They keep the tapes of those calls for three years, Delbert. I heard your voice on them. You knew Ronnie Lewis. You knew Ronnie Lewis was down at the end of the road when you went there."

"I did not." Tillis voice quivered as the impossible became the inevitable.

"Delbert, you couldn't see the car from the road. You had no reason to go down there unless you knew someone was there." Kincaid stopped. "This is important, Del. This is premeditation. This isn't positive policing, this isn't street initiative. You went down there to meet a man you already knew. We're waving goodbye to negligence, hello murder two."

"Murder two? Are you nuts, man? I told you I shot the guy. It was an accident. I didn't mean it."

"That's the beauty of it, Delbert. I believe you, I really do. Have from the beginning. It was an accident, *and* it was murder."

"You're crazy, man. I don't have to listen to this bull-shit. I want my union rep here. If you're so damn certain of all this, why hasn't Homicide picked me up? That dyke bitch would love nothing better than to bust my ass. I was with her at the academy. She was a ball-cutter then, she's a ball-cutter now."

"That was the hard part, Delbert: motive. Motive and intent, that's what I needed. You can stop the interview now if you want. We can wait for your union rep to get here. I don't care if you don't say another word. You might want to hear what I have to tell you alone, though—without him here. See, I don't think they're go-ing to be too eager to rush to your defense. Are they?"

Tillis stared back, impassive, defiant, but wondering if Kincaid could back up his words.

"I wanted you to be a simple schmuck, Delbert. A poorly trained, unqualified guy who had no business be-ing a cop, sent to do an impossible job without the tools. I could have pounded on your failures like a drum while I preached my personal brand of truth. You were almost as big a victim as Lewis. That's what I wanted to see, but you wouldn't let me. No, you're anything but simple, Del-bert. You've failed to qualify twice. Once more and you're out of a job. I'll bet you're not independently wealthy. Your friend Ronnie Lewis is not a captain of industry ei-ther. How do a small-time hood and a marginal cop turn that around? Work with what you've got. Here's the best part, Delbert. I'll even spot you being careful about your

162

plans, but you should have used a better quality target than Ronnie. He called an attorney to represent him in a shooting. Last week. So Ronnie's either clairvoyant or incredibly stupid. I'll go for number two." Kincaid watched Tillis try to stifle his disbelief at Lewis's stupidity and greed.

"You like that, huh? What a fool. Couldn't wait to get shot first, then line up the lawyer. Who knows, maybe all the good ones would be taken. Here's where your accident becomes murder. I see an insurance fraud here. You shoot Lewis. He sues the city for what? A million dollars? Isn't that typical these days? You two split the proceeds. Your ineptitude and lack of training provides the necessary element of negligence. Hell, my report would have been your best piece of evidence. This shooting was definitely unjustified. In fact, let me tweak this one a little bit. You get a lawyer and sue the department for negligence in your training—you shouldn't have been allowed out on the streets with a weapon. Hell, I'll stipulate to that. You double-dip your ineptitude and walk away a millionaire. Now that's a golden parachute. Every other cop on the force pays your severance pay. I don't think so."

"You haven't said a word about murder, Sergeant. It's what it always was—an accident." Tillis even smiled a bit, confident that Kincaid was blowing smoke and couldn't prove the points he was making.

"Murder it is. A person killed in the commission of a felony is murder two. Fraud's a felony. You knew him; you went to a secluded place to meet; your partner had lined up an attorney to represent him in a gunshot case. That's a conspiracy. You were to provide the bullet. And you did. That makes it murder. And an accident. You meant to shoot him, not kill him. I said I believed you."

The door to the interview room opened and Detective Seymour walked in. She had her right hand extended toward Tillis. She moved her index and forefinger together like scissors and went, "Snip, snip.

"Delbert Tillis. You have the right to remain silent, anything you say can and will be used against you in a court of law. . . ." The Miranda warning went on as Tillis shook his head.

"What tipped you off? Why even bother to look into this? I mean, what could have been more open and shut?"

Kincaid knew that all violent deaths were best approached as open and shut: with an open mind and a shut mouth. "It was something you said, Delbert. From the very first, you said it was a mistake. You didn't mean to kill him. That's right. It was a mistake. You didn't mean to kill him. That's right. It was a mistake. You didn't mean to kill him. But you never said you didn't mean to shoot him. That's what bothered me."

This one is for Adam, who when he saw the light, his spirits rose and he was young again.

Dan A. Sproul

"Oh, Mona"

Horseracing has been the favorite sport of mystery
writers as well as kings. Some, like Dick Francis, feature
the owners, trainers, and jockeys; others, like William
Murray, view the sport from the bettor's perspective. In
the latter category are Dan A. Sproul's short stories about
Miami private eye Joe Standard. The following is one of
the best racing mysteries in short-story form.

Miami is a seasonal city. Things tend to diminish in the summer. Traffic jams are smaller; so also is the price of a hotel room. Calder racetrack produces scrawny race cards and puny mutuel handles. The private detective business suffers, too. Like everything else, the P.I. business goes into a wait-and-hold mode until the first snowflake plummets earthward in Canada, New York, and New Jersey. Then things pick up.

The pivotal date is October fifteenth. Along about then begins a direct corollary between the influx of visitors and the increasing day rate at the Miami Beach hotels. Horses begin to ship into Calder for the Tropical meet. Life gets a little less laid back.

At Standard Investigations we gear up for the season by making sure the phone bill is paid. I use the plural pronoun *we* strictly in an editorial sense. There is only I, Joe Standard, sole proprietor, except on those rare occasions when my good friend Frankie Swinehart, or Swine as he prefers to be called, comes in to assist me. Normally Swine toils as a security guard at Calder Race Course. It works out for him, since he can get paid and lose it back without leaving the premises, thus embracing the economy of saving time and mileage. Swine is incapable of winning any kind of substantial bet on a horse. And worse, he's been unable to absorb this awful truth even though it has been demonstrated relentlessly by more than twenty years of betting with both hands.

Along with the lack of mental acuity necessary to master the fine art of handicapping, the fates dealt him a vicious blow in the looks department as well. Swine confronts the world with hyperthyroid, cue-ball-like eyes and teeth with a crooked and pronounced buck. He never had much luck with the girls. What he did have was honesty, loyalty, and a tender-hearted simplicity that belied his looks. I guess that's why it was so difficult for me to believe Ordway Crook when he called to tell me that Swine had been arrested for the murder of his girlfriend, Mona Phillips.

Ordway Crook, as you might guess from his name, was a lawyer, a divorce lawyer to be precise. We had a sort of business relationship. Certain of my cases produced a disgruntled spouse from time to time. I referred these unfortunates to Crook. He in turn paid me a small referral fee.

"They got in a fight," said Crook over the phone. "He beat her up pretty good. The cops at the scene say it looks like she might have cracked the back of her head on the corner of a small refrigerator in his room when he knocked her down."

"What does Swine say?" I asked.

"Says he didn't do it. What else? That's what they all say." There was a slight pause. I half anticipated what was coming next. "You know I don't do pro bono work," he continued. "The court will appoint him a public defender. But I promised him I'd call you. He said you were tight with Donk Nolan, the bondsman. He wants you to arrange bail."

"How much?"

"A hundred thousand."

At the onset there were several things that went contrary to all reason, the first being that Swine had a girlfriend; the second, that he was able to get *any* female inside the gopher hole he lived in.

I'd done skip trace work for Donk Nolan. Tight wasn't the way I'd have described our relationship. We weren't tight. We were loose. I didn't particularly like Donk. He demonstrated with enduring passion that he liked me even less, but rarely to my face. Bitterness, mistrust, an unrestrained caustic disposition—it was in his genes. Possibly these attributes are a requirement for any successful bail bondsman.

Donk would require ten percent up front to post the bond: ten thousand. I had the money. Business had been good. My interest in Down and Out Stables was paying off. Best of all, I'd quit betting the gimmicks at the track. Win bets only—good money management. I was pulling it in steadily. In The Bag Boyd had set me up a stock portfolio. Last I looked, it was near thirty grand. But the thing was, I'd been tapped out most of my adult life. Whatever the odds are that the Second Coming will happen next Tuesday, double them. That's about the chance of my handing ten thousand of my own money over to Donk Nolan. There was another way. I picked up the phone.

"Standard? It must be Halloween. What the hell do you want?"

"I need a favor."

"That's rich," he said, and hung up the phone.

I called him back.

"Nolan Bail Bonds," he answered.

"Kyle Breen," I said. "What's it worth to you if I bring him in?"

"Standard, my old buddy. You said you wasn't interested in Breen. I got Golby on it."

"Golby puts his shirt on backwards," I said. "Breen's too mean for him. He'll hurt him bad and enjoy the hell out of it. Golby knows it. He won't go anywhere near Breen. You know it, too. Why do you think I didn't want to fool with him? But things change. How much are you on the hook for with Breen?"

"What you want to know for?"

"I want to make a deal."

"A deal? You want a deal? Okay, I got his mother's house, but it's only worth about a hundred and sixty G's. Kyle's bond is a hundred and seventy-five thousand, and I'm gonna lose my fee. There ain't much time. What kind of deal you talkin?"

"Swine's in the Dade County lockup. I need you to go down and post his bail—a hundred thousand. And I want you to waive the ten thousand fee."

"Yeah right. So when that little bug-eyed jerk takes off and you don't show up with Breen, I'm out of business."

"Think positive. I'll get Breen. If I don't, I'll work the ten thousand off. Swine won't go anywhere. I'll make sure of that."

"If I weren't desperate, I'd tell you to shove it."

"I know you would."

A brief pause ensued. "All right, it's a deal," said Donk. "But you only got three days."

I told Donk to bring the papers on Kyle and meet me outside the courthouse. Kyle Breen, six foot six, two hundred seventy pounds, played backup tight end for the Jets for six years. He was kicked out of the NFL because of a manslaughter charge for killing a man in a barroom fight. After that, he turned ugly—arrested for assault during the commission of a crime. Served only about three years. One detective lost an eye trying to take him the last time.

I'd educated myself on Kyle's history when Donk offered me the job originally. It's always a good idea to know what you're dealing with. I turned Donk down because I'm not that young any more . . . and not that hungry. Besides, you don't stay all that fit if the only exercise in the sport you enjoy involves flipping pages in the *Form* and walking back and forth from the track parking lot. Then too, the idea of Donk, the greedy little weasel, dropping fifteen or twenty thousand kind of gave me a warm feeling all over. But . . . things change.

Outside the county jail Swine was jubilant. He gave me an awkward hug. Donk handed me the sheet on Kyle. "A bench warrant's been issued," Donk said. "There's the arrest authorization—there in the blue envelope. You got to get this miserable #%@*&t%$, Joey."

"Don't call me Joey," I said, studying the documents he gave me. "What's this address you have listed for him?"

Donk shrugged. "That's the address Kyle gave me. It's his mother's house. But he ain't there, I can guarantee you that."

I took the picture of Kyle from the packet. Ugly bastard, even his face had muscles. Donk continued his dialogue of hand-wringing despair as Swine and myself piled into my vintage Mustang.

Donk shouted at our departure: "Remember, you only got three days before the bond forfeiture to the state!"

"What's got him all excited?" Swine wanted to know.

I explained the arrangement I'd been forced to make with Donk to get the bail for his release. I went on to tell him what I knew about Kyle Breen. Then I asked him what happened with Mona Phillips.

"I didn't do it, Joe. You know I couldn't do nothin' like that."

"What happened, then?"

Swine was in the dark. He told me that Mona Phillips was a seller at Calder, a dispenser of pari-mutuel tickets. He said that he took her a cup of coffee now and then when she was on the job. But they weren't lovers, he insisted. He asked her out once. She refused, so he never tried again. Sometimes they rode the bus together. She had an apartment just down the street from his efficiency.

"So what was she doing in your apartment?" I broke in.

"I ain't sure. She knocked on the door, so I let her in. She said she ran out of cigarettes and wanted to know if I had any. Well, you know I don't smoke. Hell, *she* knew that. She . . . she acted like she was kinda coming on to me. She asked me to go down to the corner and get her a pack of cigarettes . . . said that while I was down there maybe I should pick us up a six-pack of beer."

"So what did you do?"

"What the hell do you think? I took off down the street for the corner store."

"Hmmm. What about when you got back?" I prompted.

"I was gone maybe fifteen minutes tops. When I got back, I was gonna knock for her to let me in, but the door looked busted in. It was partway open, so I pushed it open all the way and walked in. Bang, the lights went out. Somebody conked me on the noggin."

"Then what?"

"Then nothin'. Old man Chainy comin' back from the liquor store stuck his sorry drunken face in my open door and called the cops."

The yellow crime-scene perimeter tape still stretched across the broken door to Swine's apartment. We tore it down and went inside. The dwelling was dark, *Racing Form*-strewn, and decorated in antique chipped enamel. A lone hundred watt bulb suspended from mid ceiling on a scraggly cord illuminated, but failed to overpower, the utter dinginess.

"This place gets worse every time I come in here," I commented. "Did you ever get the drains fixed?"

"Everything works fine," said Swine, stepping carefully over the chalk outline of Mona in the middle of the concrete floor. "You think it's okay to erase that?" he asked.

"I imagine it'll wear away in a day or two," I told him, an answer he accepted eagerly. On the floor near the chalk outline was a cereal box with cornflakes spilling out. Half a dozen pari-mutuel tickets were strewn about on the countertops and floor. An unopened box of Rice-A-Roni lay conspicuously by the door along with a six-pack of beer. I pointed out these items to Swine and asked if he remembered their being there when he woke up.

He pointed at the six-pack by the door. "Yeah, that's the six-pack I bought. The cops took the cigarettes. I had them in my pocket. And I know the cornflakes was there. Every time the cops stepped in them there was a crunching noise."

"So, except for the six-pack, how do you explain the rest of the stuff?" I asked. "Who scattered the tickets all over? Who put the cornflakes on the floor and tossed the Rice-A-Roni over there?"

"Hell, I don't know. It wasn't me."

"Okay if it wasn't you and it wasn't the cops, it must have been Mona or the killer. Don't you figure?"

"Uh, yeah, that's right," Swine said. "But why would Mona want to dump my cornflakes on the floor?"

I pointed out to Swine that he was failing to grasp the essence of the picture presented here. Obviously somebody was looking for something. It appeared as if they stopped before they got into the search in earnest. Either they found what they were looking for or they were interrupted. Otherwise there would have been a lot more stuff dumped from the shelves and cupboards.

"Can you tell if anything is missing?" I asked him.

Swine did a quick perusal of the tiny room. "I don't see nothin' missing," he said.

I picked up one of the mutuel tickets from the top of the small refrigerator. It was dated two weeks before. "What's these tickets?" I asked.

"Oh, I keep all my losing tickets in a shoebox for the year. Then when I hit the biggy I got some losers so's I don't have to pay the income tax. You was the one that told me to save 'em."

"It might have been a needless precaution," I told him. "I don't remember you ever hitting a payoff big enough to get near the IRS window. Where's the shoebox?"

Swine pointed to a small floor shelf in the corner. "I keep it right over ... damn. It's gone."

Before I had time to absorb this new turn of events, a small mouse scooted in little spurts across the floor. We stood stock-still and watched it make its way to the pile of cornflakes and begin to nibble away.

"Don't move," said Swine. "That's Martha."

"Martha? How do you know it's a female?"

"She's got her babies behind the refrigerator," Swine explained.

"Jeez, are you nuts? How the hell can you live like this?" I asked.

"Like what?"

Now you understand why it was hard for me to believe that Swine could kill anything with malice. I told him that he was on me for the next few days until I could find Kyle and figure out what happened with Mona. I convinced him that if we were going to clear him it would take both of us to unravel his predicament. Which was true. But mainly I wanted to make sure I could find him. I trusted him not to jump bail, but if things should turn sour—well, you never know.

I have my office in the back of the Sunbelt Realty Building. It's only one room with a community toilet down the hall, but it works for me. While Swine was calling Security at Calder from my office to explain why he hadn't shown up for work, I supplied Bonnie in the Sunbelt Realty office with Kyle Breen's Social Security number and the address from Donk's documentation. In a matter of a few minutes I handed her twelve dollars, and she handed me a credit report on Kyle Breen. It was standard procedure. Sometimes it paid off, sometimes not. I took the report with me into the office.

Swine was stretched out on my cot beneath my gigantic photograph of the matchless Seattle Slew edging away from Cormorant approaching the far turn in the 1977 Preakness Stakes.

"I told them I was gonna take a coupla days vacation," he said. "Where we gonna start at?"

"Don't know yet," I mumbled, studying Kyle's credit

rating. The report was about what you would expect. No-body was going to sell this guy a used car. There was one item that caught my eye: Kyle had an active credit card. And it wasn't yet maxed out. It was a beginning. I explained my plan to Swine.

"What kinda weirdo are you?" Swine asked. "We can't break into his mama's house."

"We're not going to break into her house," I reassured him. "Hopefully she'll just hand it over if we play our cards right."

On the way Swine issued relentless warnings about the cruelty of harassing old ladies, posing various scenarios: she could get excited and have a heart attack, or fall and break her hip, or call the cops. All this needless concern rushed from memory when Mrs. Breen opened the door. She was anything but frail. Old but tall and big-boned, she filled the doorway. "What do you punks want?" she asked.

Meeting Mrs. Breen could only add to the wonder of how nasty Kyle must be. But I forged onward.

I pointed to Swine. "This is Mr. Squeege. My name is Colbert. We are representatives of Visa, the credit card company." I waited for her reaction, but she simply stared at us in sinister silence. I struggled on. "There is a credit card for a Mr. Kyle Breen listed at this address. We are here to pick up the card for non-payment."

"Kyle's not here, neither is the card," she told us. "Anyway, I sent a payment in on his card two weeks ago—so hit the bricks."

I put my hand against the door she was about to slam in our face. "Well, if you have a statement from us that reflects the card as being current, I guess there could have been a mix-up at the main office. Have you got your last statement?"

She swore and thudded across the living room, leaving us in the open doorway.

"Jeez, ain't she a load," Swine commented in her absence.

She returned with the smirk of virtuous right on her side and thrust forth the vindicating document. "Here's the statement," she said. "See for your ownself. Then get the hell out. Never heard of such a thing . . . Visa got their own police. World's goin' to hell."

The statement was only eight days old. "We'll need to keep this," I said. "You know, to straighten things out back at the main office."

"Well, you can't have it," she shouted back. She made a grab for it but missed. She might have been big, but she was slow. Me and Swine were in the Mustang halfway down the street before she even got to the sidewalk.

Back at the office Swine sat on the cot while I studied Kyle's credit card statement. "When we gonna work on my case?" he asked. "I got a preliminary hearing in a few days."

"First things first," I said. "I had to find out if Kyle was still in Miami. According to his credit card statement he was still in town ten days ago. But since you bring it up, let me ask you a few questions."

"Shoot."

"Were you still knocked out when the drunk looked in the door and called the cops?"

"Yeah, one of the cops woke me up. Chainy was standin' in the doorway yellin' at the cops, tellin' them what a vicious bastard I was."

"You told the police what happened?"

176

"Yeah, I told 'em. I showed 'em the lump on my head. They booked me anyway."

"How did they identify Mona?"

"Whaddaya ya mean?"

"I mean, did they check in her purse for an I.D. or a driver's license, or what?"

"No, I told them who she was," said Swine. "Come to think of it, there wasn't any purse."

"Mona didn't carry a purse?" I asked in surprise.

Swine was thoughtful for a moment. "No, she had a purse. One of them bag things that hung on her wrist. But it wasn't there when the cops was diggin' through my stuff. At least, I don't remember seein' it."

"I'll check with Crook and see if we can persuade him to get some details from the D.A. Sounds to me like there are a lot of holes in their case. Cops usually take the path of least resistance. In this case you were it. As far as I can tell, the facts are as follows: Somebody struggled with and killed Mona. Somebody attempted to search your apartment. Not necessarily in that order. The killer took with him or her your box of losing pari-mutuel tickets and Mona's purse. He or she might or might not have found what they were looking for. My guess is, they didn't. If the killer had the item and knew it, only the item would have been taken...whatever the item is. There would have been no reason to take your tickets and Mona's purse, unless they thought the item was in the purse or the box. So, they were in a rush and not sure they had it. Now we need to determine what 'it' is. What have you got in your crappy apartment that somebody would kill for?"

"Nothin'. And you can believe that."

"If that's true, Mona must have had something on her

that she hid in your apartment while you were off at the store . . . something somebody wanted pretty bad. Something that fit in her handbag."

I could just make the eleventh race at Calder. I ripped off a piece of notepad, scribbled a phone number, and handed the slip to Swine. "That's the number to my new mobile phone. I got something I want you to do."

"Get out," said Swine. "You got a cell phone! When did this happen?"

"I'm trying to move into the twenty-first century here," I told him.

Kyle's credit report showed that he had used the card recently four different times at the same restaurant, The Boathouse in north Miami. I explained this to Swine. I handed him the photograph of Kyle that Donk had given me. "Stake out the restaurant. If you spot Kyle, follow him when he leaves and give me a call on the mobile phone." I handed him two twenties. "Here's busfare and some lounging money."

"What are you gonna do?" he wanted to know.

"I'm going to the track," I told him. "Maybe I can get filled in on Mona—talk to the other sellers, see if I can pick something up. Where was her window?"

Swine instructed me as to where in the large Calder racing plant Mona did business.

It was twelve minutes to post for the eleventh race when I went through the grandstand turnstile. One of the benefits of a well-run and beneficent racetrack like Calder, they let you in free after the seventh race.

The crowd had thinned; most were probably busted out by now. I grabbed a discarded program from a trash barrel and did a quick survey of the eleventh race: seven furlongs on the main track for two-year-old fillies. It was a long race for young, inexperienced contenders. A smart handicapper should be looking for a horse that had at least been the distance or gone longer.

After digging a little deeper in the trash barrel I managed to salvage a *Form* and ripped out the page with Calder's eleventh race. It was in bad shape, damp with what I hoped was coffee, but still legible. Number three, Dainty Lady, had gone a mile and a sixteenth last out—a terrible race. But there were no worldbeaters entered, and she was the only entry that had gone more than six furlongs. The trainer was good with two-year-olds. The jockey was competent and usually sober. Dainty Lady was nine to one. It was a chance to get back the forty that I'd given Swine.

I went to the third window in from the University Drive side, the north entrance on the ground floor of the grandstand—Mona's old window. There was a Cuban woman there now, with orange hair.

"Ten and ten on the three horse," I said to her. She punched up the tickets and grabbed the twenty I offered. "Did you know Mona, the gal who used to work this window?"

She told me in broken English that she had worked upstairs; this was her first time in the grandstand. I moved over to the guy working window two from the north entrance. "How about you? Did you know Mona?"

He was Cuban also, but his English carried only the faintest Latino trace. I explained that I was a private investigator looking into her death. "Yes, I knew Mona," he told me. He seemed cooperative. I asked him what kind of person she was.

"She was okay," he responded. I waited several seconds for the expanded version.

DAN A. SPROUL

"What does that mean?" I asked, in an effort to draw him out. "She was a good seller? She gave to the Salvation Army? She didn't pick her nose? What?"

One window to my right and four windows to my left were open with no customers. So you can imagine my consternation when an old nimrod with a cane poked me in the back.

"Hurry up," he said. "I want to make a bet."

"Go over there," I instructed him, pointing to the woman with the orange hair.

"I ain't goin' over there," the old man shouted hysterically in my face with beer-stained breath. "This is my lucky window. Bet, or get the hell out of the way."

This I well understood and let him pass. He bet twenty to win on the six. The horses were out of the gate as he turned from the window. We both stood stock-still watching a nearby monitor as his six horse broke on top and drew off to a two length lead. Dainty Lady, my three horse, was last into the first turn.

"*Come on, Cholee!*" he shouted. "*Open up with that six horse, Benny, open up!*"

Cholee had already gained a five length lead at the far turn. My three horse had only beaten one horse.

"Come on, three," I muttered with faint heart.

The old man cackled gleefully as Cholee entered the stretch turn still holding four lengths in front. "*You got it now, Cholee! Pour it on, Cholee!*"

After the stretch turn Cholee began to take baby steps. Her lead diminished rapidly. Only one horse was now moving with any energy. And that horse was . . .

"*Come on, Dainty Lady!*" I screamed as the filly came six wide into the stretch and commenced to gobble up contenders.

"Keep going, Cholee," the old punter beseeched in a whisper of desperation as the front runner strained unsuccessfully to maintain her slim lead.

As Dainty Lady sailed past the old man's selection, I screamed: *"Drop dead, Cholee!"* The old bastard turned rapidly and rapped me on the shin with his cane. I grabbed my leg to stem the pain and missed the finish.

"Damned communist," he spit at me before tottering away.

I presented my winning ticket to the old man's lucky seller, the one I had been quizzing before I got into it with the old maniac. Dainty Lady paid $20.20 and $6.40. My ticket was worth a hundred and thirty-three bucks. As he counted the cash out, I asked again about Mona.

"I don't want to say anything bad about the dead," he commented.

"Why not?" I asked. "The odds are pretty good the dead can't hear you."

My leg hurt like hell. I could feel a large knob beginning to rise on my shinbone. Raul was the name of the lucky seller of the old lunatic who'd rapped me with the cane.

It took awhile to drag the information from him. Mona had only been on the job a little over a month. She kept to herself, Raul told me. Didn't have any close friends except maybe Swine, who was obviously sweet on her and brought her coffee down from the second level every day. He then alluded to the fact that she was probably a thief, explaining that the track had warned her numerous times because of shortages in her cash drawer. When I asked if any thing unusual had happened in the last day or so, I hit pay dirt. He told me about the superfecta ticket.

Raul had forgotten which race, but the superfecta had paid over thirty-six thousand and there was only one ticket sold. "The guy got in Mona's face," Raul told me. "He was screaming at her that he'd hit the superfecta. Claimed that he forgot to take his ticket and she still had it."

"How could the guy be so sure that he hit the super?" I asked.

"He was screaming at her: *I always bet my address, one, three, two six—that's my house number, one, three, two, six Alexander.* Then he called her names and threatened her. When he tried to climb over the counter, Allen and Brody from Security dragged the guy away still screaming."

Hobbling to the parking lot on my swelling leg, I put a call in to Ordway Crook. I needed to confirm my suspicions. It appeared obvious that the guy at 1326 Alexander had an excellent motive to stalk Mona; add to that the missing items from Swine's apartment—a shoebox full of spent pari-mutuel tickets and Mona's purse—and it hung together. It was even money that Mr. 1326 Alexander broke in, hammered on Mona, and was searching Swine's hovel for his superfecta ticket when Swine showed up with beer from the corner store.

Ordway Crook was still the attorney of record in Swine's case. He returned my call to give me the information gleaned from the D.A.'s office. And also to remind me that he was now on the clock at two hundred fifty dollars an hour. If Swine didn't pay, it was going on my tab. He reported that there was no information from the police that Mona Phillips' apartment had been searched when they did their investigation. And he confirmed that Mona's purse had not been found at the scene.

Back at the office, I checked the charts in the *Racing Form*. It was the sixth race two days back at Calder. There was only one ticket for $36,384.60.

I called the head of Security at Calder, Jimmy Cox, a personal friend. I explained to him my suspicions concerning the death of Mona. It only took him a few minutes to find out that the ticket had not been cashed.

I'd just hung up when the cell phone in my pocket rang.

"Joe, I found Kyle," Swine said excitedly. "I watched him go into the restaurant and followed him when he came out. He's got a room a block from the restaurant in the Goodman Hotel." Swine gave me the address. I told him to stay there until I picked him up.

It took a half hour to get to the Goodman and find Swine. He slid into the Mustang and had to slam the door a couple of times before it closed properly.

"I even got his room number," Swine reported. He watched me do a U-turn and head back south. "Where the hell you goin'? Ain't we goin' in to get him?"

"Something we need to check first," I said. When we got back to Swine's neighborhood in Hialeah, I had him direct me to Mona's apartment. The door had been jimmied. It took only a cursory look through a window. The place had been thoroughly tossed. Even the couch and chairs had been cut open and the stuffing strewn about. It meant only one thing: Mr.1326 Alexander hadn't found the ticket at Swine's dump. He must have figured that Mona's place was too hot last night for anything but a quick search. He just waited until the cops cleared out.

I explained my discoveries concerning the superfecta ticket to Swine. "We need to check out your place again," I added. "Also, we need to pick up Leroy." Leroy was

Swine's name for his handstitched blackjack. A nifty tool in hand-to-hand tussle situations.

I followed Swine into his pigsty. "How come you're limping?" he asked.

I told him about the old man with the cane. I pulled my pants leg up to take a look. The spot on my leg was angry and swollen. It hurt like hell. "I got somethin' that'll help," Swine told me. "Just a minute." He went to a makeshift medicine cabinet that resided in a plastic container he pulled from beneath his bed.

"What is it?" I asked him.

He pulled out a can and popped the lid. "Poultice," he said, "I got it from Oslo Corbett. He says it'll draw out the infection and reduce the pain and swelling. I'll just smear some on the wound and wrap it with this vet wrap he gave me."

"That's for a horse," I pointed out.

"It'll work on you the same," said Swine. He tore the retaining band from the vet roll bandage and began to unravel it. The ticket that had been inserted in the center hole of the roll fluttered to the floor.

It was a superfecta ticket. It was *the* superfecta ticket. The date and the numbers were right. I was holding thirty-six thousand plus in my hand.

I allowed him to put the stuff on my leg. I didn't figure it could hurt any worse.

"Maybe you ought to let me hold the ticket," Swine suggested, clamping the bandage off.

"Never mind that. Get Leroy."

Kyle worried me. With the bum leg it was going to be doubly difficult to take him . . . maybe not even possible. As for Swine's situation, we had gleaned some circumstantial evidence. But outside of a motive for 1326

Alexander, there was nothing to tie the guy to Mona after the track incident. We needed more.

To confront Kyle head-on would be very dangerous. I needed a plan. We were on our way to the Goodman Hotel to apprehend him when an idea began to bubble around in my brain. I explained everything to Swine. I asked him if he could go inside and see if Kyle was still there without tipping him off.

"Not a problem," he said. "The desk clerk is Eddie Sloan. I already talked to him. I told him I'd let him into any vacant owner's box in the clubhouse free for the rest of the year."

"You mean Odds Board Eddie?" I asked.

"Yeah."

Odds Board Eddie, a fixture at the track for the late races, was a bettor with a particular angle. He added the weight the horse carried to the final odds on the toteboard, and whichever contestant had the lowest number was his selection—sort of an oddball, and aptly named.

Once Swine reported back that Kyle was still in his room, I told him to plant himself in the lobby and keep an eye out. I headed the Mustang farther north and about ten blocks east to where the map on the wall at Sunbelt Realty indicated I would find Alexander Street.

It was there all right: one, three, two, six in black letters stuck on the mailbox. And the little red arm was up. I checked the return address on the mail inside. Mr. 1326 Alexander had a name: Jorge Cumal.

I put the mail back in the mailbox and limped up to the porch. I punched the doorbell and stood back. The door opened almost at once. A small, pudgy woman with two different-colored eyes and no teeth gave me the once-over. She rattled something at me in Spanish.

I bedazzled her with the tried and true: *"No hablo español."* She backed out of the doorway and waved to someone inside.

Jorge was big, maybe an inch taller than Kyle's mama, and probably a lot quicker. His mustache was meager; his English was good and direct. "What do you want?" he asked.

"You're looking for your superfecta ticket," I said. "I can tell you where to find it for twenty percent."

He closed the door behind him and joined me on the small porch. "What you talkin', man?"

I didn't want to make it too complicated because I didn't know how smart he was. One thing for sure, I had his attention. I told him that Frankie Swinehart, Mona's boyfriend, had told me in confidence that Mona had given him the ticket. I told Jorge that Swine, short for Swinehart, still had the ticket. And I knew where he was staying. I told him we had to move fast before Swine cashed in when the track opened tomorrow.

Jorge didn't even pretend that he didn't know what I was talking about. "Why hasn't he cashed it before now?" he wanted to know.

"He's been in jail. Don't you read the papers? He just got out late today."

He nodded. "Oh yeah . . . I read about it. I—I ah—I think I know where he lives. What I need you for?"

"He's moved," I said quickly. "He's in a hotel in north Miami." Jorge was a bit sharper than I'd first surmised. But he was greedy. I knew that he had already made up his mind to screw me out of my percentage should he get the ticket back. Given that, and driven by desperation and greed, he was ready to buy into anything. I was counting on it. But he kept surprising me.

"Why didn't you just get the ticket yourself?" he asked, catching me by surprise.

"Bum leg," I said feebly, pointing to my leg. "Swine's a pretty good-sized guy. It'll probably take both of us. Besides, you got a rotten deal. It's your ticket."

"A big guy?" Jorge muttered, obviously puzzled. I remembered too late that he had conked Swine on the head. Evidently his impression was that Swine wasn't a big guy. Of course he was right. Swine wouldn't go more than a hundred sixty pounds wearing a scuba belt. But Jorge dismissed it, possibly considering me a weenie.

"Let's go," he said. "I'll follow you in my car."

Jorge drove a vintage Cadillac DeVille with its common trademark: that is, the eroded-away space between the rear fenders and the large, vertical taillights. He tailgated my Mustang with unrelenting enthusiasm, allowing no chance that I might lose him in traffic. When we entered the Goodman Hotel in lockstep, I spotted Swine behind a newspaper in the corner of the tiny lobby. Jorge kept his eyes on me as we proceeded to the stairs. Odds Board Eddie behind the registration desk ignored us.

"Second floor," I told Jorge.

Swine had given me Kyle's room number. As we started up the stairs, I was getting a little apprehensive. For this to halfway work, I had to rely heavily on Jorge's demonstrated greed and Kyle's intrinsic savageness. I was praying that neither would let me down. It had been a long time since my Golden Glove days. Just to play it safe, I decide to send Jorge inside while I waited in the doorway.

I stood alongside the door. "Two oh five, this is it," I told Jorge. "You think we should knock or what?"

"The hell with that," said Jorge. "We take this little

[Spanish expletive] by surprise." With that he rammed his huge frame into the door. The door flew open with negligible resistance. The momentum of his charge carried Jorge partway into the room, where he came to an abrupt stop as the six foot five inch, two hundred seventy pound Kyle, clad only in his underwear, rose to his full imposing height from the bed.

Jorge said nothing for a brief second, he simply stared. But if faces could speak without a mouth, his face would have shouted *whoa!*

Kyle stood unmoving, using the interlude to marshal and focus his nastiness.

Jorge realized that something seemed to be wrong. But he made two fatal errors. The first was not running out the open door. The second was: "You're Swine?" he said to Kyle.

When Kyle lunged, he was much, much quicker than his mom. He grabbed Jorge's shirt with a large fist and lifted him off the floor. He cocked his other fist back as Jorge began to jabber profusely.

"Wait! Wait!" shouted Jorge. "I thought you were Swine..."

The blow knocked Jorge across the room. I pulled my head from the doorway to take a position against the wall in the hallway. From inside I could hear Kyle shouting.

"You little piss ant. You break into my room and call me a swine. I know you're workin' for that #@bail bond guy."

I chanced a look around the door jamb. Kyle was holding Jorge upright with one hand. His other hand was full of Jorge's black hair. He was gleefully hammering Jorge's head against the wall.

Thud ... thud ... thud.

Kyle's back was to the door. While he was occupied, I

drew Leroy out and took five or six big steps into the room. I smacked him a good one on the back of the head. He let Jorge collapse, unconscious, to the floor and turned slowly to face me. Then his eyes fluttered, and he sort of melted into a pile.

Of course I'd had plan B if Kyle hadn't ignited on his own. I had thought I might get things under way by announcing to Kyle that Jorge was working for Nolan Bail Bonds. Just as well I hadn't had to use it. It made the rest of the plan possible.

I took the superfecta ticket from my shirt pocket and put it under the corner of the lamp on the table by Kyle's bed. I got a glass of water from the bathroom and doused Jorge. His nose looked broken, and he had a front tooth missing.

"You all right?" I asked as he came around.

"My face," he moaned. He spit the missing tooth onto the carpet.

I handed him a wet hand towel to press on his nose.

He nodded toward Kyle, who lay unmoving nearby. "What happened to him?"

"I took care of him while he was busy with you."

"I don't think that's Swine," said Jorge. "I mean, that's not the guy I remember . . ."

"I don't know who you're thinking about. That's the only Swine I know. And look there on the table—isn't that the ticket?"

With the mention of the ticket, the glaze evaporated from Jorge's eyes. They fixed on the bedside table. He attempted to rise, fell back, then scrambled forward on hands and knees to grasp the ticket. He studied it carefully, smiled wickedly, and put it in his shirt pocket. About then Kyle groaned.

"We better get the hell out of here before he comes around," I said. "You cash the ticket when the track opens tomorrow. I'll be at your house at noon for my cut."

Jorge got awkwardly to his feet. "Yeah, right," he said. He shrewdly chose not to add the word stupid to his confirmation. He beat me through the doorway by two steps.

We raced down the stairs to the lobby. Jorge continued out the lobby door. I went into the street and watched him wheel away in the Caddy, then stepped back inside and motioned to Swine.

Kyle was still out when we got back to his room. Swine took a piece of clothesline from his pants pocket and bound his ankles tightly together. I used plastic handcuffs to fasten his hands behind his back. Because of my bad leg, it cost an extra thirty dollars to have Odds Board Eddie help us carry him down to the Mustang. With the top down we laid him on the trunk and rolled him into the back seat.

On the way to the main lockup downtown, I used the cell phone to cell Donk Nolan and tell him that I had Kyle. I told him to meet me downtown. He gushed euphoria and praised my abilities. None of which could mask the fact that he was still an offensive little jerk.

Back in the office Swine plopped on my cot in protest. "You got to be an idiot boob for givin' the superfecta ticket back to that killer—thirty-six grand—what the hell you thinkin' of?"

"Look, try to get it straight. I got a call in to Jimmy Cox. When the track opens tomorrow and Jorge tries to cash that ticket—which he will surely do—track security is going to grab him and hold him for the police. Ordway Crook has talked to the D.A. and explained that Jorge killed Mona to get the ticket back. Raul the seller and track security will testify about the confrontation over the ticket at the track. When they catch Jorge trying to cash it, it'll be all tied up for them—open and shut."

Swine shook his head. "Yeah, but thirty-six thousand, Jezz."

"The price of freedom is high," I reminded him.

"What about Jorge? How much time you think he'll get?"

I opened the *Form* to the first race at Calder. "Hmm, that's a tough one," I muttered, my attention fixed on one of my key horses that had drawn the rail sin the first race. "Depends on the jury. Killing someone who stole your superfecta ticket might be considered justifiable homicide in some circles."

Mat Coward

"Tomorrow's Villain"

Crime fiction can embody any value of general fiction, including satire and social criticism. In the story that follows, Mat Coward—humor, gardening, or book review columnist for numerous British periodicals—has a great deal to say about publicity, prejudice, and public opinion. Coward's first novel is *Up and Down*, published by Five Star in 2000.

Flat Coward

"Tomorrow's
Villain"

For a short while, following the death of my daughter, I became something of a national hero.

It helped that I was an ordinary bloke—a self-employed electrician—and not what the papers call a 'toff'. The papers hate toffs, which is odd, given that the papers are staffed almost exclusively by toffs.

It helped even more that I was a lone father. Lone mothers are, even these days, still subject to a certain moral ambiguity: is she in that position deliberately? Or did she at least bring it on herself? But a father, struggling bravely against both nature and society to raise a child all on his lonesome—why, he's halfway to being a saint already.

So when Nadine (named for the Chuck Berry song) died in a back street in the West End of London, all I had to do was fight back the tears on live TV and I was instantly canonised.

I made the usual press conference appeal for witnesses, remembering with some guilt as I did so that whenever I'd watched such performances on TV in the past, I'd always assumed that the person making the appeal was the guilty party.

Nadine died one week after her eighteenth birthday, of

a rare allergic reaction to the chemicals contained in an anti-rape spray. Normally, so the coroner later declared, this would not have led to a fatality; however, there was evidence at the death scene of a scuffle, during which, it was surmised, her assailant had held the canister close to her face and emptied its entire contents directly into her mouth and nose. Her death, essentially from respiratory failure, had followed rapidly. I was astonished to learn that Nadine carried such a spray—she loathed all weapons—but I supposed that no parent ever knows their children as well as they think they do.

Within seventy-two hours of my daughter's death, the police made an arrest: a 21-year-old, black, male shop assistant, Horace Jones. The next day's papers described him variously as Nadine's "live-in lover" and "steady boyfriend". I'd never heard of him.

A black, male killer, a white, female victim; a brave but grief-stricken dad. We were news, the three of us.

These events happened in November, so they were still fresh in the public's mind when a national radio station ran its annual "Man Of The Year" phone-in poll. I won. That made me laugh. I mean, *really* laugh—laugh with real amusement. I was the Man of the Year for having lost my daughter. If I'd had two daughters, and they'd both been killed, would I have been elected Pope?

Horace Jones denied all charges, both at the time of his arrest, and a few months later, during his trial. His denials were not believed, and he was duly sentenced to life imprisonment.

His trial put me back in the headlines, and my heroic status was confirmed and even enlarged. I really believe that, at that moment, I could have stood for Parliament with some hope of success. Nadine was a victim, Horace Jones was emblematic of all that was wrong with modern Britain, and I was . . . well, I seemed to be, for no reason that was ever clear to me, the symbol of all that was *right* with modern Britain.

Jones' lawyer lodged an appeal against the conviction. As it happened, I knew the lawyer, Teddy Edwards; had known him, at least, some years earlier, when we'd served together on a local anti-apartheid committee here in Maidstone. About a week after Jones began his sentence, Teddy phoned and asked to see me. I agreed; I was still in that stage of grief where I wanted more details, more information, more understanding of what had happened.

"He's not guilty, Jack," Teddy said as we sat drinking tea in my empty kitchen. "I'm sorry, I know that probably isn't what you want to hear, but I have to tell you: I have no doubt in my mind at all that Horace Jones did not kill Nadine."

It wasn't what I wanted to hear, of course, and it wasn't what I'd expected to hear. "You have to say that, don't you, Teddy?" I replied. "A lawyer—you've got to believe your clients are innocent. That's how it works, surely?"

He shook his head. "Not at all, Jack. Not like that at all. Ninety-nine per cent of my clients are thieves and liars and worse. I have to *accept* that they're innocent if that's what they choose to tell me, but I'm not required to *believe* it. I represent them to the best of my ability, because that's my job—and because," and here he paused for a self-deprecating chuckle, "and because, now that I'm a middle-aged, middle-class solicitor, I actually do believe in the system. I'm not the radical I once was, Jack. Well, which of us is? I think our system of law is, over all, a good system. And it can only work as long as even the most heinously guilty arsehole gets the best defence the system can provide him with. But no, I don't usually believe their pathetic fairy stories."

"So what's different this time?" I asked.

He sat forward in his seat, and started ticking off items on his fingers. "OK. Right. Basically, I think Horace has been lynched. He's black, Nadine was white. She was a lovely girl training to be a nurse, he's just some inner city nobody with a petty criminal record; possession of drugs, some minor thieving. It's a match made in Hell."

"Just because ignorant people wanted him to be guilty doesn't mean he *wasn't* guilty," I said.

"No, sure, good point." Teddy looked tired and sweaty. He'd aged a lot in the few years since I'd last seen him. Much of his hair had gone, and his suit was irreversibly rumpled. It was a reasonably expensive suit, so I assumed the rumpling came from within. He took a packet of cigarettes out of his pocket and waved it at me. "Do you mind if I smoke?"

"No, of course not."

"Really," said Teddy, "say if you do."

I shook my head, and stood up to find him an ashtray. "Nadine smoked."

"They all do, don't they?" he said, lighting up gratefully. "Teenage girls. My wife says the ones you want to worry about are the ones who don't smoke. You can guarantee they're doing something much worse."

Teddy went back to talking about the case, putting forward his arguments concerning Horace Jones's innocence, but after a while he noticed that I wasn't hearing him.

"Christ, Jack, are you all right?"

It was the smell of the cigarette. Before Teddy, the last person who'd smoked in that house had been Nadine. For

some reason, when everyone came back here for the funeral meats, all the smokers were careful to take their cigarettes out into the garden, even though there were
ashtrays on every surface in the kitchen and living-room.
A kind of bizarre, turn-of-the-century mark of respect for
the dead: don't let them see you smoking.

When the snake of aromatic grey and white smoke
from Teddy's cigarette coiled across the table between us
and up into my brain, I instantly and absolutely broke
down. From a man of flesh, holding things together, I
turned into a bowl of dry cornflakes: shattered, jagged,
formless. And then soggy, as the tears flowed. I wasn't
sobbing: I was just sitting there, staring straight ahead,
while the tear-water poured out of my eyes like beer from
a tap.

Teddy helped me through to the living-room. He drew
the curtains, put the lights on, poured us both a scotch
from an almost full bottle on the sideboard. I'd hardly
been in the living-room since Nadine died. I felt out of
place, almost a visitor in my own home, and I think that
helped me regain control of my tear ducts.

After a while, I was ready to resume the conversation.
Teddy wasn't smoking any more.

"I don't know how much of the trial you took in,
Jack. I don't imagine legal niceties were uppermost in
your mind, but let me tell you—and you don't have to
take my word for it, I'll get you a transcript of the trial—
there was basically no evidence against Horace. No serious evidence."

"Then how did he get convicted?" I asked. "You said
just now you believed in our system of law."

"Yeah, sure, but compared to *what*—that's the question." Teddy rubbed his hands over his scalp, making the

little hair he had left stand up in tufts. He looked like a baby that's just woken up grumpy from an afternoon nap. "To an idealist, a thing is either perfect or terrible. But a realist sees things in context. All I'm saying is, if you were an innocent man, with no money, charged with a terrible crime, where would you rather be tried: Britain or America? Britain or China? Britain or Spain?"

"But this time the system got it wrong. That's what you're telling me?"

"I'm sure of it."

"OK," I said, the details of the evidence given in court coming back to me. Teddy's assumption was understandable, but wrong: in fact, I had taken in, and retained, every word of that trial. As long as the trial went on, Nadine still existed. People still spoke of her, and what does being alive mean other than being talked about? "As I recall, there were two main pieces of physical evidence. First of all, the wounds to your client's face . . ."

"Right," said Teddy. "The nail scratches. The wounds were the right age, and they came from a woman's hand, or to be precise from false nails—fun nails, they're called these days—we didn't contest that, but remember that the prosecution was unable to say that they came from *Nadine's* nails. And that's not just a technicality, Jack."

"The wounds were said to be made by a woman of Nadine's height."

He shrugged. "She was of average female height. Means nothing."

"All right. What about the fingerprints?"

"The clincher, as far as the jury was concerned," Teddy admitted.

"Horace's prints were on the canister of anti-rape spray. Nobody else's, not even Nadine's. He says, as you'll remember, that he and Nadine had met in a pub in Covent Garden a month before her death, right?"

"And that they'd seen each other 'as friends only' several times during that month. Yes, I remember." So much for the press reports that she'd been killed by her 'Black Live-In Lover'. "But when your barrister asked him in court if, during that time, he had handled the spray can, he couldn't say, could he?"

"Not *couldn't* say," said Teddy. "Wouldn't say. And that's crucial, Jack. You know that barristers never ask questions they don't already know the answer to?"

"I've heard it said."

"Well, we thought we knew the answer to that one. We thought Horace was going to reply that Nadine had spilt her handbag once when they were out together, and that he had helped her re-pack it. Hence the single set of his prints on the spray."

"So why didn't he?"

Teddy shook his head. "Don't know. Actually, yes, I think I do—because it was a lie. I don't think that is how his prints got on there, and he is the kind of bloke—something of an innocent, religious upbringing—that he's just not willing to tell a lie. Even to save his neck."

Now I shook my head—the scotch was clouding my mind a little. I hadn't had a drink since the day of the funeral. "But if even you think he's lying about the anti-rape spray . . ."

"My guess is that he knows something about what happened, but he's not willing to say it. So, to avoid lying, he just says nothing. Or else, *I don't know, Sir*, which amounts to the same thing." Teddy stood up. "Look, Jack, I'm sorry. I've given you a bad evening. I'll let you get some kip, now. But can I talk to you again? I really think it's important."

"Of course you can," I said. "I'm always happy to talk." *About Nadine*, I didn't need to add.

Teddy sent me the trial transcript, and I read it, feeling a jet of life squirt up through my body every time I saw the word *Nadine* in print.

The prosecution's case was straightforward. Horace and Nadine first met in a pub in Covent Garden. They went out together several times over the next few weeks, to pubs, clubs, ethnic restaurants. They did not sleep together. They chatted about the things they had in common: football (she was a West Ham fanatic, my daughter), exotic food and 1960s rhythm and blues music.

On the night of her death, they had been drinking in a pub off the Charing Cross Road. At closing time, they walked towards Leicester Square Tube station, taking a short cut through an unlit alley. There, Horace demanded sex. Nadine refused. Horace persisted, to the point of attempted rape (her clothes were in disarray when she was found). She tried to use the anti-rape spray on him, but he took it from her and turned it on her, forcing it into her mouth and nose. When he saw the effect this had on her, he panicked and ran. She was found dead by an off-duty ambulance driver about forty minutes later. At around that time, a blood-splashed black youth was seen running in a nearby street.

Horace Jones was a suspect from the start of the investigation, according to the prosecution's version of events. Detectives learned of his existence from some girls at Nadine's college, and heard from the same source that he and Nadine had been seen "arguing violently" in a Covent Garden wine bar the night before her death. He was described as "a big, strong man" which caught the detectives' attention, since it had already been noted that the method of death probably ruled out a female killer, a short man, or a weakling.

When taken in for questioning, Horace denied killing Nadine, or fighting with her, or attempting to rape her, but he declined to give an account of his movements during the crucial hours. He also refused to explain the scratches on his face, and when, on the second day of questioning, he was confronted with the fingerprint evidence, he offered no comment. At the end of the second day, he was charged with murder.

The police did everything by the book: no doubt about that. It's clear from the interview transcripts that they went to great lengths to persuade Horace that he ought to be represented by a lawyer—"Don't need a lawyer, man. I got no lies to tell"—and the interviews were interrupted repeatedly for tea breaks, and on three further occasions so that Horace could be seen by the duty surgeon, "as the prisoner appeared to be in a state of considerable emotional shock".

They'd got their man, and they weren't going to lose him through a procedural error. Or else maybe they were just good cops, trying to do the job properly. I suppose that's not impossible, after all.

"Have you read it?" said Teddy on the phone.

"I have."

"Great. Thanks. Listen, sorry to have to, you know, put you through—"

"That's OK. Don't worry."

"OK, great." A pause, during which I wondered whether there were any cigarettes in Nadine's room. I'd never smoked, not even as a kid, but it would be nice to smell that scent again. "Listen, Jack—I'd like you to meet him. Horace: I'd like you to talk to him."

I almost dropped the phone, as my heart stopped pumping and my limbs froze. *Meet him?* "Is that... would that be allowed?"

"Oh yeah, yeah, listen—yeah." Teddy was gabbling. In gratitude, I suppose, that I wasn't screaming at him. "I mean, you know, a prisoner's allowed visitors. Up to him who they are."

"And he's willing?"

Teddy laughed. "About as willing as you are, Jack! But, yes, he'll see us. If you think you're up to it."

How much easier it must have been in the days of capital punishment, I thought. At least back then the ghosts were all dead.

"So you've read the evidence, what do you think?" We were in Teddy's car, driving to the prison. "There's not much to it, is there?"

"I agree it's a bit thin," I said. "But if Horace didn't do it, and he wasn't there, then why wasn't he able to offer a more convincing defence? Some sort of alibi, or something."

"I'm hoping," said Teddy, who seemed a lot more nervous than I was, "that we'll find that out today." I, by contrast, was not hoping for anything in particular. Why was I there? The usual reason: to prolong the existence of Nadine.

"You won't get a word out of our Horace," said the prison officer who checked our papers. "He's the tall, dark, silent type." When the guard clocked my name, he gave me a look that only just fell short of naked contempt. That was an omen, if I'd been in a state to notice it. But all such thoughts fled my head the moment I sat down opposite Horace and looked into his eyes for the first time.

I knew straight away that he hadn't killed my daughter.

It wasn't anything to do with him. It wasn't that I looked upon Horace and knew him incapable of murder. It was rather that I looked at Horace and knew *Nadine* to have been incapable of being murdered by him.

Nonsense, of course. Irrational, meaningless. I understood that then no less than I understand it now, but that understanding didn't change what I knew. One thing that having your daughter murdered does for you—did for me, at any rate—is it liberates you from the rules of rationality. If you know something, you just know it, and you don't ask how or why. I had already accepted the utterly impossible fact that my only child had predeceased me; after that, accepting any lesser impossibility was child's play.

Teddy introduced us—as if we needed it!—and then sat with his chair slightly behind mine, leaving the two of us alone in a room full of chattering, grieving men and women.

"All right, Horace," I said, without preamble. "You didn't kill Nadine. So who did?"

Horace said nothing, just stared at me with the eyes of a disinterred corpse. He didn't blink, and he didn't look away.

"Do you think your need not to tell is greater than my need to be told? Is that it, Horace? Because if so, then there's nothing I can—"

He blinked. Once. It was one of the most effective interruptions I have ever been subjected to. I stopped talking, and waited.

At last, he said: "I don't want to tell you. Being in here is better than telling it. It's terrible in here, but it's better than telling it." But he did tell us his story, even so. Not all of it—not even then—but enough.

A week later, Teddy and I held a press conference. Teddy gave a broad outline of the case for an appeal hearing, while I answered follow-up questions from the reporters—all of which were of the idiotic "How do you feel?" variety. My well-rehearsed answer was simple: I felt it was wrong that a man should be in prison for a crime he hadn't committed. I felt that those actually responsible for my daughter's death should be brought to justice. Beyond that, I had no comment to make.

The Campaign For Justice For Horace Jones was formally launched, with Teddy as its Treasurer and me as its Secretary—and thus, within the space of a day, I passed from being yesterday's hero to being tomorrow's villain.

To the newspapers, I was no longer an ordinary working bloke; I was a "self-employed businessman". I was no longer a brave lone father, struggling to raise his beautiful daughter; I was now a "divorcee loner," who had raised a "wild child". (The fact that my ex-wife had died in a motor accident shortly before our divorce had been finalised, and that I was therefore technically a widower, went unmentioned).

I was, above all, no longer that quiet, unassuming dad who bore his bereavement with solemn dignity. Now, I was that crazy do-gooder who wanted to let a murdering monster out of jail to kill again. (A *black* monster. The word was always there, even though it rarely appeared in print.)

One journalist—who I later discovered was all of 22 years old, fresh down from Oxford, and a niece by marriage of the proprietor—wrote an op-ed piece in the *Daily Telegraph*, telling the world (and, incidentally, me) precisely what it was that I was doing, and why. The *what* was putting my "white liberal conscience" and "knee-jerk pro-ethnic bias" before the "natural love a proper father feels for his child". And the reason I was doing this was, as far as I could make out, because that was what white liberals did.

It was all a case of "political correctness gone mad," the writer concluded (demonstrating that what she lacked in empathy she made up for in cliché-mongering), and furthermore it was this "false prioritisation, born of middle-class guilt and enforced by the liberal theocracy," that had led to the breakdown of family-based, Christian society. And so on: I'm sure you're familiar with the script.

Daft, I know, but it was that word "liberal" that annoyed me most. I have never been *remotely* liberal; I am a socialist son of socialist parents. My daughter was a socialist. My great-grandfather was arrested seven times during the General Strike. If Lucinda Buckteeth-Jodphurs, or whatever the silly little bitch's name was, wanted to get into a liberal-despising contest with me, she'd better be prepared for a heavy defeat. My wife, now, she *was* a liberal. Probably one of the reasons we split up—I don't mean because we argued about politics, but because, being a liberal, she had no moral impediment to abandoning her husband and child to pursue self-fulfilment.

Smart comedians, bored with their usual diet of bent politicians and ugly TV celebrities, made neat little gags at my expense. They couldn't be accused of racism, of course, because they were being *ironic*.

It wasn't only the mass media that took an interest in me. Someone painted "Wog Lover" in large, ironically black letters on my garage door. Of the two attackers, I found I had more respect for the spray-painter than for the *Telegraph* girl. They were both saying the same thing, after all—*exactly* the same thing, make no mistake about that—but at least the painter didn't try to disguise himself with the false-beard-and-moustache of education, privilege and logorrhoea.

I left the legend on the garage door, didn't try to clean it off. I decided instead to treat it as a compliment. "Wog Lover"? Sure, why not? I *do* try to love my neighbour: that's how I was brought up. It's how my daughter was brought up.

Besides, if I'd cleaned it off, someone would only have put it back, wouldn't they? I could have been out there with a bucket and scrubbing brush every day for the rest of my life.

There was much more in a similar vein, but it's not worth listing. No-one actually hit me or put a bomb through my window. As for the rest—well, if you want the truth, being a national villain was considerably less irritating than being a national hero had been. At least I could get my car out of my garage without first clearing several dozen bouquets of damn lilies away from the door.

"I'm really sorry," Teddy said one night over a beer, in my living-room. The campaign to secure an appeal hearing went on for two years—a much quicker process than it had been in the recent past, Teddy was always at pains to point out. In America they bury their mistakes, he'd say. At least Horace is still alive.

"You're sorry for what?" I asked, though I knew what he meant.

"All this. If I'd known it was going to be so hard on you—"

"You'd have done it anyway," I said, putting an end to the discussion. Because he *would* have done it anyway, and he'd have been right to do it, so what was the point of pretending otherwise?

The appeal hearing revealed the usual tragic, tawdry story of errors and evasions. It wasn't so much a case of evidence being deliberately hidden in order to frame the innocent—more a case of facts which didn't fit being ignored, so as not to ruin a good theory. Evidence, for instance, suggesting that there had been more than two people involved in the scuffle which led to Nadine's death. Evidence which showed that Nadine's death might have been caused by one strong man, or by a number of smaller, weaker people acting together.

Everyone does that, don't they? Leaves out the bits that don't fit. Cops do it, politicians do it, school teachers, scientists, sports commentators.

In the dock, this time, Horace told the story that he had told me when I visited him in prison.

"Nadine and me, we were friends, OK? Nothing more. I don't care if you all believe that or not, that's the truth. That is the *truth*. I'm not gay or nothing, but she already had a boyfriend. She was seeing a married man."

That was the bit he hadn't wanted me to hear, because of what had happened between me and Nadine's mother. He was right: I didn't want to hear it. I didn't want to hear evidence, in a court of law, that I had raised a daughter who was merely human, not perfect.

"The night she died, the night they killed her, she and I had a drink, and then she went to meet this fellow, John."

Don't call her *She*, I wanted to say. If you call her Nadine she still exists.

"He was supposed to be at a meeting in Birmingham, but he wasn't, he was meeting her at a hotel in Hampstead. But when we split up after our drink, and she was going to one Tube and I was going to another, I followed her. I decided to follow her, because . . ."

During a long pause, no-one in the court tried to prompt him.

". . . I wasn't her boyfriend, OK? Whatever everybody thinks. I just followed her because I was—because I decided to follow her to see if, you know. Just to *see*. When she turned into that alley, near the Tube, I saw that I wasn't the only one following her. There was four girls, four young women, and they were following her too. I saw them. They had this can of spray, I didn't know what it was then, just a can of something. The main girl, the leader, she was wearing gloves. I saw what they did, and I ran up to them and I was shouting at them to stop and I tried to grab the can, but one of the girls, she raked my face with those long nails. I couldn't see too good, there was blood all in my eyes, and I . . . I ran off to get help. To get some help, you see? For Nadine."

That was the bit he hadn't wanted *anyone* to hear. That was why he had gone to prison for a crime he hadn't committed: to avoid telling the world that he had run from four girls.

"I don't think they meant to kill her. I think they just meant to beat her up. But she . . . Nadine collapsed when they sprayed that stuff in her face." Another long, uninterrupted pause. "I ran off to get help."

A young black man—a young black *male*, as the newspapers always say—running through the streets of the West End, blood running down his face, shouting about murder. He couldn't find a policeman, and no citizen was brave enough to help him. Are you surprised?

By the time he got back to the scene, Nadine was dead.

"I went home," Horace concluded. He was asked by the Crown's barrister and by his own why he had simply gone home, why he hadn't stayed with the body, called the police, called an ambulance? I don't know why they asked: surely the answer was obvious. The poor kid was ashamed.

Horace Jones did not receive a proper pardon, but he was released on a technicality. He went to live, Teddy told me, with a distant relative somewhere in the Midlands. He changed his name. He refused to sell his story to the newspapers, which means that if the reporters ever do catch up with him they'll consider it their solemn duty to rip his life to shreds. I only hope that by then he's got a life worth ripping.

I never saw him again, except for briefly in Teddy's office, immediately after his release, when I just had time to ask him one question.

"People saw you and Nadine arguing the evening before she died. What were you arguing about?"

He gave me that dead stare. I didn't know if he was going to answer, until he spoke. "Football," he said.

"Football?"

"I don't like football. I like cricket. In cricket you get fair play."

I've no idea if that was the truth. Could have been, I suppose. Funny thing is, Nadine and I used to have that same argument. I'm a cricket man, myself.

* * *

On the steps of the appeal court, a police spokesman announced that "as far as we are concerned the case remains
closed"—police code for, "Of course the bastard was guilty—
we wouldn't have arrested him otherwise, would we?" But
they were humiliatingly forced to abandon this position
only a few days later, when one of the girls involved in the
attack on Nadine broke ranks, and turned herself in at her
local police station, accompanied by her family lawyer.

She hadn't been directly involved in the violence, she
said. Leading the attack had been her best friend, the wife
of the man Nadine was seeing, along with the wife's two
sisters. They'd set out to teach Nadine to "keep her filthy
hands off other women's blokes" but "it had all gone horribly wrong" and she could "no longer live with the guilt."

She was charged with a lesser offence; the other three
were charged with murder. Their case is due to be heard
early next year. And I, naturally, am a public hero once
again. I am the courageous, loving father who fought for an
innocent boy's freedom against the forces of bigotry and
ignorance. My drive is full of bouquets again. I hate it. I'm
thinking of moving, changing my name, going abroad. But
I'm afraid that to do so would be to surrender to cynicism,
and I am determined not to do that. Cynicism is the triumph
of death and futility, and I won't willingly become its ally.

Of course, to some I am still a "Wog Lover," and poor
Horace is still a murdering savage who got away with it.
A Conservative MP, hiding behind the parliamentary
privilege of immunity to the laws of slander, told the
House of Commons that in his opinion the police had
acted correctly throughout, only to have their actions
"second-guessed by subversives," and that Horace Jones
was "a guilty, guilty man with a soul as black as tar."

To my astonished delight, the MP's party leadership

disowned him, his local activists turned against him, and his career fell into a terminal decline. So, then: there *are* still good people in the world. Perhaps I'm even one of them, since the campaign to free Horace began, for me, as a means of keeping Nadine's name alive—but somewhere along the way it became something else: a desire to prove that in a world full of shrugged shoulders, it is still possible to give witness to the simple, concrete difference between right and wrong.

I try to remember that, I mine that thought for whatever comfort it contains, now that the whole business is over and done with, now that my daughter Nadine finally does not exist, and can never exist again.

James Powell

"Honeydew Wine"

Like Edward D. Hoch, Canadian-born James Powell is a rare example of a writer who has based a long career almost entirely on short fiction. Humor is his trademark, as in this story of an unusual small-business enterprise

James Powell

Honeydew Wine

Toward evening a van pulled into the driveway of a substantial house of tawny brick on a fringe of Toronto's Rosedale district. On the vehicle's side panels the words "Cozy Disposal" arched above an old-world scene of a country gate decorated with hollyhocks and delphiniums.

The driver, an elderly man with a brush-cut and sun-burned face got out pulling soft leather briefcase after him. He wore a crisp white short-sleeved shirt and a modest tie. Coming around to the passenger side he opened the door for a stoutish woman perhaps a few years younger than he was. She had henna-colored hair, a good-natured face and a flowered dress. As he stood for inspection she brushed his shoulders for dandruff making the bangles on her arm jingle. Then they turned as one and came up the walk.

The door opened before they reached it. A small woman armed with a cigarette stood there, a graying blonde in a painter's smock. "Mr. and Mrs. Cozy?" she asked.

The man grinned. "Boy, do we get that a lot. I'm Lorne Mullins and this is Muriel my wife. 'Cozy' is more our business philosophy." Then he nodded at the car in the driveway. "If you're having visitors, Mrs. Wilmot, we can call at another time."

The woman waved her cigarette like a magic wand and the car vanished into unimportance. "That's ours. Leland, my husband, is painting the inside of the garage. Please come in. You people are very prompt."

"Oh, we try," said Muriel Mullins as they followed the woman inside. "But business keeps us hopping. Sometimes we don't know if we're coming or going." Then she exclaimed. "What a wonderful house! I admire the colors!"

Mrs. Wilmot thanked her and ushered them down the hallway. "I thought we'd talk in the garden. If you've something to say in private never get between a man and the liquor cabinet."

As they passed the archway into the living room, Muriel asked, "Is that a Rookwood vase? How beautiful."

"I'm a bit of a collector," admitted Mrs. Wilmot.

"Before Cozy Disposal Muriel here decorated show windows for Eatons," said Mullins.

French doors led outside into the flower garden. Grouped over by a tall hedge were three wicker armchairs with corduroy pillows and a small iron table. Mrs. Wilmot offered them the chairs tucked in behind a hydrangea bush and took the seat by the ashtray.

The yarrow was tall and yellow. The daisies shone in the fading light. The lilies glowed like blood. "What a lovely garden," said Muriel. "June is certainly our month for lightning-bugs, isn't it just?"

Mrs. Wilmot looked vaguely at the drift of blinking creatures and spoke as if her mind was elsewhere. "We always called them fire-flies."

"Same difference, right?" said Mullins, taking his

order book and a small pocket-mirror framed in plastic attached to a key chain from his briefcase which he then propped by the chair.

His wife disagreed. "Only the males fly. The females just flash around in the grass. So the 'fly' part is sexist."

Mrs. Wilmot liked that. "Lightning-bugs, it is then."

Mullins leaned over, placed the key chain beside the ashtray and started to speak. But Mrs. Wilmot stopped him with a raised finger. Then she uttered a theatrical little sneeze.

"God bless you," said a man's voice from the other side of the hedge.

"Thank you, Mr. Lockridge," Mrs. Wilmot replied, keeping her finger in the air. Then they heard the sound of her neighbor pulling himself out of a lawn chair. After several moments a screen door slammed and Mrs. Wilmot lowered her finger.

"That key chain's our free gift to you for requesting a Cozy Disposal estimate," said Mullins.

Mrs. Wilmot picked up the pocket-mirror and read the message on the back out loud. "Time to Call Cozy Disposal."

"And there's our phone number," said Muriel. "Night or day."

"Let me make it clear from the start, I really haven't decided if your services will be required," said Mrs. Wilmot. "Or what I'm going to do. That is *if* I do anything." She stubbed out her cigarette and lit another. "I just decided why not look into it, the cost and everything." She waved her hand as if clearing a path through the smoke for her words. "I'm really not comfortable talking to strangers about personal matters. But, well, the fact is my husband Leland and I haven't been getting on too well since we sold the business and retired."

"No need to explain," Mullins assured her.

"Though sometimes it helps," suggested Muriel. "After all, we've been there, too, Mrs. Wilmot."

"That's how we got into our line of work," added her husband. "Retirement ain't what it's cracked up to be. Twice the spouse and half the money."

"The stress and strain of husbands underfoot all the time," said Muriel. "Talk about couch potatoes."

"Talk about honeydews," countered Mullins. "Honey, do this. Honey, do that. And both parties knowing it's all busy work to get the other party out of the way. The boys at Henderson Motors. . . ."

". . . . where Lorne worked as second-best mechanic for thirty years," added Muriel proudly.

"The boys at Henderson Motors warned me about retirement," continued Mullins, "when the voice of the honeydew is heard through the land."

"But, bravo, Mrs. Wilmot, getting your husband to paint the inside of the garage," said Muriel with admiration. "Where'd you ever come up with that one?"

"Actually it was his idea," admitted Mrs. Wilmot. "Out of the blue. Strange, I guess, because I'd given up on— uh—the honeydews about six months ago when Leland turned moody and thoughtful on me. I'd catch him sitting with his elbow on his knee and his chin in his hand and a brow so furrowed it made your head ache. And when he saw me he'd jump like I'd fired off a gun beside his ear and pretend he wasn't thinking at all. Or I'd come around the lilac bush and there he'd be like garden statuary. The Thinker."

"I know that one," beamed Mullins.

"Next thing I knew watching TV I'd catch him staring at me with these big sad puppy-dog eyes. Or I'd be reading and he'd give this wet and windy sigh and when I looked over there'd be that stare again. Or out of nowhere he'd reach over and pat my arm, 'Thirty-one years, Eunice, old girl. Thirty-one wonderful years,' he'd say. And I'd say, 'What the hell's gotten into you, Leland? Quite frankly a lot of those years weren't all that wonderful. Besides, it's been thirty-three, not thirty-one.' And he'd say, 'Whatever' and look like he was going to cry." She shook her head. "There's only so much stuff like that a person can stand."

"I'm with you," agreed Mullins. "A year into retirement I was honeydewed out and ready to strangle Muriel and bury her in the basement. I even started on a list of what I'd need: Sledge hammer, shovel, gravel, sand, cement, one of those trowels for smoothing out.

"This particular night I came to the dinner table trying to figure in my head how the drainpipe ran before I started digging. Suddenly Muriel said the sweetest thing she's ever said to me." He prompted his wife with a smile.

"I said, 'Don't eat the shepherd's pie, Lorne,'" said Muriel.

"Well, I dropped that fork like a red hot poker. And she came clean about how I'd driven her so crazy hanging around all the time she was going to poison me. And I came clean about what I had in mind to do to her. Then and there we knew if our marriage was going to survive we needed an outside interest. So we decided to go into business for ourselves. Muriel said, 'Let's do something nobody else is doing. Let's find our own niche.' and I said. . . ."

"And he said, 'A niche that hasn't been scratched,'" laughed Muriel.

"But what?" said Mullins. "That was the big question. But what? Suddenly there it was, plain as the nose on your face, Cozy Disposal, a boon to our fellow golden agers. Or so we hoped."

"Lorne was afraid there wouldn't be call enough call for it," said Muriel. "But I told him, 'Provide the service. The need will follow.'"

"Darned if it didn't," said Mullins. "And all by word of mouth."

"You're right," said Mrs. Wilmot in amazement. "This morning when I decided to kill Leland I never gave a thought to what to do with the damn body. Because I'd heard about Cozy Disposal."

"Good for you," smiled Mullins and took a paper from his order book. "Now here's our rate card. That first figure's our standard service. We remove Mr. Wilmot's remains and you will never be troubled by them again."

Mrs. Wilmot studied the card for a moment. "It seems so expensive."

"Have you priced a funeral lately?"

Mrs. Wilmot cocked her head thoughtfully as if conceding his point. "And what happens to the body?"

Muriel leaned forward. "Nothing disrespectful, I assure you, dear."

Mullins leaned back in his chair so his wife couldn't see him. Showing his well-calloused palms he winked at Mrs. Wilmot and made the motion of shoveling air over his shoulder.

Muriel asked, "Am I correct that you mean to do the dirty deed—or the 'event', as we like to call it—yourself?"

"*If* I do it. It's certainly not the sort of thing to leave to strangers."

Mullins agreed. "Muriel only brings it up because if you so desire we can put you in touch with an individual who does that sort of thing and who offers Cozy Disposal customers a special discount rate. This option, by the way, comes at no extra charge. We are recompensed by a finders fee paid by this individual."

"He's also familiar with the Cozy Disposal way," said Muriel. "We like to think our name evokes wisteria-covered cottages. Teacups. The vicarage down the lane. The polite constable at the door. A world where murder acts with taste and restraint. Think Agatha Christie and you won't go far wrong."

"In other words," Mullins chimed in, "Cozy Disposal doesn't do dismembered bodies. Or corpses done in with uzis at close range or hammers in a fit of jealous rage."

"We recommend the old heave-ho down a carpeted staircase," said Muriel, "Or off the belfry tower if you're churchgoers. We will also accept a shot from a small cal-iber revolver with mother-of-pearl handle or a single thrust with a dagger from the display on the wall. But nine times out of ten what we get is poison or the trusty blunt instrument. Women go for poison. I guess it's a nurturing thing. Men are blunt instruments."

"I was never handy in the kitchen," confessed Mrs. Wilmot. "In my mind's eye I saw myself hitting him with something."

"And why not, dear?" smiled Muriel. Then she paused and turned to other matters. "Now here's a bridge you should cross before you come to it. Have you given any thought to how you'll explain your husband's disappear-ance?"

"I guess I was going to tell people he was visiting his sick sister in Vancouver. Leland is definitely an out-of-sight-out-of-mind sort. After a bit I'd rather hoped his name just wouldn't come up any more."

"Chancy, dear. Chancy."

Mullins murmured agreement and leaned over to point at the rate card. "We at Cozy Disposal offer our clients some helpful extras in that regard. Like the 'Party Animal' option there."

"To make a long story short," explained Muriel, "I allow myself to be picked up by your husband. He then wines and dine me for a week or two where your friends will see us. Bingo games, dancing behind the waterfall at the Cataract Lounge on senior citizen night. That sets the stage. Afterwards you simply announce that Leland's run off with another woman."

Muriel patted her husband's sleeve, adding, "When it's a woman who's about to disappear the lucky lady gets to go on the town with Lorne wearing his European suit and the cutest little mustache."

Mrs. Wilmot fretted over the rate card. "This is all so expensive." She chewed her lip, brightened a bit and asked, "I don't suppose you offer a widow's discount."

The Mullinses laughed. "Hardly," said Muriel. "But let's move down to our economy option there, the mock around-the-world cruise. Give us a sample of your husband's handwriting and we'll even arrange for postcards mailed from various ports of call along the way. It's customary to top the whole thing off with a death certificate from Smyrna in Turkey."

"Which we don't recommend if a life insurance policy is involved," said Mullins. "Something about a Smyrna death certificate really gets insurance people's hackles up."

Here a side door to the garage opened spilling light into the garden. A man with a healthy head of gray hair in portly, paint-spattered overalls emerged. As the Mullinses leaned back so they were hidden by the hydrangea the man hurried along the patio to the French doors. There he stopped and called, "Eunice, I could use your help in a few minutes, okay?"

"I didn't forget," she called back. When the man disappeared into the house she said, "Leland asked me to hold the ladder for him while he paints the ceiling where it peaks."

The night deepened and the crickets started up from the damper corners of the garden.

"Well," continued Mullins, "that's how we can help you. Now here's what you can do to make our job a little easier. First, we recommend the actual 'event' take place with the subject standing on a six-by-eight-foot sheet of heavy plastic."

Mrs. Wilmot looked as if she didn't understand.

"It saves on clean-up," he explained. "There's bound to be some bleeding, either during the 'event' or when the victim hits the floor. That's why the plastic. No blood on the rug."

"I'm clear on that," she said. "What I meant was how do I get him to stand on the sheet of plastic?"

"Hey, he's your husband. I bet you'll think of something. Anyway, we arrive, roll him up in the plastic, cover it with old carpeting and wheel it out to our van on a gurney. Anybody spots us will figure you're getting new wall-to-wall."

"I believe Leland bought plastic to use as a drop-sheet in the garage. The roll said 4 mil. Is that thick enough?"

"Just what the doctor ordered," said Mullins. "Second,

please make sure the subject is really dead. That's why the little plastic mirror is our free gift to you. If it doesn't fog up under his nose it's time to call Cozy Disposal. If it does, he's still breathing and you'll have to try a little harder. Many's the time we're on our merry way only to hear groans and have to come back so the client can finish the job right."

"Well, that's it, dear," said Muriel. "Take all the time you need to make up your mind." She sat back and folded her hands in her lap. Her husband looked away and drummed his fingers lightly on his order book.

Mrs. Wilmot stared down at the ashtray for several minutes. Then she raised her head and looked around at the garden. It was just that moment when the colors of the flowers brightened and stepped forward as if to upstage the darkness.

She turned back to her visitors with her face at peace. "I appreciate your coming," she said. "And I thank you for your little gift. I'm sorry. It isn't just the money. When you come right down to it I guess I don't feel right about the 'event.'"

"But you haven't even heard about our sign-up premiums," coaxed Mullins. "Either a bottle of Mother Mullins' Shepherd's Pie Helper or—and I know you're going to like this one—our own blunt instrument, the ever-popular Mullins Sock-'O-Sand." From his briefcase he pulled a black nylon stocking stuffed with an eight-inch sausage of sand, then knotted tight. Mullins demonstrated, wrapping the empty pigtail of material around his hand.

"Take it, dear," Muriel advised her. "You don't want your Rookwood vases ending up what the police call 'blunt weapons of opportunity.'"

"So that's what the damn thing is." said Mrs. Wilmot,

her voice suddenly hard and deliberate. She pulled an identically stuffed stocking from beneath the pillow of her chair. "I came across this one months ago hidden at the back of Leland's sock drawer. Never knew what it was for. Never cared enough to ask. I forgot all about it until this morning when I needed something blunt to kill him with."

"Yipes," said Mullins and turned to his wife. "I knew we'd been here before. But it was daylight and wintertime. And we talked to a guy. Out in the garage. Remember? Boy, is our face red!"

"I remember him now," said Muriel. "Took the world cruise option. And the Smyrna death certificate. Said it would be nice for cloture."

"I'll show him cloture," shouted Mrs. Wilmot, jumping from her chair. Then she lowered her voice and started wrapping the Sock-'O-Sand around her hand. "This is what he went back into the house for. Well, I've got it now."

Mullins stood to block her way. "Listen, Mrs. Wilmot, hear me out," he said earnestly. "Maybe you two still have a chance. Muriel and I have been talking about selling Cozy Disposal what-do-you-call-'ems. Franchises. A little money up front and you and hubby could get in on the ground floor in an emerging field using proven sales techniques. Might save your marriage. It's happened before."

"It's too late for that, Mr. Mullins. It's him or me."

Mullins' briefcase chirped amid the crickets. He pulled out a cell phone. "Cozy Disposal," he said. "Lorne speaking. How can I help you? Yes, sir. Yes, sir. I understand. No need. We have your address on file. We'll be there in half an hour. Thank you for calling Cozy Disposal."

Mullins shook his head and said, "Maybe Mr. Wilmot doesn't have his Sock-'O-Sand anymore. But he sure talks like he's found himself a blunt instrument of opportunity."

"Oh-ho," said Muriel.

"That's fine with me," announced Mrs. Wilmot.

Muriel lay a hand on the woman's arm, thought for a moment and said, "Dear, Cozy Disposal finds itself in an embarrassing situation here, business-ethics and conflict-of-interest-wise. Since snap decisions are my department, here's what we're prepared to do. Promise not to mention this little contretemps to anyone ever again and we at Cozy Disposal are prepared to consider our agreement with your husband to be an agreement with you, too. On a which-ever-comes-first basis. If you follow me."

"Cozy Disposal's got itself a deal." Mrs. Wilmot strode across the garden slapping the business end of the Sock-'O-Sand in her one hand into the palm of the other.

As she disappeared inside the garage Leland Wilmot emerged from the house with a wooden rolling pin under his arm. The Mullins's watched from behind the hydrangea bush. When he saw his wife's empty chair Wilmot gripped the rolling pin in his right hand and marched purposefully toward the garage.

Mullins grimaced. "That honeydew wine is a bitter, bitter wine," he remembered.

"My money's on her," said Muriel. "But either way, let's get the gurney."

Laura Philpot Benedict

"The Hollow Woman"

In its 70-year existence, *EQMM* has introduced hundreds of debut stories by new writers. One of the most recent additions to the Department of First Stories is the first commercial publication of a Roanoke, Virginia, book reviewer and copywriter, Laura Philpot Benedict. It is an intense and gripping psychological study.

I watched as the old woman on the other side of the road pushed her mower back and forth, back and forth across the scorched August grass, the mower's yellow cord snaking over the ground like some living thing. At the end of each careful row, the old woman stood a moment, her head tilted back as though she were balancing an invisible book on her helmet of red-dyed hair. In those brief pauses, she closed her eyes and stood perfectly still, as though she were already dead, a corpse propped up in the sunlight like some ghoulish lawn ornament, an undertaker's sight-gag.

The baby squirmed in my arms, arching his back to look up at my face. He reached for my chin and scratched, an untrimmed point on his thumbnail digging into my skin.

I grabbed his hand and squeezed it. Not hard, but hard enough for him to get the message.

"Bad baby," I said. "Don't scratch Mommy."

His eyes widened and I saw fat tears form in their corners. The guilt washed over me in a wave of heat. Guilty because I was angry that he'd taken my attention from the old woman.

He began to cry in earnest and I held him close. The rattle and hum of the mower muffled his sobs.

"There, there," I crooned. "Mommy's sorry."

He pulled away with a fierce cry, aimlessly waving his gathered fist. His eyes were closing in sleep, sleep that rarely came peacefully to him. He slept only in self-defense, when he no longer had the strength to keep it away.

I took the baby inside the house, holding his head against my shoulder, imagining that my closeness would keep him asleep. I lay him in his crib, pulled the single window shade down against the vibrant sunlight. When he was settled, I pulled the door to and went into the living room to sit in my chair beside the front picture window.

The old woman was still out there, walking the fifty paces or so of each sunburned row and back again. Every so often I would lose sight of her as she passed behind the wide trunk of a silver maple, but she would emerge almost immediately, the body of the mower first, then the old woman's hands gripping the mower's handle, her canvas-clad feet and finally, her ramrod frame, thin as a cancer victim's.

I sat at the edge of the window, my head leaning against the back of the chair, peering at the old woman through half-closed eyes, so that if she did see me she might think I was sleeping or meditating. Doing anything but watching her.

Every so often she would brush at the air around her face, which I could see was, as always, heavily made-up. But mostly she just walked behind the mower, the grass behind her always shorter and slightly less brown than the grass ahead.

I watched until my own eyes closed and I drifted off to sleep.

I was born into one of those cozy, middle-class suburbs where a new family's arrival was an event. When a house changed owners, I would stand with the other neighborhood children at the back of the moving van and watch the furniture come off. We must have imagined ourselves invisible because we were always in the way of the moving men, who cursed us and repeated, time after time, "Step aside kids," and "Move or you'll get hurt." And we always did step away, but only for a minute, and then we were back again, crowding each other for a look at what was coming out next.

The first time I ever saw a king-size mattress it was coming off the back of a moving truck. I remember how we all gasped at the sight of it and how Jill Parker said that it was a bed for giants and that the new people must be freaks from a circus. When I told my parents about the bed over dinner, my father raised his eyebrows and exchanged a look with my mother that told me that people with king-size beds must not belong in our neighborhood. All the same, my mother sent me over with a chocolate-pudding pie the very next day. The man who had bought the house and his pale-haired teenage daughter had come to Kentucky all the way from California, but after six months, another moving truck came and the house was empty again.

When Barry and I moved into our house, there were no children gathered at the back of our moving van, no offers for the use of a telephone, no promise of a tuna casserole. Our house was only one of two on a small, dead end street. A friend of Barry's had bought the lot and cleared it and started building the house. Nothing special: three bedrooms, one-and-a-half-baths, vinyl siding, a vaulted ceiling and a brick fireplace in the living room to give it some character. But he'd lost his job and couldn't pay to finish it and Barry made him an offer.

I didn't see the old woman until we'd been in the house a week. I was painting the mailbox, lavender paint splattered on the t-shirt of Barry's that was stretched over my huge, pregnant belly. I heard the front door of the house across the street close, firmly, and the old woman, her hair alarmingly bright against the creamy brick of her house, walked slowly toward the Buick parked in the driveway.

"Hello," I called to her. I waved. She didn't turn to look at me.

"My name's Cathy," I said. "Cathy" came my own voice back to me, echoing off the brick of her house. I wondered for a moment if she might be deaf.

I placed the paintbrush on the edge of the can. Thinking that the old woman hadn't seen me, I started across the road to her driveway, which was poured concrete and expensive, Barry had told me.

"Hi," I said, again.

The old woman got into her car, started it. I stopped in the middle of our small road. A thin stream of gray exhaust came from the back of the Buick; it dissipated as the car rolled slowly backwards. The car paused at the end of the driveway, its bulbous taillights staring at me like two comic eyes. The old woman wasn't looking over her shoulder, or even moving that I could tell. I realized then that she was waiting for me to move, that I was merely an object blocking her way, some kind of nuisance to her, like an obstinate stray dog, or a bad-mannered child.

I started walking backwards, to my own driveway, thinking, pitifully, that there must be some misunderstanding between us, that she surely couldn't mean to ignore me. But as the car sped away, all I saw of the old woman was the shadow of her profile: oversized sunglasses, small, straight nose, gloved hands gripping the steering wheel through her closed-up window.

I awoke on the telephone's first ring. The shadows of the silver maples in the old woman's yard stretched into the road. The old woman had finished the mowing. Her Buick was gone from the driveway.

Barry was on the phone. "Cathy," he said. "What's wrong? You weren't sleeping, were you?"

I heard accusation in his voice. This child, his only one, wasn't normal. He would only sleep a few hours a day, almost exclusively in the daytime, like a miniature vampire. Barry, who could lie on the bed or the couch, close his eyes, and be dreaming in thirty seconds. Barry, who needed twelve hours sleep at a time and would spend the night in his truck to get it if the baby cried too loudly or too long. Somehow it was my fault.

"I tried to put him down early last night," I said. "I thought that maybe if it was still light outside, he would sleep."

"They want me to move on to the next one straight from here," Barry said. "Down to Trimble County." The next one. The next Taco Fiesta. Barry installed the special Mexican floor tile the restaurants used, traveled with a construction crew. He'd been working on Taco Fiestas for months.

"How long, Barry?" I said. "I'm tired of you being gone." I wanted him home, to feel his warm body next to me in our bed, even if I had to lie awake, listening, listening, listening to the baby make toneless noises from his crib while Barry slept. But another part of me, a small voice in my brain was saying "This is good, Cathy. This is easier, Cathy. This is for the best."

"Two weeks," Barry said. "Maybe two and a half."

We sat, quiet, the hundred miles of phone line humming between us.

"Take him back to the doctor, Cathy. Find out what the hell is wrong with him."

Suddenly I hated Barry, this man who'd given me this damaged child, who'd left me here in this godforsaken house with its unfinished garage and treeless yard. This man who said he didn't know if he was ready to be married, even though we had the house, the kid, the bills. Even though he'd said that he loved me a thousand times.

"You're not here, are you, Barry?" I said. "I'll do whatever I damn well please." I slapped the phone into its cradle. I knew I would regret doing it. I always did.

The baby howled from his bedroom. Days like this when he slept for three or four hours in the afternoon were the worst. It meant maybe one or two cat naps in the night, twenty minutes, nothing more.

I lifted him from the crib. He gave me a small, hesitant smile. At six months old, he was too young to reach out. But it was enough that he was happy to see me.

"You're lucky you're so cute," I told him. "Or we'd have pitched you out with the trash a long time ago." And he was cute. He had a peachy, old-fashioned look to him, round cheeks and blue eyes. Blue eyes bright like carnival glass Christmas ornaments with a sparkle that let you know that he would soon be up to mischief. "That boy's got the devil in him," my mother said. But she was wrong. The devil wouldn't waste any time on a darling like my baby. If the devil were to come on the earth, he would take the form of someone with an empty heart, someone cold like the old woman.

I fed the baby his heated oatmeal and a jar of peas for dinner. I cleaned his hands and face and put him in the stroller that sat waiting on the front porch. There was a thing I'd been wanting to do for a long time.

The old woman's Buick was still gone. Wednesday evening. She was always dressed up the same way on Sunday mornings and Wednesday evenings—tiny hat, white gloves like I wore when I was five years old (I could imagine the plastic pearl buttons at their tops), carefully ironed dress, matching handbag and shoes—which told me that she must go to church. Baptists go to church on Wednesday nights, I know. Barry's parents are Baptists.

More than six months we'd lived across the street from the old woman and I didn't even know her name.

Nervous, I pushed the baby up the road some, just short of the next house nearly a halfmile away. I walked back on the old woman's side of the road and stopped at her mailbox. Going into another person's mailbox was some kind of crime. My hand shook as I pulled at the latch.

A pile of mail lay inside. I pulled it out carefully and fingered through it. Nutter was her name: Mrs. Charles Nutter; L.E. Nutter, the Nutter Family. One piece from a mail-order steak place (imagine—mail order steak) was addressed to The Natties at 125 Elm Grove Lane.

Nutter. *Nutty. Nut Case. Nutty-as-a-fruitcake.* I laughed out loud, startling the baby who was pulling at a flowering vine that the old woman had trained around the mailbox post.

I couldn't find her first name on any of the envelopes.

The Boston Shoe Company catalog, with the initials L.E. in the address, was the closest I could get to it. I tucked the shoe catalog into the stroller's pocket and slipped the rest of the mail back into the box.

Nighttime. The coffee maker shorted out when I tried to put a second pot-full of water into its already-filled reservoir. There was a loud *pop* and the kitchen lights flickered. Water splashed onto the counter and my feet, soaking my socks and the kitchen rug. Coffee, with a little splash of Bailey's Irish Cream, was my comfort. Now there was no coffee and no comfort. Just me and the night and the baby and the old woman.

The old woman's lights went out at twelve fifteen. First, though, she walked through the house and secured all the window latches. I watched as her hand reached through the curtains, window after window, her fingers feeling for the lock and then disappearing. I don't know why she did it every night. I never saw her open windows except to clean them, which she did, every single one of them, every two weeks. After she'd secured the window locks, she switched on the floodlights planted in the yard. They bathed the house in light like it was some sort of palace. Every shutter, every gutter, every nook was outlined in broad light and shadow. Except for one space on the right side of the house. That bulb had been burned out for several days, but I don't think she knew it.

Now that I had her name, I could look up her phone number in the book and call her to tell her about the burned out light: "Hi, Mrs. Nutter. It's Cathy ... Sure you know me. I live across the street ... No, I really do. We haven't met. I'm the one with the baby ... Sure, I'd love to come over sometime ... Can I bring anything? Coffee

cake, maybe? . . . Your really are too nice . . . Well, I just
called to let you know that one of your floodlights is
burned out . . . Yes. Neighbors do have to watch out for
each other."

The baby was calm, lying on the floor, watching the ceiling fan spinning overhead. I lay down beside him and
stroked his arms and legs, his soft, soft skin. I massaged
him gently with my fingertips like the baby book said
and he lay almost hypnotized with the quiet whir of the
fan and the touch of my hands. It was so peaceful in the
house, I wondered that he could resist sleep.

I slept for one minute, maybe five. I dreamed that I
lived in a one-room cabin that had no ceiling. Storm
clouds sailed over in the sky above, but never rained on
me. My mother came to the window and handed me pies
and baskets of soap until there was no longer any room
to move around. I cried for her to stop. When I awoke, the
baby was staring at me, his curls ruffling lightly in the
fan's breeze. He stared and I wondered what he saw in my
face. I wondered if he would remember how my face
looked at this moment years from now.

He began to cry.

Two A.M. The lights in the old woman's house had been
out for almost two hours. The Home Shopping Channel
played on the television. The baby's swing clicked back
and forth beside my chair. I drank a cup of strong tea to
make up for the coffee. If they'd been selling coffee mak-
ers on the television, I'd have bought one.

At three, I gave the baby a bottle and he fell asleep in
the middle of it, his fists balled up under his chin. But as

I lowered him into the crib, his eyes opened and he screamed as though I were doing him some harm.

When the newspaper came at five, tossed onto our porch from a rusting Datsun that was sorely in need of a new muffler, I was strapping the baby into his high chair for his next bowl of oatmeal.

I wasn't hungry. I ate a couple of spoonfuls of the baby's prunes from a jar just to taste their sweetness on my tongue.

I thought about the old woman across the road. She was probably still in bed. Alone, like me. There had been a husband. Had there been children? Had she ever sat in a creaking rocking chair feeding a baby who looked up at her with eyes that had never held a look of fear? Maybe she was the sort that scared children. Maybe I wouldn't like her at all. She was cruel the way she never waved back at me. I always waved when I saw her. It was unfair of her not to give me a chance. Thinking about her made me angry. Maybe she was waiting for me, waiting for *me* to break, to beg for her friendship. What kind of person was she? What made a person mean like that?

The baby sat spinning the bright blue and green clown toy that was suctioned to his highchair tray. Such an angel. Truly one of God's miracles. He was innocence itself. Why would the old woman reject him, too? The bitch.

Standing at the kitchen sink, I saw several bursts of light in the window, brief, high flashes that streaked through the receding dark. *Shooting stars*, I thought. A present for me. A chance to make a wish. Then I saw more bounce off the stark white kitchen cabinets that Barry had installed by himself. I knew then that the flashes were in my head.

* * *

I heard the phone ringing in the house as I buckled the baby into his car seat. I was sure it was Barry, worried that I hadn't called him to apologize. *Let him wonder*, I thought.

As I opened the driver's door, the old woman came out of her house, pulling the front door shut, hard, so that the knocker clanked once behind her. Out the front door, in through the side door. Like she was superstitious. She also kept her house key under a flower basket next to the side door. A stupid, old-fashioned habit for someone who double-checked her locked windows each night.

Why did I choose that morning to follow her? I don't know. I'd meant just to run to the grocery to pick up some formula and diapers.

I followed her down our street and through the surrounding neighborhood. She drove with a heavier foot than I would have expected, barely slowing at curves where I had to downshift to stay on the road. Once, I let another car come between us so that she wouldn't become suspicious of seeing my Honda constantly in her rearview mirror.

We ended up at the big Baptist church in town. When I saw her put on her turn signal, I slipped into the lot of the dry cleaner next door. I had a clear view of her as she parked and got out of her car. She took off her sunglasses before she opened the front door and went inside.

I waited a good twenty minutes. I wanted to know what she was doing in the church. Was she a Sunday School teacher preparing lessons? Maybe she was giving the preacher advice. Old women liked to give advice. How galling, then, that she could see me every day, struggling with this angel-darling baby, and not want to rush over to help, to tell me what I should be feeding him, how often to change his diaper, how to make him sleep like other babies.

When she came out, she was carrying a Manila envelope, which she dropped onto the passenger seat of her car. The baby started fussing and I reached backward, feeling for his mouth to stick the pacifier in it. I almost wasn't able to catch up to the old woman, who had sped out of the parking lot.

She went next to a copy shop, where she walked in with the envelope and came out empty-handed.

The baby began howling and pulled at his hair.

"Go on," I said. "Go to sleep." I rubbed his foot as we drove, letting go only when I had to shift gears. It was a danger letting him sleep in the car. At home, he might sleep for two to three hours, his longest sleep of the day. My only chance to sleep. But sleep didn't matter. I needed to be close to the old woman. I needed to know what she was doing. I was hungry with the desire to know, to be there. My heart was pounding the way it had when I would wait at my apartment for Barry to pick me up for a date. It was the anticipation that something was going to happen and I wanted to be awake and alive to it.

I knew in my heart that there was something not quite right about this, that maybe the old woman might be unhappy if she knew what I was doing. But I had a right to do this, to make up for her lapse, to give her the chance to be a better person.

We drove to a shopping center across town. The roads were unfamiliar and I had to follow closely. I really wanted to stop for coffee and maybe a donut. I was getting hungry despite the nervous state of my stomach.

The old woman pulled into a space in front of a dress shop that had a small fountain out front and no clothes at all in the window. An expensive place.

I parked two rows over and shut the engine off. The baby was asleep, his mouth slightly open, the pacifier in his lap. His finger twitched.

I rummaged in the glovebox for some crackers or something but came up with only a packet of ketchup. I nipped the edge of the package with my teeth and tore off the corner, careful to put the plastic bit in the ashtray. The ketchup was warm on my tongue. I sucked at it. I was thirsty, too.

I thought about Barry. Maybe we would break up. Perhaps I hadn't loved him as much as I thought I did. We used to spend hours, whole days together in bed. Days like dreams that had no purpose, no reason to them. Just aimless happiness. Days when we would sleep and eat and make love. But I was having trouble imagining myself having days like that again. Everything had become difficult, complicated, new. Hard: The harsh morning light that flooded our white (blindingly, damnably), white kitchen; the unflinching bitterness of the old woman's soul; the brittle ring of the telephone; Barry's voice, cold and accusing.

The old woman came out of the store. A saleswoman carried out something on a hanger, a dress, maybe, or a suit (the old woman wore a lot of brightly-colored suits, despite her garish hair) covered with an opaque plastic bag. She hung the bag in the Buick and nodded to the old woman. Then the old woman smiled.

The bitch actually smiled.

All at once, I felt that the months of waiting were over. I backed the Honda out of its space and drove right up behind the Buick, blocking the old woman in. My foot slipped off the clutch and the car shuddered to a halt. I felt my pulse beating in my ears. Now was the time! I imagined myself getting out of the car, walking up to the old woman and shouting at her, telling her what a mess she'd made of my life. How her cruelty had hurt me.

How they stared at me. Did I seem crazy to them? The saleswoman's slender face wore a look of frank curiosity. Disdain, too, I thought, for my old car. But the old woman just hid behind her sunglasses, her lips pursed. Uninterested.

I looked away and started the car and drove home as quickly as I dared.

Barry left three messages that day.

Pleading. "Cathy, pick up the phone. Talk to me, Cathy."

Angry. "I've taken about all of this shit that I'm going to take, Cathy. I'm sick of your games," he said. "Bullshit, Cathy. This is bullshit."

The third call came about midnight. He sighed into the phone, a long, drawn-out breath that sounded sad, regretful. He hung up.

We ran out of baby formula about two in the morning. I thought about Marie Antoinette and her words, "Let them eat cake." The baby was laughing at a shadow on the wall. We had plenty of grape juice.

The shooting lights that I'd been seeing showed up again and again, falling like a shower as I sat in my chair and watched the old woman's house through the night.

I filled the useless coffee carafe with water to its ten cup mark and drank from it until the water was gone.

The old woman turned the floodlights out sometime early in the morning. But her curtains stayed drawn.

Around noon, the baby started screaming. I held him

in my arms and tried to give him a bottle of grape juice, but he turned his head to the side and pushed my arm away. It wasn't me he didn't want, I knew. It was the old woman's fault that I'd forgotten the formula. The baby's screams faded in my ears, becoming just a background, like roughly textured music.

The old woman left her house in the late afternoon. She turned her head ever so slightly to look at my house, my window, my face.

Click. Click. Click. The baby slept in his swing, the sun warming his tired little body. My angel.

The phone rang. My mother's voice on the answering machine. "Cathy. Barry called me. You've upset him terribly, Cathy. Call me," she said. "How's my baby boy?"

It was late when the old woman came home. She checked the windows and turned on the floodlights.

The phone rang about one in the morning as I opened the front door. Barry's voice on the answering machine. "Don't, Cathy," he said.

The key, of course. The key like an invitation for welcome friends. The kind of friend I would be. Would have been.

As I put my hand on the old woman's doorknob, I thought of gloves. Plastic kitchen gloves were all I had, orange rubber things that would have been clumsy and overlarge. If I'd worn gloves, it would have said something about intention, wouldn't it? I was just visiting. I wasn't intending anything.

The door felt solid against my hand. Everything about the house felt solid. Old. Settled.

I stood in the old woman's kitchen. It was dark and cool. Neat. I tiptoed quietly, as though I were in a church.

I would be respectful even if the old woman didn't deserve it. I found the light switch and flipped it on.

The kitchen cabinets were knotty pine, matching the paneling on the walls. Matching, like her shoes and purses. I lifted the teakettle on the stove and found it full of water. I lit the burner beneath it. I discovered an uncut pound cake under a ceramic cover painted to look like a strawberries-and-cream layer cake. Like she'd been expecting me.

How many times had my mother sent me to a neighbor's house, my arms aching under the weight of her heaviest casserole dish, filled to the top with fragrant noodles or a chicken and rice bake? Here I'd come to the old woman's house empty-handed. I felt ashamed and mean.

I took a long, serrated bread knife from a block on the counter and green china plates and teacups and saucers from the cupboard. I put the dishes on the table and cut a piece off the pound cake.

"Charles?" The old woman spoke from down the hallway. "Charles, are you home?"

I quickly sliced another piece of pound cake, thinner this time. Less generous. Old women don't eat much. I put the cake on the waiting second plate. Fat, honey-colored crumbs dropped from the knife. I touched my fingers to them and put them to my lips. *Heaven.*

"Charles?" The old woman sounded worried now. Definitely not the way a hostess should behave.

She stood in the doorway, looking much smaller to me than she had from a distance. She was really quite petite. Her hair was disheveled, odd. Up close, her skin was less wrinkled than I'd imagined. Perhaps she wasn't such an old woman.

"Cake?" I said. "The water will boil in a minute. Where do you keep your tea?"

She took it all in—me, the cake, the crumbs on the table. "The police," she said. "Get out, or I'll call the police." But she was frozen where she stood. Her eyes looked wild, a little crazy. I was just a woman, a mother, no one to fear. It was a hell of a welcome.

I reached out for the phone hanging on the wall just a foot or so from the old woman's head. She flinched. I took the receiver in one hand and jerked on the cord, breaking it free from the phone. The plastic connector skittered across the floor. It seemed such a silly, dramatic thing for me to do that it made me laugh.

"Oh, no," I said. "I think I broke your phone. I'm sorry."

"You did break my phone," the old woman said. "Now get out."

I carefully hung the phone back on its cradle. I could have left then. I probably should have. But there was the cake and the tea I hadn't yet made. I was hungry. So hungry.

"I just wanted to sit down," I said. "I'm tired. Can't you just sit with me and have some cake?"

The old woman eased her way into the kitchen, keeping her distance from me. "Have all the cake you want," she said. "Take it. Just take it."

"You don't understand," I told her. She didn't understand. And suddenly, I was so profoundly tired that I was having a difficult time driving the words from my mouth. "Sit," I said. "Please." My head felt heavy.

"I wouldn't sit at a table with a piece of white trash like you in a million years," she said. She pointed at me, her arm shaking in the long, apricot sleeve of her robe. "I know you," she said. "I know who you are."

"But we haven't met," I said. "My name is Cathy." I heard my voice speaking, but it seemed to come from far away, somewhere far below me.

"You're going to get out of here," the old woman said. "And they're going to take that little bastard child of yours away from you when I tell them what you've done."

My angel. She was talking about my angel-baby. What was she saying? I couldn't see her very well. My face felt cool and wet. Rain? I looked up, but there was nothing but ceiling above me.

The shriek of the tea kettle's whistle shook me from the daze into which I had drifted. The old woman lunged for the door, but I grabbed her around the waist before she could pull it open. She was light, so light, as though she were hollow. She flopped forward, over my arm. A rag doll.

"Sit down!" I screamed. I pulled out a chair with one hand.

The old woman didn't resist. She slumped into the vinyl seat, her shoulders resting against its back.

I slid the plate with the slice of pound cake on it into the space in front of her.

"Eat it," I said.

She was still, looking down at the floor. "I won't," she said.

"Eat the goddamn cake!" I was shouting at her.

When she made no move to take it, I picked up the piece of cake in my hand. I jerked her head back by her hair and the red hair—I saw now that it was a wig—came off in my hand. The old fraud. A bitch and a fraud.

When I pitched the wig across the room, the old woman tried to get up out of the chair, her head pitifully small now, and gray. But I was too fast and too strong for her. I pushed her back down.

The old woman began to wail. A high, mournful quaver.

"You have to eat the cake," I told her, firmly, as though she were a child. I pushed the piece of cake into her open mouth. She gagged, tried to spit it out again. When she tried to close her mouth, I pulled her jaw down. I tore more cake from the loaf, a handful, and pushed it, too, into her mouth. She struggled, turning her head from side to side. We fell to the floor, but I had the entire cake in my hand now. I fed her and fed her. I filled the empty, old woman with the rich, buttery cake. Finally, she stopped struggling. She was full of sweetness.

Standing in the old woman's driveway, I could see into my own living room: the baby (my darling, sweetest angel) sleeping in his swing; the flickering glow of the television. Like looking into my own life.

Inside, I stopped in front of the gold-framed mirror that my mother had bought and made me hang by the front door. "To touch up your lipstick on the way out the door," she said. But I didn't recognize the woman I saw in the mirror. Was I this haggard witch with the deep, purplish circles beneath her eyes? When had my hair lost its color of fluid sunshine and taken on that steely tone? Why couldn't my eyes meet themselves in the mirror?

I sat down in my chair beside the front window and dialed the number of Barry's motel. "Hello," he said. "Cathy?" He sounded awake, as though he'd been waiting.

"Come home," I said. I put the phone back in its cradle, gently, quietly, so as not to wake the baby. Leaning my head against the back of my chair, I closed my eyes and fell into a hard, dreamless sleep.

Dana Stabenow

"Missing, Presumed . . ."

Of several writers setting mysteries in the State of Alaska, the best-known and most prolific has been Dana Stabenow, author of novel series about Liam Campbell and Kate Shugak. In a rare short story, she offers a view of the legal system in the 49th state.

One

Sec. 09.55.020. **Petition and inquiry.** If a petition is presented by an interested person to a district judge or magistrate alleging that a designated person has disappeared and after diligent search cannot be found, and if it appears to the satisfaction of the judge or magistrate that the circumstances surrounding the disappearance afford reasonable grounds for the belief that the person has suffered death from accidental or other violent means, the judge or magistrate shall summon and impanel a jury of six qualified persons to inquire into the facts surrounding and the presumption to be raised from the disappearance. If no one submits a petition within 40 days, a judge or magistrate may submit the petition from personal knowledge of the case.

—Alaska Statutes, Code of Civil Procedure

Eli Sylvester Horrell, fisher, husband, father, went overboard halfway between Dutch Harbor and the Pribilof Islands. Weather conditions that day in January included fifteen-knot winds and twelve-foot swells. The crew of the *Jeri A.* had seen Horrell go in. In spite of an intensive search by the United States Coast Guard, the *Jeri A.*, and three other crabbers, his body had not been recovered.

Now it was June. Horrell's widow, two sons, and one daughter were seated in the front row. The widow, daughter, and youngest son were weeping. The oldest son stared at nothing, white-faced and without expression.

Magistrate Linda Louise Billington, known to friends, defendants, and bar patrons as Bill, was new to the state, new to the town of Newenham, and new to her job. The hearing had come less than six months into her first term of office. It was a balmy spring day, sixty-three degrees with sunny skies and a light breeze. The last of the snow had melted, the last of the mud had dried and the birch and the diamond willow and the alder all showed tiny leaves of a bright, vivid green. She wanted to be outside, catching her first monster king salmon, or climbing her first Alaskan mountain, or taking her first ride in a float plane with a real bush pilot, or even slapping away her first horde of the infamous Alaskan mosquitoes. She looked around the cramped, windowless courtroom lodged in a forgotten corner of the prefabricated building that served as the seat of the third judicial district of the state of Alaska, and thought, How I Spent My Summer Vacation.

In the six months since she had been sworn in she had stumbled through her first arrest warrants, fumbled through her first search warrants, and muddled through her first arraignments. She had figured out how to set bail, and how high. She had issued half a dozen restraining orders, and had taken emergency action in one case of child abuse that still gave her nightmares. She had tried, convicted, and sentenced no less than sixteen drunk drivers. She had tried and convicted one fisher of fishing without a permit, a second for fishing past the end of the period, a third for harvesting female opilio, a fourth for harvesting undersized kings, and a fifth for fishing outside the district to which his permit restricted him. She had learned to discount most excuses offered by fishers, because if all the engines alleged to have broken down in her courtroom really had, half the Bering Sea fishing fleet would be in dry dock.

She was beginning to build a reputation. The night before in the bar she'd heard one fisher mumble at her approach, "Gawd, here she comes, Hanging Bill." No compliment in her life had ever tasted so sweet.

This, however, was her first presumptive death hearing.

Sudden, violent death was no stranger to Alaska, especially the Bush. Pilots wrecked planes. Hikers disappeared into national parks. Climbers fell down mountains. Snow machiners started avalanches. Cross-country skiers fell into glaciers.

And, as in this case, fishers fell overboard. Alaska had thirty-six thousand miles of shoreline. Much of its living was made on the water.

Many of its missing people were lost on that water.

When it became obvious that the missing was dead, a presumptive death hearing was held to engage the machinery of the state to issue a death certificate.

The two-by-four folding table that stood in for a judicial bench was stacked with the necessary tools as specified by the Magistrate Correspondence Course: the case file, the list of witnesses, no exhibit list as there were no exhibits, her jury instructions, a log sheet, a blank verdict form, paper and pencils, and a box of Kleenex. There was a copy of the Presumptive Death Hearing Script, extracted from the correspondence course binder, held between her knees and the bottom of the table in case she forgot what she was doing midway through the process. She'd already checked the tape recorder twice; she checked it a third time on the principle that it was a mistake to allow any mechanical object to realize its own importance. Hattie Bishop had been sworn in as bailiff. The jury was impaneled. The witnesses were waiting.

One of the fluorescent lights flickered overhead behind a plastic lens yellowed and cracked with age. Her back brushed against the standards bearing the American and

Alaskan flags. Metal chair legs scraped the floor when someone shifted his weight, somebody else coughed. The second hand on the plain white face of the clock over the door clicked loudly up to twelve: 9:00 A.M.

She cleared her throat and restarted the tape recorder. "We are again on record. This is the district court for the state of Alaska at Newenham, Alaska, Magistrate L.L. Billington presiding." She noted the date and the time, the name of the deceased, and the case number. "Ladies and gentlemen of the jury, Eli Sylvester Horrell, deckhand on the fishing vessel *Jeri A.*, went into the Bering Sea somewhere between Dutch Harbor and St. Paul the night of January 12 of this year. His body has not been recovered. It is your duty to decide if sufficient evidence is available to presume that he is dead."

She paused, and peeked at the papers in her lap. When she looked up again the sixth juror was staring at her, as he had been staring at her pretty much unblinkingly since she had sworn in the panel. She straightened in her chair and frowned at him to dispel the notion that she'd been caught cheating. "The standard of proof is probable cause, which means you must find it to be more reasonable than not"—she underlined those last four words with her voice—"that Mr. Horrell is dead."

Mrs. Horrell gave a gasping sob. Bill held out the box of Kleenex. Mrs. Horrell took one with a damp and grateful look.

"You may ask questions of the witnesses; indicate that you wish to do so by raising your hand after the witness has finished testifying. You may take notes." She gestured at the pads and pencils. "Once all the witnesses have testified, you will retire to deliberate your verdict. That verdict must be unanimous; that is, all six of you

251

must agree on the verdict." She paused. "Are there any questions?"

There weren't. Hiding her relief, she said, "Very well. The court now calls its first witness, Alaska State Trooper Daniel Reynoldson, to the stand." Trooper Reynoldson, whose uniform had seen better days, stood up and came forward, hat under his arm. "Raise your right hand. Do you solemnly swear or affirm that the testimony you will give in the case now before this court will be the truth, the whole truth, and nothing but the truth?"

Trooper Reynoldson's voice was thin and reedy, unexpectedly so coming from such a large, barrel-chested man. "I do."

"Please be seated." Reynoldson sat and straightened his spine as if to counterweight the bulging belly sitting in his lap. "State your full name, your mailing address, and your occupation." He did so, declared he had no relationship to the deceased, and told the jury what he knew about the circumstances of Horrell's disappearance, which wasn't much. When the *Jeri A.* had docked, Captain Quinn had called the trooper post. Reynoldson had been catching that day and he had responded to the call, taking Quinn's statement, talking to the other three deckhands, and talking to the family about the deceased's state of mind (code for whether he was suicidal; he wasn't).

"Thank you, Trooper Reynoldson. Does the jury have any questions for this witness?"

They hadn't. Bill called Captain Enrique Quinn to the stand. Captain Quinn, a tall, wiry man in his mid-forties with elegant Latino features and nervous hands, took the oath and described the night (dark, temperature and barometer both dropping, twelve-foot swells, wind blowing out of the northwest and creating spray that turned instantly to ice), the crew's activities (hot on the crab, pulling one pot after another, the hold half full and less than twelve hours left in the fishing period), and his last sight of Horrell. "We were moving from one string to another when we started to ice up. Eli got a bat out of—"

"Excuse me," Bill said, "a what?"

"A baseball bat."

She was new to the place and the job, so she was careful to keep the incredulity out of her voice. "You use a baseball bat to fish for crab?"

Everyone looked tolerant, even the jury. "We use them to break ice off when the deck starts icing over." When she continued to look blank, he added helpfully, "If we don't, the weight of the ice might pull the boat over, make it turn turtle." He paused. When she didn't say anything, he added, "So then we'd be in the water and—"

"Thank you, Captain Quinn, I've got the picture," Bill said, and wondered how long it was going to take her to learn everything she needed to know about the fishing business. She wasn't sure but she thought the sixth juror winked at her.

"Mick, Joe, and Harlen"—Quinn nodded at the three scruffy young men sitting at the back of the room—"baited pots while Eli beat ice."

"What happened then?"

"He slipped," Quinn said. His voice was suddenly weary, his face drawn. "He just—he slipped. He skidded right across the deck, came up hard against the gunnel, and somersaulted right over the side." He ran a hand through thick black hair. "It all happened so fast, I—"

He stopped, and into the silence that followed Bill prompted, "What did you do?"

"I stopped the engines, tripped the beacon, took a

bearing, yelled 'Man overboard' on the loudspeaker." Quinn's voice dropped.

"Captain Quinn," Bill said, gently but firmly, "I'm going to have to ask you to speak up."

"I'm sorry," he said. His voice deepened, his words becoming more clipped. "I stopped the engines, marked our location, triggered the emergency locator beacon, yelled 'Man overboard' on the loudspeaker. We already had all the deck lights on. Everybody ran back to the stern, we heaved life rings and a raft over the side, hollered Eli's name. There was no answer." A pause. "I called the Coast Guard"—he nodded again, this time toward a trim young man in a crisp blue uniform—"and told them what happened. We sat there until dawn, about nine, nine-thirty, I guess. Some other boats showed up to help look, the *Sandy C.*, the *Rhonda S.*, and"—he thought—"oh, yeah, the *Dixie G.* Search and Rescue showed up about then, too. They couldn't find him either." His voice dropped again. "We looked for two days. There was—he was just—gone."

"And then?"

"And then we went back to Dutch. The period was over, the quota was met, we couldn't do any more fishing."

"Thank you. Does the jury have any questions they would like to ask this witness?"

One man, portly, grizzled, raised his hand. "Was Horrell wearing a survival suit?"

Quinn shook his head. "No."

"Were any of your crew?"

"No."

"Do you have survival suits on board?"

"Yes."

"Enough for everyone?"

Quinn's expression hardened. "Yes."

"Where?"

Quinn bit the words off. "In the portside galley locker."

"Everybody know where they are?"

"Yes."

"Everybody know how to put them on?"

"I run a survival suit drill the day before the season starts. I always do."

"Then why wasn't Horrell wearing one?"

"You know damn well why, Warren," Quinn snapped. "They're too bulky to work in."

This was what came of holding a jury trial in a town small enough for everyone to know everyone else. "Gentlemen," Bill said.

"I'm done, Your Honor," the juror said, sitting back in his chair with the air of a righteous pigeon.

One at a time, Bill called Horrell's fellow deckhands to the stand. One by one, they corroborated Quinn's testimony. As the third left the stand, the Horrell daughter buried her face in her mother's shoulder.

Bill consulted the witness list. "Lieutenant Commander Richard Klessens?"

The man in the blue uniform came forward to take the oath. He had round pink cheeks and wide-spaced round blue eyes. He didn't look old enough to drive a car, let alone a helicopter, but a pilot he was. In command of the Search and Rescue helicopter that had flown to the scene of Horrell's disappearance, he testified that they had spent the daylight hours of the better part of two days searching for Horrell's body. They had spotted two of the *Jeri A.*'s life rings, an empty plastic bottle of Coke, and a homemade buoy made of a Clorox bottle painted fluorescent orange, but no Eli Horrell.

Next up was paramedic Joe Gould, a thin, intense young man with the fanatical look of a medieval martyr. He spoke in a laconic monotone that negated the impact of what he had to say. Two minutes was his estimate of how long Horrell would have had in the Bering Sea in January without a survival suit or a raft. "After that, hypothermia sets in, the victim becomes disoriented, can't tell which way is up, loses consciousness, and drowns." It was Joe Gould's educated opinion that Eli Sylvester Horrell was dead a minimum of twenty-two minutes after he went into the water. At that point the youngest Horrell son left the courtroom at a run. Mrs. Horrell looked at the older son and he followed his brother.

Gould was the last name on the witness list. The clock showed twenty minutes after ten. Bill felt as if it ought to be much, much later. "Ladies and gentlemen of the jury, you have heard the testimony of the witness in this case. Do you have any questions?" She was beginning to feel restive beneath the steady gaze of the sixth juror, who hadn't looked away from her once during the testimony of the witnesses. She consulted the jury list. "Mr.— Alakuyak?" She stumbled a little over the name.

His gaze unwavering, showing no shame at being caught staring and no perceptible alarm at being confronted, he said, "Nope. No questions."

Ruffled but determined to retain at least the facade of impervious judicial calm, she said, "Anyone else?" No one else. "Very well. You may retire to the jury room"—a glorified reference to the conference room reached through the door in the wall on her left, which was even smaller and dingier than her courtroom, not to mention less well furnished—"to deliberate your verdict. Court is in recess."

She waited until the jury had filed out. To Mrs. Horrell she said, "I don't think they'll be long, ma'am. Why don't you take a break, get yourself a drink of water, stretch your legs?" She nodded at the daughter. "There are pop and snack machines down the hall to the left."

Mrs. Horrell managed a smile. "Thank you." She and her daughter waited for Bill to rise and then stood and shuffled out, heads together, arms around each other, moving like two old women. The paramedic had already left, as had Horrell's three crewmates, immediately following their testimony. Trooper Reynoldson, Commander Klessens, and Enrique Quinn sat where they were, Reynoldson and Klessens conversing in low tones, Quinn staring at the floor over folded arms. His face was pale beneath its outdoor tan and there were shadows beneath his eyes. Bill paused in front of him. "Are you all right, Captain Quinn?"

He started, and stared up at her. "What?"

"Are you all right? Do you feel ill?"

"Oh. No. No." He sighed. "This is the first time I've lost a member of my crew. I keep thinking there was something I could have done."

"Was there?"

He looked startled again by her blunt question. "No," he said quickly. "No. There wasn't."

"Well, then?"

The lines of his face eased a little. She turned to walk away, and to her back he said, "Your Honor?"

She looked over her shoulder.

"Thanks."

Bill retired to her chambers, another tiny, airless room with just enough space for a desk, a chair, and a filing cabinet, and busied herself with paperwork.

When she looked up again, it was ten to twelve. She frowned, and rose to open the door.

The widow and her children were back. Reynoldson was gone; Klessens looked impatient. Enrique Quinn was now sitting next to Mrs. Horrell, patting her shoulder with a kind of helpless awkwardness as she wept silently into a Kleenex. The kids looked miserable, but they were also young enough to begin to be bored, and restless with it.

In the chair next to the door into the jurors' room, Hattie Bishop dozed, her head against the wall, her mouth slightly open, a soft snore issuing forth. Bill let her own door close with a loud thud and when she opened it again Hattie was sitting upright, blinking. "Bailiff," Bill said, beckoning. Hattie, looking sheepish, got to her feet and crossed the courtroom. Bill closed the door behind her.

"Any messages from the jury?"

"No," Hattie said, relieved that she wasn't going to be chewed out for sleeping on the job. "No, Your Honor," she added hastily.

"Hmm." Bill pursed her lips and tapped her foot. "Go knock on their door, ask them if there is any testimony they would like to review, or if I can help them in any other way."

She waited. The jury probably wanted lunch on the state, and were drawing out their deliberations to include the noon hour. Not in my courtroom, she thought.

The door opened and Hattie looked in, bright-eyed and bursting with news.

"Well?" Bill said.

"They say they're deadlocked, Your Honor!"

Bill stared for long enough to make Hattie fidget. "They say they are what?"

"Deadlocked!" Hattie repeated in the same thrilled accents. This was better than Court TV off the satellite.

Bill's lips thinned. "Call them into the courtroom. Now."

The jury filed back in and took their seats. Bill looked at the portly juror. "Is there a problem, Mr. Foreman?" Her tone indicated that it would be better for them all if there wasn't.

The portly juror—what the hell was his name? She consulted the jury list. Warren Ollestad. Mr. Ollestad shifted uncomfortably in his chair.

"Well?" she demanded.

Ollestad cast a fleeting look at his fellow jurors. "I'm afraid so, Your Honor."

Bill felt rather than saw new tears forming in Mrs. Horrell's eyes. "Explain," she snapped.

"Well, we seem to be deadlocked."

"Really," Bill said. "How extremely interesting. Deadlocked on what, precisely?"

"Well—" Ollestad floundered for a moment. "Five of us are willing to sign the verdict. The sixth isn't."

Bill looked down the row of jurors with a sense of fatalism. Yes, the sixth juror was still staring at her, that dark, intense, irritatingly knowing stare. She'd never seen him in her life before this day; what right did he have to that look of possession, that air of knowledge? "Mr. Alakuyak—"

"That's Ah-LAH-coo-YAK," he said.

"Mr. Alakuyak, what's your problem?"

"I don't have a problem, Your Honor."

She resisted the impulse to glare. "Then why can't you

join the other jurors in a reasonable presumption of Mr. Horrell's death?"

"It's not his death I can't agree to," Alakuyak said, "it's the manner of it."

"What?" gasped Mrs. Horrell.

"What the hell?" Captain Quinn said.

"Your Honor," Klessens said in protest.

Bill waved them all to silence. "'The manner of it.' Mr. Alakuyak, four people saw him go over the side of the *Jeri A.* in high winds and heavy seas halfway between Dutch Harbor and St. Paul Island. An extensive search by four boats and one helicopter failed to locate him, alive or dead."

"I know that. My voices tell me something different."

Bill stared. "Voices?"

"Yes."

"What voices?"

"The voices that talk to me."

"You hear voices?"

"Yes."

The silence that followed didn't seem to weigh on the sixth juror as much as it did on everyone else. "You mean like Joan of Arc?" Bill said at last.

He grinned. The jolt of that grin nearly knocked her out of her chair.

"What the hell is going on here?" Quinn said, starting to his feet. "Who is this nutcase—"

"Sit down, Captain Quinn," Bill said sternly, recalled to her office and her sworn duty. He sat.

"Your Honor—" One of the two women on the jury spoke up, a young woman with the Tatar features of the upriver Yupik. Her voice was so soft as to be barely audible.

"Yes"—Bill consulted the jury list—"Ms. Nickolai."

"If Uncle's voices say there is something wrong, then there is something wrong," Mary Nickolai said, still in that same soft voice.

Ollestad said warningly, "Mary—"

"Warren," she said, still in that soft voice, "I let you talk me into agreeing in the jury room, but maybe we should listen to Uncle."

Moses Alakuyak kept that steady, watchful, aware gaze on the magistrate, and said nothing more.

For her part, Bill felt things were getting out of control. She didn't like it. She did what she always did when things got out of control, when she'd suffered her third miscarriage, when her husband had been laid off at Boeing, when he had hit her. She went on the attack.

She leaned forward, pressing her hands flat against the table in front of her, and fixing the sixth juror with an unyielding stare. "Mr. Alakuyak, do you have any evidence to support your feelings?"

"They aren't feelings, they're voices."

This time she didn't resist and did glare. "Then do these voices have a shred of hard evidence to back up what they have told you?"

He was silent. Mrs. Horrell was sobbing, the children looked miserable, Quinn furious. Klessens looked like he was struggling not to burst out laughing. "Mr. Alakuyak, this proceeding is solely to determine the fact of Eli Sylvester Horrell's death. Do you have any reason to believe he is still alive?" When he remained silent, she repeated, "Do you?"

"No."

"Do you have any reason to doubt the evidence given by the paramedic who testified before you this morning?

Do you think that Mr. Horrell could have survived in the conditions in which he went overboard?" Again he was silent, and in spite of her determination to remain calm and in control Bill could hear her voice rising. "Do you, Mr. Alakuyak?"

"No."

"Do you have any reason to believe that the three deck-hands and the captain of the *Jeri A.* were mistaken in their separate eyewitness accounts of Mr. Horrell's disappearance?"

"No."

"Do you have any evidence to offer that the United States Coast Guard was negligent in its search for a survivor?"

"No."

"You have no doubt, then, that Eli Horrell is dead."

Alakuyak ran a hand through a thick mane of already rumpled dark hair. "No."

Bill sat and folded her hands on the table, shoulders square, severely erect. "As I explained to you in my instructions to the jury before the hearing, Mr. Alakuyak, and may I remind you that when I asked, you had no questions about them, this jury has only to determine the fact of death, not the cause or the manner of death. The fact of death. In other words," she said, leaning forward again and for a moment forgetting who else was in the room, "I don't care if your little voices told you that Scotty beamed Mr. Horrell onto the bridge of the *Enterprise* two seconds after he went into the water. The preponderance of the evidence, evidence which you have just admitted you accept, leads us to presume Mr. Horrell's death."

The younger Horrell son was out of the room for the

second time, and Bill was recalled to the grieving family's presence. "Do you understand, Mr. Alakuyak?"

"Yes, Your Honor," he said.

"Good," she snapped. "Then get in that jury room and bring me back a verdict form with six signatures at the bottom."

"Yes, ma'am," he said.

And then he did something very odd. He smiled at her, a smile one part rueful, one part apologetic, another part something she couldn't identify but that seemed familiar to her, as if she'd seen it in her own mirror. For a split second she wondered where they had met before, and reassured herself that they hadn't. Of course they hadn't. She would have remembered that smile.

Two

Sec. 25.24.050. Grounds for divorce. A divorce may be granted for any of the following grounds: ... (2) adultery; (3) conviction of a felony; (4) willful desertion for a period of one year; (5) either (A) cruel and inhuman treatment calculated to impair health or endanger life; (B) personal indignities rendering life burdensome; or (C) incompatibility of temperament ...

   —Alaska Statutes, Marital and Domestic Relations

He aimed it at her again that evening from the open door of her office at Bill's Bar and Grill. "Hey, girl."

She sat back in her chair. "Mr. Alakuyak." She overlooked the familiarity of his address as she had laid off her judicial robes for the more casual dress of the owner and proprietor of the best bar in Newenham. There were only two, so the competition wasn't fierce.

"Try Moses," he suggested. "Easier to pronounce."

He stood about five-seven, not much taller than she was, weight about one-sixty, she thought, most of it muscle and bone. Gray eyes narrowed between Yupik folds, something she saw in many of Newenham's polyglot faces, dark hair graying at the temples. She thought he was older than she was, but she couldn't tell by how much. He was dressed in frayed and faded jeans, a blue plaid wool shirt worn at the elbows, and Sorel boots, pretty much the standard uniform for a Bristol Bay fisher.

In turn, he took his time surveying the long swath of silver hair combed straight back from her brow to fall softly around her shoulders, the full breasts barely contained by a powder-blue T-shirt with "Bourbon Street" scrawled in sparkling pale green letters across the chest, the narrow waist nipped in by a wide leather belt. He made no effort to hide his admiration; he even craned his neck for a better view of her skintight front button Levi's. "I'm going to find that black tent you were wearing this morning and burn it."

She found herself doing something she hadn't done in years, something she had thought that at fifty-three she was no longer capable of doing at all. She blushed.

He grinned. His was an angel's grin, but only if the angel's name was Lucifer. "Buy me a beer?"

Three

Sec. 25.05.0301. Form of solemnization. In the solemnization of marriage no particular form is required except that the parties shall assent or declare in the presence of each other and the person solemnizing the marriage and in the presence of at least two competent witnesses that they take each other to be husband and wife. A competent witness for this purpose is a person of sound mind capable of understanding the seriousness of the ceremony. At the time of the ceremony, the person solemnizing the marriage shall complete the certification on the original marriage certificate. The person solemnizing the marriage and the two attending witnesses shall sign the original marriage certificate and the necessary copies.

—Alaska Statutes, Alaska Marriage Code

The couple had elected to take the traditional vows, Bill noticed as she looked at the ceremony clipped to the back of the marriage license. Short and sweet, no invocations to the goddess, no praising of Allah, no chanting for Buddha. Good. "Send them in," she told Hattie, who a year into Bill's term of office had proved to be her most reliable bailiff, and who needed the extra money to supplement her Social Security pension anyway. So Hattie dozed off while the jury deliberated behind the door at her back, so what? She could be passing them newspapers with stories about the case being heard on the front page, something that had happened during a recent trial in Fairbanks. Everything was relative.

Bill waited as Hattie left the courtroom. It was the end of the day, a long, cold dark day the January following Eli Horrell's death. The luck of the draw hadn't tossed many wedding ceremonies her way; she was glad to go home on a note of optimism. She believed in marriage as long as she wasn't the one saying "I do."

And Moses returned from Anchorage this afternoon. She smiled as she thought back to the day in this very court when they had first met, when for a terrifying moment she had thought she was going to have to find out if a simple magistrate had the authority to issue a directed verdict or even declare a mistrial, all because of this half Anglo, half Yupik hearer of voices.

He'd moved into her small home on the bluff of the Nushugak River a month after that day. The only times they had been apart since was when he went to fish camp in August and this last trip to Anchorage to see the dentist at the military hospital on Elmendorf Air Force Base. He'd been gone four days. It wasn't his fault that it felt like four months.

The door opened and she looked up.

She didn't recognize them at first, as Mrs. Horrell wasn't crying and Captain Quinn wasn't looking ill or angry.

"Your Honor?" Hattie said, and Bill realized that it was the second time Hattie had said it.

"I'm sorry, what?"

Hattie looked at her, puzzled. "These are the folks who want to get married." Ever helpful at pointing out the obvious, she nodded at the license on the table.

Bill looked down and read the license for the first time. Enrique Quinn and Cynthia Horrell. She had not known Cynthia Horrell's first name before this. She didn't recognize the names or the faces of the two witnesses, although the best man gave off a strong aroma of beer and the maid of honor was flushed and giggly. It seemed the wedding party had begun without benefit of ceremony.

"Your Honor?"

She looked up again. "I'm sorry?"

"All you all right?"

Bill pulled herself together. "Of course. I'm fine—I'm

just—I'm fine." She wondered if she should say she was pleased to see them again, and decided against it. She forced her mouth into what she hoped was an acceptable smile. "You have asked for the traditional vows, I see. Would you like me to lead you in them?"

"No, Your Honor, we've got them memorized," Cynthia Horrell said, blushing.

"Then please begin."

They faced each other. "I, Enrique, take you, Cynthia, to be my lawfully wedded wife, to have and to hold from this day forward, for better, for worse, for richer, for poorer, in sickness and in health, to love and to cherish; and I promise to be faithful to you so long as we both shall live." He didn't stumble once or miss a single word.

Bill nodded at the bride. She peeped up from beneath her eyelashes with a flirtatious look better suited to a fifteen-year-old and said in a voice that was almost indecent in its triumph, "I, Cynthia, take you, Enrique, to be my lawfully wedded husband, to have and to hold from this day forward, for better, for worse, for richer, for poorer, in sickness and in health, to love and to cherish; and I promise to be faithful to you so long as we both shall live." She, too, was letter perfect.

They exchanged rings and turned to Bill with expectant faces. In a voice she did not recognize as her own she said, "By the authority vested in me by the State of Alaska, I pronounce you husband and wife."

Four

Sec. 11.41.110. Murder in the second degree. (a) A person commits the crime of murder in the second degree if . . . (2) the person knowingly engages in conduct that results in the death of another person under circumstances manifesting an extreme indifference to the value of human life . . .

—Alaska Statutes, Code of Criminal Law

"Was it one or both of them?"

"Who took out the life insurance policy?"

"She did."

"Who was it through?"

Bill sighed and rolled over to snuggle her head into Moses's shoulder. "The same people who insure the *Jeri A.*"

"Quinn's boat."

"Yes."

"How much was the payout?"

"A million five."

He whistled through his teeth. "Definitely for richer. You can split a million five five ways without anybody feeling shortchanged." He thought. "Given that Alaskan fishers are virtually uninsurable because of their high percentage of violent death, the premiums must have been astronomical."

"Not as high as the payout. And they only had to pay a year's worth."

"Yeah. How did Reynoldson find out?"

"Somebody owed him a favor who called somebody else. Moses?"

"What?"

"I'm sorry."

He was silent. She waited, listening to the slow, strong beat of his heart. "No," he said. "You were right. It was fact of death you were looking for, not cause or manner. In law, you were absolutely right to ignore anything I said.

And you didn't know me, then." She could hear the smile in his voice. "Can't say that's the case now, can you, girl?"

She sighed again. "Doesn't make me feel any better." Another silence. "How did he do it?"

Moses snorted. "Dying on a crabber is easy, Bill, it's staying alive that's hard. He probably watched, waited for just the right moment. The story they all told was probably mostly true, they were icing up, Horrell was using the bat, the rest of the crew was pulling and baiting pots. All Quinn had to do was wait until just the right moment to jerk the bow around crossways of the swell. The hull would thump down and the boat would roll and Horrell would lose his balance and go over. It happens often enough when it really is an accident. It would be easy to make it happen. Make it murder."

She flinched. "I suppose that is what it is. Murder."

"You can't prove it."

"That's what Reynoldson said. What about the rest of the crew?"

"They might suspect something, you mean? Well, so they might, especially now that the boss has married the beneficiary. Suspecting is different than knowing, though, and like I said, even split five ways, there's enough to go around with a million five."

"You think they were in on it?"

He shrugged. "The *Jeri A.* is one of the high boats in the Bering. Pulls a lot of pots, catches a lot of crab, makes a lot of money, pays a high crew share. They're not going to risk losing that by accusing their captain of premeditated murder."

She thought of Mrs. Horrell's endless tears, which in hindsight looked more like tears of guilt than tears of sorrow. Quinn's queasiness now looked like fear of discovery and punishment. She raged again at the thought that she had actually consoled him over the loss of a crewman. She felt furious and frustrated and impotent. She didn't like it. "What do the voices say now, Moses?"

He pushed her over on her back and slipped between her legs. "They're not talking, babe," he said, eyes gleaming down at her as he settled himself into her embrace. "They know enough to leave me alone at times like these."

"And when you've got a skinful of beer."

"And when I've got a skinful of beer," he agreed. "They show that much mercy." He kissed her, and it was long and slow and sweet. He raised his head to look at her. "Leave it go," he said. He grinned, the grin that said one day he would be either beatified or burned at the stake, or both, and kissed her again.

She let herself drift with the now familiar current of pleasure and when she was left, spent and gasping in extravagant satisfaction upon the shore, she remembered Cynthia Horrell, now Quinn, and her flirtatious up-from-under look at her new husband in the courtroom that afternoon.

I'll be here a long time, she thought. And so will they. I'll watch, and I'll wait. Someday.

Moses pulled her close. "Leave it go, girl."

"Okay," she said.

He knew her so well after half a year that he didn't bother calling her on the lie.

Besides, it didn't matter. The Quinns would get their due.

The voices had told him so, and they never lied.

Joan Hess

"Miss Tidwell Takes No Prisoners"

Arkansas author Joan Hess has created two long-running series of humorous crime novels, one featuring book dealer Claire Malloy and the other Maggody chief of police Arly Hanks. The same light touch is apparent in one of her rare short stories.

Ellen Tidwell, referred to by her friends from college days as "Twiddle," knew exactly why Drake had insisted on taking her out for lunch on her eighty-third birthday. Driving up to the inn at dizzying speeds could well have given her a heart attack; the ride back down the mountain would be all the more terrifying. She might keel over from a stroke, and ever-so-devoted nephew Drake would be the beneficiary of her house, her cats, Mama's silver service (custom-made in Atlanta, with a particularly elegant creamer and sugar bowl), Grandpapa's Civil War memorabilia, her collection of rare African violets, and all the money she had accumulated over fifty years of teaching school, living frugally, and investing so wisely that her broker called her for advice. Drake, her sister's boy, was the sole heir of what, she had to admit modestly, was a rather substantial estate.

When her time came, she knew perfectly well that the cats would be dispatched, the violets dumped in a trash bag, and the family treasures and homestead sold. The money, however, would be put to good use, keeping Drake and his whiny, anoretic wife in acceptable standing at the country club. Their equally whiny sons, one skulking about town on probation, the other on the verge of expulsion from the college to which Miss Tidwell discreetly wrote checks twice a year to cover tuition, would don coats, ties, and appropriately mournful expressions for her funeral. And dance on her grave forever after.

Twiddle was not stupid. She was willing to admit she was functionally blind. Resisting a walker, but dependent on a cane. Arthritic, and at the mercy of a regimen of prescription and herbal drugs to keep her fingers from curling into gnarled twigs and her knees from locking permanently. Getting old was a pain in the tush, but the alternative was nothing she looked forward to; the time would come, but she had always envisioned a sigh in her sleep. Until then, she had her kittens, her violets, her portfolio, and her friends who dropped by but were also dropping dead at an alarming rate.

"It was kind of you to come all this way just to take me out to lunch," she said to Drake as she opened the elaborate multipaged menu. "Such a nice place. So expensive and all."

"It's your birthday. I wish we could all get together more often, but the boys are so busy and Alisha spends most of her time at the hospice. There seems to be a crisis every day."

"The terminally ill can be a bother," Twiddle said as she put on her glasses and peered at the menu. "I was thinking I might just have soup and a salad. Do they have a nice house dressing?"

"Alisha intended to come," Drake persisted, "but the fund-raiser is this weekend and someone has to see to the details. She sends her love."

Twiddle took off her glasses. "I'm quite sure she sends something. Whatever it is remains to be seen, but by someone with better eyesight than I."

A figure loomed beside her. "Good afternoon," he said. "My name is Peter and I'll be your server. We have three specials today . . ."

After he'd droned on about orange roughy, chicken in some sort of soy sauce, and pasta involving sun-dried tomatoes, Twiddle prudently opted for French onion soup and a side salad.

"How are the boys doing?" she asked when the waiter at last drifted away.

"Derek was hoping to spend a year abroad in London, but it's out of the question. Tuition and expenses will run well over twenty thousand dollars. Alisha and I have made it clear that he'll have to finish up at the state college."

"I hope you don't expect me to indulge him," Twiddle said bluntly. 'He's very lucky to be able to attend college without working in the cafeteria as I did. His grades tend to indicate he does not value his education."

"But he does." Drake leaned forward and made a futile attempt to clasp her hand, which she whisked into her lap. "He would have given anything to be here today on your birthday, but his girlfriend has a solo in the concert this afternoon and he feels as though he needs to be there for her. His mother and I have always encouraged that kind of loyalty."

She would have wiped away a tear had there been one. "What instrument does she play?"

He sat back. "Ah, cello, I think, or one of those stringed things. A most talented girl. She's an orphan, as I must have told you. Very sad."

"Three months from now, you'll be telling me that Derek and Hugh are orphans, too, and therefore worthy of my generosity. It may not ring true, Drake. Are you once again experiencing financial problems?"

"It's not my fault, Auntie. The prime rate's up and buyers are reluctant to take out mortgages. I have four houses on the market and five more under construction. The finance company wants a substantial payment on existing construction loans. It's temporary—I swear it. Six months from now, I can pay you back with whatever interest you want."

"Seventeen percent?"

"That's hardly reasonable, and most likely illegal."

Twiddle touched her linen napkin to her mouth to hide her smile. "Well, then," she said, "you might do better at your bank. If you'll excuse me, I think I'll visit the ladies' room before we have our meal."

She seized her cane and made her way along the hallway wallpapered with dark flock, wondering if her suggestion of seventeen percent interest might prevent Drake from further attempts to borrow money. "Neither a borrower nor a lender be," dear Mr. Franklin had opined so astutely. At times, she felt so old that she might have heard it from him in person.

Not, of course, that he would have come south of the Mason-Dixon line (having been much too busy flying kites in France or whatever). She herself had never been farther north than Richmond, and that only for a week. Brossing County, North Carolina, had offered quite enough excitement for a lifetime. She'd been educated there, taught generations of children to read, write, and recite their multiplication tables, played the organ at her church, and buried her parents in the mossy cemetery. Her semi-cognizant friends still came by to spend pleasant afternoons of bridge, iced tea, and gossip. Her cats were content, and her houseplants flourished as if in a rain forest. Her azaleas were particularly lush, possibly in honor of her birthday.

She'd had a slight pang of regret that she had never traveled to New York City or such exotic destinations as London and Paris, but Miss Tidwell had accepted many years ago that these were not to be among her experiences. Brossing County, for better or worse, had been the entirety of her life.

She struggled down the dark hallway. Having failed to bring her glasses, the etched signs on the doors were incomprehensible. Finally, after a few moments, she decided that she had found the proper facility and went inside.

The room itself was dark, which was to be expected with the gathering clouds and the promise of a thunderstorm before the day was over. There was a rather peculiar sink, but Miss Tidwell had more pressing problems on her agenda. She made her way to a stall, checked to make sure there was adequate tissue available, and took a seat.

And heard the door open—and then, a heart-stopping few seconds later, male voices.

Her first instinct was to screech in outrage. How dare men barge into a ladies' room! She'd powdered her nose and put on her gloves in every proper ladies' room in the county. As a girl, she'd touched up her lips, patted on rouge, and straightened her nylons. Over the years, she'd listened to tales of woe, of broken hearts and schemes to take care of "certain problems" in clinics in distant cities. She'd offered many a handkerchief, squeezed many a hand, sworn confidentiality, and in some cases, slipped a few dollars in a beaded evening bag. Ladies' rooms were meant to be havens.

At that very moment Miss Tidwell came to the chilling realization that she herself—herself!—was in the men's room. She, who had never seriously kissed a boy, much less done something significant, was in a room in which grown men were apt to expose themselves. She had no idea what else they did when distanced from the ladies. Tell each other crude jokes? Make disgusting noises involving the full spectrum of bodily functions? Brag about sexual conquests? Debate anatomy, male or female?

She slid her feet as far away as she could from the stall door. She would have to suffer through whatever rituals were performed, and then, when they were gone, slip out to the hallway and never so much as relive a single second of her embarrassment.

"Nobody's ever gonna know, Peter," hissed one voice. "Dump this in the soup. I'll give you a thousand dollars now and another thousand when she's dead."

Peter, the "your server" person, sounded quite a bit more nervous than when he'd rattled on about roughy and pasta. "What about the cops? An autopsy?"

"She's old, and she has a history of heart problems. No one will think twice."

"I don't know . . ." Peter said with a groan.

Twiddle wished he had used a name, but she had little doubt that Drake had taken advantage of her absence to arrange to have her murdered. A cup of soup enhanced with a dollop of poison, and then a delightfully gooey layer of broiled cheese to hide any odd taste. A fatal heart attack. Her fellow diners would shrink back, then flee, their appetites spoiled by the intrusion of death. The next day would be business as usual.

Her sister had died under similar circumstances. Indeed, no one had thought twice. Drake and Alisha had taken Enid out to a buffet at the Holiday Inn on Easter Sunday. She had next been seen in a coffin, chalky and still for all eternity. They had claimed she had choked on a stalk of celery.

Enid had always disliked celery.

As much as Twiddle wanted to bang open the stall door, she was frozen with panic. Once Drake knew she'd overheard the conversation, he would be all the more determined to murder her before she had a chance to contact her lawyer after the weekend and arrange for her estate to go to the local animal shelter. He could merely hustle her out of the inn, claiming she was traumatized by her misguided foray. There were many places alongside the road without guardrails; all he'd have to do would be to throw open the passenger's door and give her a hearty shove. She'd tumble like a bag of garbage all the way to the bottom of a ravine.

Could she throw herself on the mercy of the manager, telling him how she'd overheard the conversation while huddled in a stall in the men's room? She tried to imagine herself sobbing with fury while Drake made remarks about her purported mental fragility due to her advanced age, and then apologized as he took her to the car. Any protests she might make would be tainted by the reality that she'd been in the men's room. If anyone had noticed him leave the table, he could say he'd made a call on the pay phone halfway down the hallway. Alisha would confirm it, just as she would the Second Coming—if it enriched her checking account.

Twiddle sucked in a breath as the door opened and closed. They were gone. She was more of a "goner" if she did not take action, but what was she to do? Allow Drake to put her down as he would her cats? Sip her soup and die in what might be a most agonizing way?

"Hell, no," she whispered, surprising even herself. Mama and Papa had never used such language, nor had they allowed their daughters to do so. The Tidwell family had not been wealthy, but decorum had ranked just below piety. Neither she nor Enid had ever missed church services or Saturday afternoons at cotillion classes.

She waited another minute, then scurried out of the stall and made it to the hallway without encountering any gentlemen intent on using the room for legitimate reason—as opposed to plotting murder. Drake was seated at the table, nibbling bread and nodding at acquaintances. Peter was nowhere to be seen.

Her salad had been served, as had Drake's. Twiddle sat down and offered a wan, apologetic smile. "I'm so sorry, but I seem to be experiencing some gastric distress. As much as I appreciate your bringing me, I simply cannot eat a bite. Will you please take me home?"

"Of course, Auntie. Do you mind waiting for a minute while I speak to the waiter?"

"How kind," Twiddle said. "I believe his name is Peter."

"And I believe you're right," Drake said jovially as he stood up and disappeared in the direction of the kitchen.

As she came up with a solution.

She was mulling it over when Peter appeared. "I'm disappointed that madam will not be dining with us," he said. "Our French onion soup has been given four stars, and our orange roughy . . . but, well, if madam is feeling ill . . ."

279

"Madam does not care to feel more ill than she does at the moment," countered Twiddle, wondering if he might have felt obliged to attend her funeral, or at least serve canapés after the services. Doubtful, in that Alisha would prefer to cut costs. Chips and dip atop the coffin, most likely. "Please do not describe the orange roughy once again. I'm feeling queasy, and I do want to be considerate of the other diners."

"Of course," Peter said, trying to sound the tiniest bit European despite his molasses-tainted accent. "Might a cup of tea help settle your stomach before your drive?"

She did her best not to gasp. "Nothing, thank you. Please let Drake know that I'll be waiting for him in the car."

"Yes, madam," he said as he glided away, no doubt chagrined that he would fail to earn two thousand dollars. Drake was penurious enough to demand back the deposit. Peter might have to settle with minimum wage and tips for the afternoon.

Twiddle wobbled her way out of the dining room and down the walk to Drake's car. Her parents, along with Enid, might have done a few flip-flops in their graves, but she was not inclined to be poisoned so that Derek could attend school in London, Hugh could purchase drugs, and Alisha could donate the flower arrangements to the hospice fund-raiser.

Drake said all the right things as he joined her. At her request, he drove at a civilized speed down the mountain, no doubt pondering his possibilities now that he had witnesses at the inn who could confirm his story of her fluctuating health. Did he think he could turn on a gas jet and leave her to die in her sleep? Did he think a well-placed napkin on the staircase might cause her to fall? He undoubtedly had a vial of some sort of poison in his pocket—a poison that would mimic heart failure.

She had no choice but to strike first. She was entirely too vulnerable, should he make a dedicated attempt to kill her. Once he was gone, she would let it be known to Alisha and the boys that everything she owned would go to the Brossing County Animal Shelter, thereby eliminating any expectations that might lead to future attempts on her life. Alisha might flourish off the proceeds of life insurance, but Twiddle suspected Drake was not the sort to keep up the premium payments.

"I do apologize," she said as they arrived back in town. "At my age, this sort of thing does happen. I should have warned you that I was far from robust yesterday. I was hardly able to sip consommé."

"Let me fix you a cup of tea before I leave," Drake suggested.

Twiddle vehemently shook her head. "I am in no way going to allow myself to be a poor hostess."

As they went inside her house, she scooped up a cat and squeezed it with a heartfelt enthusiasm, celebrating its life, if not her own. "You remember Monty, don't you?" she asked Drake as she sat down on the sofa. "He was such a hellfire in his day. Half the cats in this neighborhood have his yellowish-green glint in their eyes."

"I'm sure they do, Auntie. I'll take this opportunity to browse in the library."

"Feel free, dear; you know where it is. I'll put on the kettle."

Twiddle released the squirming cat and went into the kitchen. There, she sank down at the table and thumbed through her soul as if it were a paperback novel. Her most heinous crime to date, during her eighty-three years, was an anonymous note to the school board suggesting that a certain teacher might have been less than circumspect in areas of personal conduct. Although nothing had come of it, she'd always regretted it. "Live and let live" had become her motto; now it seemed that Drake did not share it.

If he had his way, that was.

She sat for a long while, aware that Drake was appraising first editions and wondering where to sell them. She was among the most helpless—old, easily dismissed, and should the situation arise, casually carted away to a mortuary. No one really listened to her anymore. Her insurance salesman sent a birthday card each year, spotted with saliva and signed by a shaky hand. Her accountant called every now and then, mostly to explain how well he was balancing bonds and treasury notes. The nice young woman across the street, recently licensed to sell real estate, dropped by with cookies and brochures about assisted-living facilities. None of them seemed to hear her determination to remain independent, to feed her cats and water her violets, to sit at the piano playing the sentimental songs of her youth, to relax on the porch where her parents and grandparents had sat, watching the lightning bugs flicker as the twilight darkened and the streetlights came on one by one, like sentinels protecting everything that was good and just in Brossing County.

She knew she did not have many years remaining, but she had some. What's more, the very idea that Drake would discuss her imminent demise in a men's room was so revolting that she felt acid rising in her throat. He and Peter, nearly chortling over the possibility. Giggling, perhaps. Would Drake soon be plotting other scenarios with

Alisha, who was likely to be more concerned with a funerary menu than the nuts and bolts of murder?

Eighty-three, yes, but far from the hapless victim. Drake had to be stopped. If he continued to make attempts on her life, he would get lucky, sooner or later.

And thus Twiddle made the ultimate decision to kill her nephew before he killed her. She'd toyed with the idea, but its time had come. He was a direct threat. Alisha would weep copiously, but then align herself with the overly tanned golf pro (there'd been rumors). Derek and Hugh might find reason to dance on their father's grave. She had no other option.

As the tea kettle whistled, she split a dozen melatonin capsules into a teacup, then added boiling water, a tea bag, and several teaspoons of sugar and a splash of milk. Eager to leave (and perhaps plot the next attempt on her life), Drake would gulp it down simply to escape her parchment pallor.

Or so she hoped. She sat down across from him and handed him his cup. "You are going to be so angry with me," she said. "I am old and dithery. I'm afraid I may have left my wallet at the inn. I had no reason to take it out of my purse in the ladies' room, but I wanted to powder my nose and I was digging for my compact."

Drake smiled. "Why don't I call them and ask them to keep it until I can fetch it?"

Twiddle contained herself despite the condescension dripping from his voice. "It's a bit more serious, I'm afraid. I know how much you and Alisha look forward to treasuring Grandpappy's collection, but just this morning I sold a letter to dear old Mr. Sweeny, who's been hounding me for years about it. He insisted in paying me in cash, and I intended to deposit it after the weekend."

283

"A letter?"

"Well, not just a letter. It was a letter signed by General Robert E. Lee granting my great-great-grandmother safe passage through both Confederate and Union lines in order to be with her daughter during a difficult pregnancy in Pittsburgh. A personal note from General Lee across the bottom margin seems to have made it more valuable."

"How valuable?" Drake asked weakly.

"Sixteen thousand dollars. Mr. Sweeny has coveted it for years, and, well, I've been looking at some investment opportunities."

"You left a wallet containing sixteen thousand dollars at the inn?"

She did her best to look chagrined. "I assure you that it was an oversight. My wallet is no longer in my purse, and I haven't so much as gone to the grocery since Mr. Sweeny bought the document. I objected to a cash transaction, but he insisted, and the banks are closed. What was I to do? I was not comfortable leaving it here."

"Sixteen thousand dollars?" Drake repeated. "You think you left it in the ladies' room? For chrissake, Auntie! If I call, the money will disappear into some employee's pocket. How could you do such a thing!"

"Perhaps no one has found it. It's possible it fell behind the sink."

He stood up. "I'll go back immediately."

"I cannot allow you to leave until you've finished your tea," she said, jutting out her chin. "I deprived you of what would have been a lovely lunch. Would you like to take some cookies with you, or perhaps a tuna salad sandwich?"

"I cannot believe you'd leave sixteen thousand dollars in a ladies' room."

"Drink your tea, dear."

Drake drained the cup, seemingly oblivious to what might have scalded his mouth. "You need to allow someone else to see to your financial dealings," he said coldly. "I'll have a word with your lawyer after the weekend. Living alone like this in a drafty old house, with cats underfoot, and all these steep staircases . . ."

Twiddle frowned as he banged down the cup. "That is from Mama's centennial rosebud set. It may be chipped, but it is of value to me."

"But sixteen thousand dollars isn't?"

"You sound agitated, Drake. Are you sure you're capable of driving in this condition? It's already begun to rain, and the roads can become very slick."

Drake looked as if he had more caustic remarks to offer, but grimly put on his raincoat and left. Monty crawled into her lap and purred appreciatively as she scratched his ears.

The melatonin, her favorite sleep aid, would affect him within twenty minutes. It was possible that drowsiness would overcome him to the point that he pulled over halfway up the mountain, but she suspected the specter of vanishing cash would distort his judgment. He was undoubtedly cursing her flightiness as his foot pressed firmly on the accelerator.

The lack of guardrails was disgraceful. Papa had complained to their state senator on more than one occasion. She made a mental note to write a letter to the quorum court.

When the telephone rang an hour later, Twiddle nudged

an indignant Monty aside and rose. Her heart pounding, she went into the foyer and picked up the receiver.

"Auntie Tidwell," said Alisha. "Are y'all okay?"

Twiddle battled off a sense of antipathy and maintained a pleasant voice. "Why, yes. I gather Drake has told you how I was a bit overcome at the inn and—"

"No, I just heard something on the news about how a woman was poisoned at the inn and a waiter was taken into custody. She was elderly, and I suppose . . ."

"I am not the only elderly woman in Brossing County, dear. Have you heard from Drake?"

Alisha sighed, either from relief or disappointment. "I expect him any minute now. We're having a few couples over later this afternoon, and he promised to clean the grill, although I don't see how we can use the patio if this nasty ol' weather lasts. I can't believe that the one afternoon I plan a party, it sounds like a bowling alley out there." She sighed once again. "Is he on the way?"

"He most definitely is on the way somewhere," Twiddle said. "I hope nothing happens to spoil your party."

"Me, too. I had all the carpets cleaned just last week. I don't know what I'll do if all these folks come tromping in with muddy shoes."

Twiddle murmured something and hung up, wondering how the carpets might look after the post-funeral festivities. Perhaps Alisha could rent a room at the country club. She was making herself another cup of tea when the doorbell rang.

She approached the front door with some trepidation. Through the frosted glass, she could see a figure silhouetted by the constant flash of lightning. Thunder rattled the house. Rain streamed off the roof in a gray blanket.

Her hand may have trembled as she reached for the

doorknob, but Miss Tidwell had never been one to turn faint at the sight of a mouse or to hesitate to fend off unwanted advances. The prospect of an enraged Drake or even a steely county deputy was more daunting, but she'd gone too far to falter now, especially with Monty and his feline consorts watching from the staircase.

"Goodness gracious," she said as she gestured for her caller to come inside. "You're soaked to the skin, Mr. Sweeny. You should have waited until the storm passed. I realize you're eager to buy that letter from General Lee, but you're liable to catch your death of cold in weather like this. How about a nice cup of tea and a cookie before we settle down to business?"

Mr. Sweeny nodded with his typical shyness.

"I have to admit I'm a wee bit nervous about having all that cash in the house," she murmured from the doorway.

He took out a handkerchief and fastidiously dried his wire-rimmed bifocals. "You shouldn't be, my dear Miss Tidwell. Nobody else knows of this transaction of ours, or even that I planned to come here. It's our little secret."

Even at eighty-three, Twiddle mused as she started toward the kitchen, there was no reason why she could not take up a new career. And she did seem to have a heretofore unexplored talent.

David Dean

"Whistle"

Some of the stories of David Dean reflect his professional background as a New Jersey police lieutenant. But he says the sources of this tale of mounting terror were the dream of a whistle and his ownership of a corgi.

It was Silkie's low, warning growl that brought her to full consciousness, though the ragged, frantic barking up and down the street had percolated through her dreams sometime before. Miriam lay in the warm darkness of her bed, eyes open but still unseeing, as the remnants of the dream she had been having gradually released her.

She had dreamed of her husband, though not as she had last seen him in life, but as he had been during their courting over forty years before: full of health and vigor, handsome and boyish. He had approached her with a sprightly step, smiling and whistling at the same time, and she had smiled happily back, trying to recognize the tune, only to realize that there was no tune at all. He strode by her without acknowledgment, his head swinging from right to left, his low whistle rising and falling melodically in a sad, yearning call; while somewhere outside her dreams she felt Silkie grow restless on the bed.

With a huff of breath, she shook her head to scatter the last clinging tendrils of sleep and turned her attention to her closest, and only, companion. Silkie stood on her stumpy hind legs, stretched her full long length to rest her front paws on the window sill. By the faint glow of a distant street lamp, Miriam could see that her dog's whole bearing was one of anxious inquiry, her slender head whipping to and fro, from the window to Miriam and back again, her tail curled tightly and scything the air in anxiety. (When questioned about the presence of a tail on a corgi, Miriam had always pointed out that her corgi was a Cardigan, not one of your common Pembrokeshires with their poor little stubs. She knew it was ridiculous to be proud of a dog for being what it was, but couldn't help herself.)

The dog now thrust its snout betwixt the partially raised window and the sill, squeezing its delicate skull in as far as it could go before reaching the screen, alternately growling and blowing her nostrils clear to better draft the scent so troubling her. All the while, the larger dogs up and down Miriam's winding street barked themselves hoarse from their backyard pens. She knew that Silkie was dying to join in their chorus, but held back for fear of her mistress's disapproval. Even so, she cast occasional pleading glances in Miriam's direction while dancing nervously from one paw to the next.

Miriam sat up in bed. "This is too much," she muttered. "It's getting to be a regular occasion around here!"

She heaved her small, rather corpulent frame from the warm confines of her bed and made her way to the window, glancing at her bedside clock as she did. It read two twenty-seven A.M. With a slight grunt, she bent at the waist, shouldering Silkie aside for a view of what could be causing all the commotion. Undaunted, the corgi shoved back and managed to wedge herself into a somewhat tighter accommodation at the window.

Miriam peered hard into the shadowed darkness of the yard and the street beyond, but was unable to discern anything out of the ordinary. Even with the full moon casting its soft, strong illumination, Miriam could see nothing to be alarmed about. She looked down at the corgi, who gazed up at her as if awaiting further instructions, her dark eyes and black nose glistening in the moonlight.

With an explosive bark that made Miriam's heart jump, Silkie's attention swiveled back to the window and the world outside it. The dog began a frantic effort to climb up into the window itself.

"Shush!" Miriam cried out, then clamped a hand over her own mouth. Had she seen something move out there? Something, or someone, skirting the sharp edges of the shadows that lay like spilled ink across the street in the Neufields' yard? Certainly Silkie had sensed something! Had someone been watching her the whole time she had been squinting out the window?

Instinctively, she drew back, tugging her reluctant pet with her. The barking of the Tobers' dogs just next door grew in intensity. Wasn't that in the same direction that the shadow had been moving? Silkie strained at her collar, growling deep in her throat, the fur on her shoulders and tail standing on end. After several minutes, the barking of the Tobers' dogs began to taper off and Silkie visibly relaxed. Miriam remembered to breathe and exhaled loudly into the quiet room.

With a bound, Silkie leapt up onto the bed, circled several times, and then flopped herself down with a loud sigh. Flattening her huge, pointed ears back against her skull, she squeezed her eyes shut and composed herself for slumber, her previous concerns forgotten.

"Must be nice!" Miriam chided the small creature lovingly, and proceeded to burrow back into her covers, but not without a nervous glance at the window.

As the barking faded in her own neighborhood to be picked up distantly in others, Miriam closed her eyes for a second time that night, thinking harsh thoughts of careless dog owners who let their animals roam or, worse, simply turned them out when they grew tired of them or found them suddenly unfashionable. It had not escaped her notice that the young families of her neighborhood only chose breeds that were in vogue. The current fad favored Labradors on the one hand, of which there were no fewer than five on her block alone, and more ferocious-looking types on the other, such as pit bulls. She'd heard rumors of only one such creature on her street, and had not laid eyes on it, no one had, as its master, a part-time dog breeder, kept it locked away in a secure pen behind his house. In any case, she strongly suspected that one of these unworthy owners was responsible for the near-nightly cacophony that had plagued the neighborhood these two weeks past. With the passing of years she found sleep difficult enough without the unwanted canine serenade, and if it continued, she fully intended to investigate.

The following morning was fine and brisk and Miriam arose at her usual early hour, if somewhat crankily due to last night's interruptions, in order to feed and walk Silkie. As was their custom, the woman and dog strolled to the end of their street, which terminated in a cul-de-sac. Beyond lay a small wood that separated Miriam's neighborhood from another a quarter-mile to the south. The wood line provided a convenient place for Silkie to "conduct her business" without annoying any neighbors or forcing Miriam to use the awkward and embarrassing "scooper."

It was on their return that Miriam spied her neighbor

from across the street, Elizabeth, posting her mail. Miriam hurried to catch her before she returned indoors.

"'Lizbeth, oh, 'Lizbeth ... good morning!" Miriam saluted, while Silkie strained at her leash in order to be the first to greet their neighbor. Miriam reined her in with an effort, not wishing to have the dog jump up on Elizabeth. Silkie, unlike Elizabeth's dog, was not in the least obedient to commands, and Miriam had never had the heart to properly discipline her small companion.

Elizabeth appeared genuinely glad to see them, though her smile was a bit tremulous. She even took a moment to squat down and rub Silkie's belly, as the corgi had flopped over onto its back in total submission upon reaching her feet.

The younger woman's actions secretly pleased Miriam, as she tended to judge others somewhat by their conduct with her dog, though she knew this to be unfair.

"How are you, Miriam?" Elizabeth inquired, standing once more and folding her arms across her chest against the autumnal chill.

"Well, a little worn around the edges, I'm afraid. All that commotion again last night. Were you and Gary bothered?" Miriam asked, noticing dark smudges beneath Elizabeth's eyes.

Elizabeth looked down at her elderly neighbor with concern. "It woke us up, but we got back to sleep pretty quickly. Gary thinks it's the deer setting the dogs off. This time of year they tend to raid the flower beds and shrubs as food gets scarce in the woods."

Miriam had not considered this possibility before. Had her husband still been alive, he would surely have thought of it. "Oh," Miriam responded thoughtfully. "Did Gary go out to see last night, by any chance?"

"Oh, no." Elizabeth laughed aloud at the suggestion. "You know Gary. When he's in, there's no moving him. I had to pull him by the arm to get him to leave the house that time our chimney caught fire! He would not go out in the middle of the night . . . period," she finished convincingly. "Why?" she asked, catching up to Miriam's question and becoming slightly alarmed. "Did you see someone around our house last night?"

Miriam suddenly felt foolish, and, worse, guilty of causing her young friend uneasiness. Had she really seen anything last night other than a movement in the shadows . . . maybe? In any case, Gary was probably right that it was a deer. "No . . . I guess it was the whistling that made me think that."

"Whistling?" Elizabeth looked concerned in a different way now.

"You didn't hear it?" Miriam asked shyly, noting the look on her neighbor's face and blushing with the realization that she was mixing up her dreams with reality.

Elizabeth paused, as if she were seriously trying to recall the previous night. "No, but, honey, we do sleep with the windows closed this time of year."

"Maybe I should, too," Miriam offered weakly.

"It'll help with the dogs," Elizabeth assured her.

A thought suddenly occurred to Miriam. "Where's Dakota, 'Lizbeth? I haven't seen her in days." It was their mutual distinction as the only two lap-dog owners on the street that had originally brought the women together despite their difference in years. They always inquired into the health and well-being of their respective pets and enjoyed many a curbside conversation recounting their little companions' antics and eccentricities. Neither had been favored with children.

Elizabeth's face crumpled, large tears welling up in her eyes and threatening to spill over.

"'Lizbeth," Miriam cried out in shock at her friend's distress, instinctively reaching out for her. "What's the matter? What's wrong, sweetie?"

Elizabeth had clapped both hands over her mouth as if to contain a torrent of emotion. "My puppy's got lost," she choked through her fingers. "Or run away ... I don't know!"

"No, no ... she would never run away," Miriam assured her neighbor, as sympathetic tears welled up in her own eyes. She glanced furtively at Silkie, who sat studying the two women in bewilderment, and was ashamed at her own sense of relief that it was Elizabeth who had suffered the loss and not she, though her sympathy was all the more real for it. "No, she must have got lost, honey ... She'll find her way back," Miriam concluded, giving Elizabeth a reassuring pat on the arm.

"I hope so ... I truly do ... but it's been almost two weeks now. We just let her out one night to pee, like we always did ..." She trailed off, her lips trembling. After a moment of silence, she reached out and squeezed Miriam's hand. "I'd best get in now."

Miriam watched her neighbor until she disappeared within her home, and then turned heavily towards her own. "That dog would never run away," she stated firmly to Silkie, whose fruit-bat ears pricked up at the tone of his mistress. "And she didn't get lost, either. Dakota's not like you ... she behaves!"

Silkie, however, had lost interest and was busy investigating a spot of grass that had captured her attention. Straining her stocky, muscular frame against the pull of the leash, she was able to continue her delicate and infuriatingly thorough scenting. Miriam was forced to apply both hands in order to drag the dog away, and not for the first time questioned her own wisdom in not enrolling Silkie in obedience training.

Again it was the barking that awoke her, rolling from south to north, rising in intensity as it was taken up by the dogs in her own neighborhood, while falling off in more distant ones. This time, however, it did not disturb or color her dreams, but brought her to an instant, clear-headed wakefulness. She glanced over to the window and saw that Silkie was already manning her post: head thrust forward and nose pressed to the screen, earnestly testing for the presence of whatever lay without, a deep, hesitant growl bubbling in her throat.

Miriam did not even bother to check the time, as she knew it was quite late. She had been unable to get to sleep until well after midnight, and even then it had taken several chapters of a particularly bad novel to do the trick. The news of Dakota's disappearance, as well as her dream of the previous night, had left her restless and not a little apprehensive. She longed for the decisive, no-nonsense company of her husband, who would've marched into the darkness to confront or even do battle with whatever waited there. He had been a highly deco-rated marine in the Korean War, she reflected proudly.

Somewhat emboldened by his memory, she made to rise and approach the window; the whistle froze her in mid step. Silkie's growl grew louder and more angry, and a bark was not far away. The thought of this, of Silkie bringing attention to her darkened window, flooded Miriam with a sudden terror. The idea that out there, on the moonlit street, a head would turn and a face washed white by cold luminescence would lift its gaze to her window was more than she could bear. She rushed to the dog and snatched it up as it wriggled and struggled in protest. Hugging the corgi close, she tried to shush and comfort the surprised animal, to no avail.

It wasn't just a dream, Miriam thought with little cheer. *I was right. Someone's whistling for a dog.*

The whistling stopped and the neighborhood dogs' barking grew less frenzied but did not cease. Several minutes passed and Silkie's struggles weakened, though her attention never wavered from whatever was transpiring beyond Miriam's walls. Outside, the barking ceased to be a communal effort and fell to individual voices—one dog answering another in challenging conversation. Silkie grew quiet in Miriam's lap and accepted the strokes and murmured affirmations of "good girl" with evident pleasure. The neighborhood, at last, became silent. Miriam's grip on her precious corgi loosened.

The whistle, though low and furtive, might have been an air-raid siren at a funeral for the great howl of protest it elicited. The dogs voiced their intolerance at being called to where they could not follow, and threw themselves against their chain-link pens in anguish.

Instantly, Silkie leaped from Miriam's arms and onto the floor. In a blur of speed, she made not for the bedroom window but for the stairs and the freedom of the unguarded first floor. Miriam was up like a shot as well, guessing the small dog's intent and determined to thwart it if humanly possible.

What Miriam referred to as Silkie's "perch" was only an ordinary window in the dining room that faced the street. Its attraction to the dog lay in the design, which placed the sill a mere foot off the floor. This arrangement allowed the short-legged creature to clamber in, where she just fit, to enjoy a view of the outside world in relative comfort—much like a large house cat. The aluminum screen prevented her from sliding out and falling the short distance to the earth, though its retentive powers had grown rather strained over the years by her thirty pounds.

It was to this window that dog and woman raced through the darkened house. As she hurried down the stairs, gripping the bannister in the darkness, she could hear the dog's unclipped nails clattering across the hardwood floors at high speed. "Stay!" Miriam cried out hopelessly. But Silkie, long on affection and amusing antics, was short on discipline, and hurtled, heedless of her mistress's admonition, into the window at breakneck speed. Predictably, her momentum accomplished exactly what Miriam had feared, and with a small yelp of surprise Silkie and the frayed screen vanished into the night. The whistle, just as suddenly, ceased.

Forgetting her previous terror of the whistler, Miriam gained the first floor and made for the front of the house as quickly as her plump legs would take her. She threw open the door and rushed into the yard crying, "Silkie! Silkie!"

If the neighbors' dogs had been in a frenzy before, they now were beside themselves and redoubled their efforts; some even began to howl a dismal counterpoint to Miriam's pitiful cries. Somewhere down the street a roused neighbor yelled, "Shut up!" None of this penetrated Miriam's frantic concern over Silkie's whereabouts, and she continued to call and search the yard and shrubberies . . . but Silkie was nowhere to be seen.

With a small, muffled sob, Miriam wandered onto the twisting, tree-lined street and looked both north and south. Where the trees did not obscure the newly waning moon, the blacktop appeared as oily and black as the scales of the rat snake that haunted her flower beds. In those patches where the reflected illumination could not reach, the darkness was as impenetrable as blindness. Silkie was neither to be seen nor heard.

Little by little, the neighborhood grew quiet again, leaving the old woman crying softly in the street until exhaustion and grief combined to rob her of her will to continue. With heavy steps she recrossed her moonlit yard to the waiting open door, all the while convinced that she was watched from the safety of the mocking darkness.

She fell asleep shortly before dawn in a hard dining-room chair overlooking Silkie's abandoned perch, tired and wretched, framed in the gaping hole of the screen that commemorated her little friend's inexplicable departure.

By mid-morning, only a little less tired and somewhat fragilely composed, Miriam embarked upon a door-to-door search for her corgi. Though she was not close to the families that inhabited her street, she felt certain that no one was unfamiliar with the sight of her and Silkie on their daily walks, and therefore they could be relied on to take the errant dog in and return her to her mistress at the first opportunity. It was simply a matter of alerting them to be on the lookout. She also carried a large shopping bag filled with Silkie's favorite "chewies," which she intended to distribute to each household to be used as enticements if the dog were spotted. After all, she reasoned, Silkie could hardly be expected to run to strangers just because they called.

The first thing Miriam discovered was that almost all of her young neighbors, both husband and wife, worked, and therefore no one was to be found at home. Nonetheless, fear for Silkie drove her ever forward to try each and every door.

On her fifth attempt, she met with limited success. Having pulled a rather harried young mother from her screaming toddler, Miriam set about to enlist the woman's aid, only to find herself crying as well, describing her dog and its predicament between barely suppressed sobs. With thinly disguised distaste at Miriam's performance, the young woman reluctantly accepted the baggie of dog treats and promised to keep an eye out for the missing dog. Miriam thanked her effusively and began to turn away, but not before the wailing brat snatched the bag of goodies from his mother's hand and dashed for the interior of the house. Before Miriam could protest, the door was closed in her face.

Stupid, mean-hearted girl, Miriam thought as she made her unsteady way down the drive. *Not even to invite me in . . . or offer a tissue!* She ranted inwardly as she rummaged through her purse for a handkerchief. A wadded one lay at the very bottom and she snatched it out to dab angrily at her running eyes, a hot resolve replacing her sense of humiliation and dependency on the kindness of neighbors.

Within minutes she discovered a man pushing some kind of contraption that spread a white powder across his meticulous lawn. Miriam recognized him as a teacher at the local high school and thought his name to be Ward. She had often noticed that he would be home on days when school was in session and suspected he abused his sick-time privileges. If he did, he did so without care, for he was always to be found manicuring and grooming his yard and flower beds for all to see.

Miriam strode across the carpet of lush green until she caught up to him and tapped him on the shoulder, visibly startling him. Simultaneously, his two Labrador retrievers, one black, the other white, came bounding around the corner of the house to confront the intruder they had scented from the backyard. They came at a silent lope and had almost reached her when Ward gave the shouted command, "Stay . . . sit!" Both animals came to an instant halt and sat down on their haunches, teeth bared for Miriam's benefit.

Miriam took an involuntary step backwards. "No." Ward spoke to her in a lower tone. "It's all right."

The dogs appeared as obedient as the environment that Ward had created of his property, and Miriam was a little reassured, though somewhat ashamed at the story she was there to relate of her own undisciplined dog and the trouble it had led to.

When she had sufficiently caught her breath again, and the beating of her heart had slowed enough to allow it, she explained what she wanted of him.

"That's that little dog I've seen you with, isn't it?" he inquired rather stupidly. "That's too bad . . . a damn shame. Though I don't think he'll be coming round here," Ward stated flatly, hooking a thumb in the direction of his Labs. "They wouldn't have it."

"She," Miriam corrected.

"How's that?" Ward looked perplexed. "Oh . . . your dog, right . . . she. In any case, I'll know if she shows up, that's for sure!" And he smiled proudly at his canine guardians as if he could already envision their running the corgi to ground and tearing it apart.

"Thank you," Miriam murmured and turned to go with no intention of sharing any of Silkie's treats with these brutes. A thought struck her and she turned back to find Ward smiling condescendingly at her. He quickly wiped the smile away.

"Did you hear anyone whistling last night when all that barking was going on?" Miriam asked.

Ward seemed to think it over carefully, as if somewhat embarrassed at his previous cavalier attitude. "I thought I did at one point. You know these two were puttin' up quite a racket at the time." A perplexed look crossed his face. "That wasn't you?"

"No," Miriam assured him. "That started before my Silkie got out."

"Well, it sure seemed to come from your end of the street."

"Yes," she mused. "It sure did."

With this thought in mind, Miriam made her way determinedly in that direction, passing both Elizabeth's house and her own. She knew that Elizabeth worked during the day so didn't bother to stop, but made a mental note to add Elizabeth to her after-dinner rounds. Instead, she aimed herself towards the house just next to her fellow sufferer, an idea rapidly taking place in her brain that had been suggested by Ward's offhanded observation. An idea that, as she trundled along, took the form of a suspicion.

The house that she approached stood well back from the street, its rear seemingly nestled against the wood line, though this was deceptive. In fact, the owner had cleared a long, narrow strip into the woods while allowing the remaining forest to creep up to both sides of his home. The result was that from the front the cleared area was completely unseen, while the house itself appeared in danger of being overtaken and smothered by trees and shrubs. The fact that the house, like most on the street, was relatively new only added to the atmosphere of decrepitude. Miriam thought it most unwelcoming. Even so, she clutched her shopping bag tightly to herself and marched on, for this house had become the locus of her suspicion.

The facts had formed a pattern in Miriam's mind: The owner, a taciturn and unlikable fat man who worked only intermittently, raised hunting dogs—pure breeds that he advertised for stud services. (It was also rumored that he raised fighting dogs for less humane and legal purposes.) These animals were the reason for the cleared property behind his house, and it was there that he had erected their pens and runs. This much was known.

What was also known was the time frame of the almost nightly eruptions of the neighborhood canines. These had begun almost two weeks before. What was not so well known was the mysterious disappearance of Elizabeth's Pomeranian, which occurred during this same reign of barking, possibly even signaling its onset. Miriam's own loss also occurred under these circumstances.

Lastly, there was the whistler, confirmed now by another, whose eerie forays confined themselves to the area just north of Miriam's home. These things were known, and formed the framework of facts upon which Miriam draped the newly woven garments of her deductions.

With all the conviction of the convert, and a burgeoning sense of hope, Miriam waded through the rank, yellow grass of the yard to beard a dognapper in his den.

The fat man opened the door to Miriam's knocks as if he had been standing just behind it all the while. Startled, she took an involuntary step back, as he took a baby step forward, crowding his enormous bulk into the doorway, completely blocking her view of the interior. With a grunt of effort, he twisted slightly to pull the door shut behind him, taking yet another step onto the porch and forcing her almost to the edge. "Yeah?" he wheezed.

Miriam took a steadying breath and addressed the towering, unshaven mound of flab. "You raise dogs, do you not?" she opened.

He regarded her steadily through tiny, unfocused eyes. "Uh-huh." A scent of old food wafted unpleasantly from his frayed clothes, and Miriam wished desperately there was a way to stand further from him.

"Do you sell them?" she queried, her heart beating fast.

"S'what?" he mumbled.

"Sell them. Sell dogs?"

He seemed to mull this over, turning it from one side to the next. "Yeah . . . sometimes. Why?"

"I'm in the market," Miriam stated emphatically.

"S'at so?" He seemed to think it over, absently fingering a piece of lint from his almost invisible belly button, which lay exposed as a result of his inability to button the last few holes on his shirt. Miriam thought she might retch, but steeled herself for Silkie's sake. "Nothin' you'd want," he opined. "Only big dogs. Hunters . . . and such."

"That's exactly what I want," she responded immediately. "Let's take a look at what you've got."

"No," he shot back, for the first time evincing some animation. "Don't have any."

"No dogs," Miriam snapped angrily. "You just said that you sell them."

The fat man looked worried and ran a hand through the slick, thinning strands of hair that barely covered his giant head. "None right now," he insisted, backing up a step towards the door. "All sold."

Miriam was desperate. "I'll order one from you, then," she pleaded. "A corgi! A Cardigan corgi! I'll pay good money! You just see about getting one and I'll pay for it, no questions asked!"

The fat man opened his door and stepped up into the doorway to escape the desperate old woman. "No small dogs," he announced loudly.

"So you know what a corgi looks like," she accused, then quickly reversed herself upon seeing him closing the door. "But that's good, then. You know what I want. I'll pay the going price! Whatever you ask!" she cried out as she heard the metallic snap of a deadbolt slide home.

Full of anger and desperation, Miriam turned from the porch and began to hurry around to the side of the house. She would see for herself!

The front door flew back open and the fat man shouted out to her, "Get off my property right now or I'll call the police!"

She didn't believe for a moment that he would risk calling the police, but she knew she would never be able to reach the pens before even he could stop her. Wilting beneath the heavy limitations that age had imposed upon her, she nonetheless pointed an accusing finger in the direction of the fat man. "Give me my dog back," she hissed. "You give me my Silkie!"

"Get outa here, you crazy old bitch. . . . Now!" he thundered, and glared at her as she turned away defeated and frightened. When she reached the street once more, he slammed the door so hard that it reverberated off the neighboring houses like a farewell cannonade.

Miriam knew with the certainty of divine revelation that the fat man had taken her Silkie, and what she must do.

The thought of the house-bred corgi languishing in one of his feces-strewn pens, deprived of the affection she was accustomed to, drove Miriam to desperation. She had read disturbing stories in the papers of pets being used as bait to hone the killing skills of fighting dogs. Could that be the reason for the disappearance of Silkie and Dakota? She couldn't allow herself to think of such a possibility. Come nightfall, she would act.

As she lay on her bed trying to rest and regain her composure for the task ahead, she reviewed the events of the previous evenings, her left hand absently stroking the small depression in the mattress left by her absent companion. All that had happened pointed the finger of suspicion, nay, accusation, at the odious, obese neighbor. He raised dogs for income and therefore understood the value of them. More important, he was in a position to find buyers. And buyers were something he would be in great need of since his wife had left him, taking both the children and, according to neighborhood gossip, the greatest portion of his income. "My God," she chuckled bitterly. "His grocery bill alone must demand a six-figure salary."

In any case, his house was just across the street and one north of her own—the exact location of the whistling. And now that she had stood close enough to the man to fully appreciate his enormous girth, the whistling itself proved a more understandable piece of the whole. There was no way that the fat man could even consider physically abducting a dog. The very thought of someone of that bulk attempting stealth was ludicrous. No, Miriam mused angrily, he relied on tempting and luring the poor beasts into his clutches. No doubt after driving the animals to distraction with his eerie call, and relying on their strength, or ingenuity, to find a way out to investigate, he waited in the safety of his own yard with a tasty reward and a stalwart leash or, worse yet, one of those hideous pole-and-noose contraptions that the dog wardens use. After that . . . what? Could there really be some kind of market for middle-aged dogs of unpopular breed? The alternative was too awful to contemplate.

"Dear God," Miriam prayed aloud to the empty room. "Please don't let him have hurt my little Silkie."

Moments later she fell asleep and began to grind her teeth.

When she awoke, the day had long since slipped away and the darkness it left behind confused and alarmed her. Miriam sat up in a panic to check the time, astounded that she had slept so long, and perplexed by the ache in her jaw. The clock read eleven-forty P.M. Almost the witching hour, she thought uncomfortably.

Nonetheless, she hurried downstairs, not wishing to turn on any lights and possibly betray her intentions. Finding her good walking shoes and a light jacket, she fumbled these on. Scurrying into the kitchen, she risked turning on the light over the stove just long enough to find the large metal flashlight her husband had always kept in a state of readiness there. Flicking off the stove light, she nervously switched on the torch. Miraculously, it seemed to her, a brilliant beam shot forth across the room, throwing a kitchen chair into sharp relief. Miriam hastily switched it off, not wishing to waste the batteries. Her husband had been a very careful and thorough man, but little of this had worn off on Miriam and she feared for the life of the batteries, unable to remember the last time she had thought to replace them. Just before letting herself out the back door, she retrieved Silkie's leash from its nail, coiled it tightly, and shoved it securely into a pocket. Within moments, she was making her way cautiously to the front of the house, confident that she made her way into the night world unseen.

She angled across her own front yard, making a beeline in the dark for the fat man's property. With satisfaction, she noted that not a single light shone from that direction, and her confidence increased. All she need do was make her way down his driveway in the darkness. With the small aid of the distant streetlight, she felt that this was something she could accomplish without too much chance of revealing herself. Once she reached the end of the drive, however, she would be at the wood line and it was at this point that it would be necessary to use the flashlight in order to find the path to the dog kennels. In addition, and the thought made her mouth go suddenly dry, the odds were that the fat man's dogs would not let her incursion go unnoticed. Even so, the thought that she might recognize Silkie's voice amongst them steadied her, and she marched on.

But when she stepped into the winding, deserted street, it was not the fat man's dogs that rose in protest, but a distant chorus of canine voices to the south that rolled like an ocean swell towards the dark shore upon which she stood. Puzzled, Miriam stopped to listen, an inexplicable sense of alarm having claimed her. Momentarily, the rolling sound of doggie protests and alarms traversed the small woods that separated her neighborhood from that to the south and entered her own, the neighborhood dogs taking it up with gusto.

Something niggled at her brain, disturbing her earlier thought processes: The barking disturbance arrived from the south, as it had on previous nights, she now realized.

Yet the whistle came from the north . . . the fat man, undoubtedly. But the barking preceded the whistling. That didn't make sense if it was the source of the disturbance. Hadn't the whistle preceded the barking before? Or had she got that wrong? There was no whistling now and still the dogs were frantic.

As if in answer, the whistle began, low and clear. It was almost sweet in its plaintiveness; more like a plea than a demand. Miriam began to walk rapidly in its direction, more sure than ever of its origin, yet less sure now of its meaning. She thought she could just make out the hulking outline of the fat man in the darkness of his front porch.

She paused, uncertain of just how to proceed now that confrontation was inevitable. At the same moment, she became aware that the clicking sound had ceased also. It wasn't until then that she realized she'd been hearing something just beneath the barking and baying. Something almost inaudible beyond the blood rushing in her ears. A steady click, click, click that almost, but not quite, mimicked her own steps from the moment she had entered the street.

She took several more steps to test her theory, a surge of hope welling up in her chest that was rewarded with a soft, repetitive clatter. She recognized the sound! It was the unmistakable noise of unclipped nails striking the asphalt. The nails of a spoiled little brat dog who hated the clippers!

With a cry of joy, Miriam spun about, switching on the flashlight and instinctively pulling Silkie's leash from her pocket. The cry died, stillborn, as the light framed the creature, its eyes glowing green and pinpointed by the harsh illumination, its stalking arrested by the sudden aggressive display of its intended prey. The leash slithered from Miriam's paralyzed fingers to coil uselessly on the tarmac.

Miriam suddenly understood everything and mourned for her Silkie. The beast's gray muzzle curled to bare its deadly array of wares in silent acknowledgement of its intent, while the beam of light that seemed to hold it at bay suddenly dimmed and winked out. Miriam, remembering quite clearly now that it had been several years since she had replaced the batteries, turned mechanically towards home for more; behind her there came a low, menacing growl.

The fat man closed the door behind him as quietly as his quaking bulk would allow and eased himself down onto his splayed sofa, breathing heavily through his nostrils. He feared an asthma attack was imminent.

It was not his fault, and if the old woman had left well enough alone, he might have succeeded and all would now be well. But he had seen the sudden flash of light on the street and the awful tableau it revealed, and had heard the terrible yet strangely quiet struggle that ensued. And he knew, without seeing, the inevitable conclusion. All over a stupid little dog! If she had just kept clear, he might have lured the animal back in.

He shook his head violently, spraying the cluttered room with droplets of sweat. What a mistake! What a stupid mistake he had made in buying the wolf! Besides being illegal, it had been incredibly wrong-headed. The damn thing just would not cooperate in his scheme to breed hybrids—a hugely profitable enterprise by all accounts.

It would not mate with any of his dogs and had eventually killed them all. To add insult to injury, it had resisted all attempts at even rudimentary training, responding only to his whistle for dinner—gliding out of the crate it dwelt in to glare at the fat man with baleful, challenging eyes through the chain links of its confinement, as if daring him to reach through or enter. Wisely, the fat man had contented himself with simply heaving chunks of raw meat over the fence.

Several days after it had slaughtered the last of his dogs, the wolf had demonstrated its contempt by escaping, leaving a silent, barren kennel in its wake.

Since then, every effort at surreptitiously recapturing the animal had failed. Taking his cue that the wolf was near from the uproar of the neighbors' dogs, the fat man had left trails of raw steak and lamb leading to its repaired pen, then whistled to let it know that dinner was on. In the beginning, the wolf had eaten the offerings, though avoiding the last, which lay inside its former prison, as if well aware of the clever, spring-loaded gate. In time it spurned even those, finding its skills at hunting undiminished by its confinement and game . . . abundant.

After the death of his dogs and the escape of the wolf, the attendant monetary losses, and this last unfortunate incident, the fat man could take solace in only one thing—he had told no one of his unlucky purchase, and certainly never would.

Jon L. Breen

"Justice Knows No Paws"

What kind of conceit and vanity leads an anthologist to sneak in one of his own stories? In this case, none at all, simply the compulsion to mount his hobbyhorse while letting a cat speak for him.

The judge asked the fourteen citizens seated in the jury box all the expected questions. Did they know the plaintiff, Iris Stapleton Goodhew? (Of course they must have heard of her—she's a celebrity; but it was doubtful they had the pleasure of knowing her personally as I do.) Did they know the defendant, Elmo Gruntz? (Some of the cruder looking male members of the panel might have been acquainted with that low creature and his work, but most of them looked far too civilized.) Did they know the lawyers on either side of the action, the lovely and highly capable Andrea Frost for the plaintiff, the slickly unpleasant Forrest Milhaus for the defendant? Had they or any of their family members ever sued someone or been sued in this overly litigious society? Had they ever worked in the publishing field? Had they ever written anything for publication? Had they ever been party to a plagiarism case? Had they read about the case of Goodhew versus Gruntz in the newspapers? Were there any for whom serving more than a week as a juror would be a severe hardship?

Then the judge got to the really important question, or at least the one it seemed to give him the most smirking pleasure to ask. "Are any of you allergic to cats?"

That question was indignity number three for me in the sessions leading up to the trial. What, I ask you, could be more prejudicial than to ask the jurors, "Are you allergic to the plaintiff?"

Yes, I realize technically a cat doesn't have status as a plaintiff in a human court. That had been explained to Iris and me at length by our lawyer before we even entered a courtroom. But in-court indignity number one had come a few days earlier when even my presence in the courtroom was being questioned by Gruntz and his sleazy lawyer. After a lot of wrangling and some superbly well-reasoned argument by Andrea, I was allowed to sit in (or sometimes lie or slink in) on the proceedings.

I suppose I must introduce myself, in the unlikely event you don't know me already. I am Whiskers McGuffin. Yes, yes, *the* Whiskers McGuffin. You have undoubtedly seen my name and photograph on numerous dust jackets, even seen and heard me on the TV talk show circuit, as co-author of a very successful series of detective novels with my longtime human companion Iris Stapleton Goodhew. If you are a true collector, you may also have acquired an autographed copy with my distinctive paw print on the flyleaf. They are called novels, but in truth they are only lightly fictionalized accounts of my real-life exploits as a feline detective. While I, in the tradition established by Ellery Queen, appear in the novels under my own name, Iris adopts an alias, as the younger, slimmer, but no more beautiful and charming Winona Fleming.

The dubious juror question also reminded me of indignity number two. Though Iris via Andrea successfully insisted that as a full collaborator on the books, I had the right, nay the duty, to be present, there was some talk of requiring me to stay in a cage on or under the counsel table, as if I were some kind of wild animal whose freedom to wander the courtroom would somehow endanger human life or otherwise subvert the cause of justice. No sooner was that battle won than the defendant Elmo Gruntz asked for similar rights for his own animal companion, Fang, a huge and fierce German shepherd on whom he said the attack dog Rip in his novels was closely modeled. That led to a long legal confab as well, precipitated by the possibility that Fang really could be a danger to others in the courtroom, though Gruntz claimed he only ripped the flesh of drug lords, child molesters, and other human scum, leaving the pure of heart alone.

What weighed most heavily in the decision that I could attend the trial and Fang could not was the fact that I actually had a collaborative byline on the novels in which I appeared and Fang did not. Either Gruntz was less prone to share credit or, more likely, members of the canine species lack the necessary intelligence for literary achievement. I hope you won't take that as an instance of dog-bashing. Dogs have many fine qualities, and in some respects may even be the superior of cats. I don't think a dog could commit premeditated murder, do you? But I'm sure a cat could.

Anyway, back to the courtroom. I'll leap forward, though. A lot of trial action really is boring; in fact, I don't know how people can sit still for it all. At least I could wander around the room and explore without missing anything important. Once the jury had been seated and opening arguments presented, Andrea Frost called to the stand the expert witness who would lay out the basics of our case against Elmo Gruntz. He was the renowned crime fiction critic and historian Merv Glickman, a kind and cheerful man who seemed to know every author, every title, and every continuing character in the history of the form.

I confess I had been dubious about making Merv Glickman our major witness. He is on record as not loving cat mysteries, though he seems reasonably fond of cats, and some of the points he would make in his testimony would not be wholly complimentary to our work. But Andrea assured us that his obvious objectivity could only make our case more persuasive, and Iris seemed to agree.

Andrea spent some twenty minutes establishing Merv's credentials: the publications he'd reviewed for, the books he'd written or edited, the university courses he'd taught, the awards he'd won. Had I been less keyed up, I might have catnapped through much of this. Then Andrea got to the key questions.

"Mr. Glickman, are you familiar with the works of Iris Stapleton Goodhew and Whiskers McGuffin?"

"Yes, I am."

"And are you also familiar with the works of Elmo Gruntz?"

"Yes."

"Did I ask you to make a close study of one novel from each of these, uh, bylines?"

"Yes, you did."

"And what were those two novels?"

"*Cat on a Hatpin Pouffe* by Goodhew and McGuffin, published in 1997 by Conundrum Press, and *Devour* by Elmo Gruntz, published in 1999 by St. Patrick's Press."

"Did you find any points of similarity in the two novels?"

"I found many."

"Could you summarize them for us?"

"Certainly. I'll begin with the more superficial. Each of the books has a title that fits in with a pattern the author has established to create brand recognition. Each of the books has exactly 450 pages and 26 chapters. Of those chapters, in each case half are told from the point of view of an animal character. Every other chapter of *Cat on a Hatpin Pouffe* is narrated by the animal companion of the heroine, free-lance journalist Winona Fleming. That, of course, is Whiskers McGuffin." Merv smiled in my direction, and I meowed in gratitude at his politically correct (because sensitive) choice of words.

"Every other chapter of *Devour*," he went on, "is told from the viewpoint of Rip, the dog belonging to unlicensed homeless private eye Abel Durfee." I knew, of course, that the distasteful imputation of animal ownership embodied in this second identification was no accident. Gruntz and his character would naturally think in terms of ownership, master and slave, rather than equality.

"While the chapters about Rip follow his thoughts," Merv went on, "they are not actually written in his voice but from an omniscient narrator. Third dog rather than first dog, you might say.

"Both novels are, of course, whodunits. And in each novel, about twenty of the 450 pages are devoted to advancing the plot."

Andrea raised a disingenuous eyebrow at that. "Twenty pages out of 450? What did the two authors do with the other 430 pages?"

"Well, in the case of *Cat on a Hatpin Pouffe*, there is much attention to descriptions of the scenes, how the various characters are dressed, landscaping, interior decoration, meals, including recipes for selected dishes, things like that. And of course everything must be described twice, once from the viewpoint of a human character and once from the quite different and distinctive, and I might add frequently entertaining, viewpoint of Whiskers McGuffin."

Frequently entertaining? I bristled at the faint praise.

"The approach in *Devour*," Merv went on, "is quite a bit different with much of the needed page filling provided by descriptions of physical action: fistfights, car chases, menaces in parking garages, sex, torture, rape—and of course the vengeance finally taken on the baddies by Durfee and Rip is described in loving detail, without a cracking bone or a bleeding wound neglected. Also, Gruntz can go on for pages of monosyllabic macho posturing dialogue between Durfee and one or more of the villains. Enough speeches of one word to a paragraph and those 450 pages fill up fast."

Forrest Milhaus made some kind of an objection to the slighting tone of Merv's description of Gruntz's repellent novels. Really quite mild, I thought, and he *had* been accepted as an expert witness.

"Please go on, Mr. Glickman," Andrea said, after the judge had quite appropriately overruled the objection.

"In both books, there are several chapters made up of the detective summarizing the previous action, all of it well known to the reader, for the benefit of another character. And of course each series has a number of continuing characters who must recur in every book, even if they don't really have anything to do with story."

"How many continuing characters are there in the series about Winona Fleming and Whiskers McGuffin?"

"May I refer to my notes?"

"Certainly."

Merv drew out a vest-pocket notebook and flipped a few pages. "Seventeen," he replied. "That's not counting Winona and Whiskers."

"That seems like a considerable number."

"They do mount up."

"And how many continuing characters are there in the Abel Durfee and Rip series?"

"Remarkably enough, the same number, seventeen, apart from Durfee and Rip."

"Could you briefly list them for us?"

"From both series, you mean?"

"If you would."

"Well, in the Goodhew/McGuffin series, you have of course Winona Fleming's police contact and on-and-off boyfriend Detective Lieutenant Brent Hooper; her upstairs neighbor and best girlfriend Adele Washington; her elderly protective landlord Iggy Lamplighter; veterinarian and on-and-off boyfriend Dr. Curt Hamilton; gossiping hairdresser cum cat groomer Sadie McCready; Winona's loving but eccentric parents Hank and Minerva Fleming; her somewhat wild sister Stacy Fleming Tracy; her sister's abusive ex-husband Lester Tracy; her lovable but troubled teenage niece Morning Tracy; her priest brother Father Phil Fleming; her sometime editor and former boyfriend Axel Maxwell; the demented cat psychiatrist Dr. Ephraim Entwhistle; cat food manufacturer Ingo Dominguez and his domestic partner, cat sculptor Fred von Richtofen, who also by the way is Brent Hooper's police partner; wealthy and snobbish cat breeder Muffin Esterbrook; and nosy neighborhood druggist Pops Werfel."

"And in the Abel and Rip series?"

"Let's see now. There's Abel's main police contacts good cop Lieutenant Al Corelli and bad cop Captain Ed

McBride; his social worker and sometime girlfriend Estelle Magdalini; his crazy-Vietnam-vet sidekick Thorn; local newspaper columnist Manny Graves; good rackets boss Claude Willis; Reggie and Pedro, Claude's two enforcers; bad rackets boss Itchy McAllister; Grog and Amadeus, Itchy's two enforcers; Livia Gravel, local madame and Abel's off-and-on girlfriend; Abel's sociologist brother, Dr. Max Durfee; his naïve and danger-prone niece Megan Durfee; bartender and A.A. advocate Clancy Esposito; lawyer Sholem 'the Shyster' Schuster; alcoholic unlicensed veterinarian Dr. William 'Carver' McTweed; punchdrunk newsy and ex-boxer Bobby 'the Bandaid' Whistler; and— did I miss anybody? No, I think that's seventeen."

"And all seventeen have to appear in each and every book?"

Merv shrugged. "As I say, when there's 450 pages to fill. . . ."

"Could you now briefly summarize the plot of *Cat on a Hatpin Pouffe* for us?"

"Yes. Winona and Whiskers are visiting Sadie Mc-Cready to get their respective fur done. Sadie says a friend of hers, fleeing an abusive husband, needs a place to stay. Sensitive to the situation because of her sister's experiences, Winona quickly offers her guest room, though Whiskers is dubious. When their boarder is found strangled with a distinctive designer necktie, suspicion falls on the victim's husband, who sells that line of necktie at an exclusive men's shop he owns. But the detective work of the human-feline team eventually pins the crime on the husband's business partner, whose amatory advances had been rejected by the victim. In the last chapter, Whiskers comes to Winona's rescue by upsetting a poisoned cup of tea served her by the murderer."

"Now tell us the plot of *Devour*."

"Abel Durfee hears from bartender Clancy that a friend fleeing out-of-town loan sharks needs a place to crash. Abel helps the man vanish into the homeless community, though Rip is suspicious. When the fleeing man is found carved to death with a broken Thunderbird bottle, the cops arrest one of Claude Willis's enforcers, who they think was working for the out-of-town loan sharks. Abel finds out the real murderer was the lone shark's apparently legitimate business partner. He had started a child forced labor and prostitution ring. The victim had found out and the killer had come after him. In the last chapter, Rip rescues Abel, who is being force-fed cheap vodka preparatory to being sent over the cliff in his car to an explosive death, and pretty much devours the killer."

"Would you say that is the same plot, Mr. Glickman?"

"I'd have to say it's pretty similar."

"I have no further questions. Your witness."

Forrest Milhaus, who had been smirking through much of Merv's testimony, rose to cross-examine. As he approached the witness chair his shoe grazed my fur and I scurried under the defense table. He apologized, but I was not fooled, nor I think were Iris and Andrea. That had been no accident.

"Mr. Glickman, may we look at some of the supposed similarities between my client's work and the plaintiff's?"

"Certainly."

"You referred to a title pattern to establish brand loyalty. I don't see many similarities between Ms. Goodhew's titles and Mr. Gruntz's."

"Their titles aren't similar. It's the use of a title *pattern* that is similar."

"Perhaps you could explain. What is Ms. Goodhew's title pattern?"

"Punning versions of famous titles or phrases including the word *cat* or a related word. For example, when Winona and Whiskers invaded Steinbeck country, the title was *The Cat and the Cannery*. A novel with a computer industry background was called *Cat and Mouse*. Their Florida novel offered a slight variation, *Kitten on the Keys*. And of course, the book at issue here is *Cat on a Hatpin Pouffe*."

"Do those strike you as good puns, Mr. Glickman?"

"Maybe some of them are rather strained, but that's not the point, is it?"

"The lawyer asks the questions, Mr. Glickman. And what is my client's continuing title pattern?"

"One word titles, as short as possible. The first in the series was *Rip*, named of course for the dog character. The others referred to what Rip and/or Abel Durfee do to the unfortunate villains. *Tear, Shred, Cut, Flay, Slice, Slash, Gouge, Gash*, and of course *Devour*."

"Not so similar to Ms. Goodhew's titles, are they?"

"Only in that they are title patterns. That wasn't one of my major points."

"No, I suppose not. Shall we move on then? Have you heard of the designations *tough* and *cozy* referring to mystery fiction?"

"Certainly."

"What do they represent?"

"Differing approaches to the crime story, or you might say different schools of mystery writing. I think the terms are self-explanatory."

"Do my client and Ms. Goodhew take the same approach or belong to the same school?"

Merv smiled at that. "Not at all."

"Would Ms. Goodhew be classified as a cozy?"

"Cozy as you can get, yes."

"And would Mr. Gruntz be a tough?"

"None tougher."

"Ms. Goodhew and Mr. Gruntz begin to sound more and more dissimilar."

Andrea was on her feet, and about time. "Objection. Counsel should ask questions, not comment." I had hoped she would call Milhaus on his continuing refusal to include my name as co-author of the books, but I supposed she knew what she was doing.

"Comment withdrawn, your honor." Milhaus picked up from the clerk's table the copies of the two books Andrea had entered into evidence. "Mr. Glickman, I am handing you a copy of *Cat on a Hatpin Pouffe*. I direct your attention to the photograph on the back of the dust jacket."

"Yes, that's a photograph of Ms. Goodhew and of Whiskers." Better of her than me, I always thought, but they don't give me jacket approval.

"What is that object that Ms. Goodhew is holding up to the camera so proudly?"

"That's a Martini."

"Really! It doesn't look like a drink."

"It's an award," Merv explained. "A sculpture of a cat named Martini."

"And what does this award honor?"

"The best cat mystery of the year."

"Why the unusual name?"

"They wanted to call it the Macavity, but that was already taken, so they named it after one of Mr. and Mrs. North's cats."

"And what organization grants this award?"

"The FCC. No, not the one you think. The Feline Crime Consortium. It's an organization of people who write cat mysteries."

"Why did they need such an organization and such an award?"

"Lack of respect accorded cat mysteries. The writers didn't feel that cat mysteries were getting sufficient attention from the other crime fiction awards. They didn't expect much of the Edgar but the more cozy-oriented fan-voted awards like the Anthony and the Agatha were ignoring them, too. So they formed their own organization and came up with their own award."

"And Ms. Goodhew has won this award?"

"She and Whiskers"—thank you, I meowed—"have won three of them. They have been nominated nearly every year."

"Is it true the same four writers are nominated nearly every year?"

"With minor variations, yes, that's true."

"Now I'd like to hand you this copy of Mr. Gruntz's novel *Devour*, the other work we are considering in this trial. And again I direct your attention to the author photo on the back of the jacket."

"Yes, there's Elmo Gruntz and his dog Fang."

"And what is Mr. Gruntz holding in his hand?"

Merv smirked. "As the caption to the photograph explains, that's called a Baskerville, ostensibly an award for the best dog mystery of the year."

"Why do you say ostensibly, Mr. Glickman?"

"Because it's a gag. There is no such award. Your client made it up and awarded it to himself because he thought it would be a funny joke on the cat ladies."

"Ordinarily, I would object to your apparent ability to

read my client's thoughts, Mr. Glickman, but let's say you're correct, that the similarity between the two jacket photographs is intentional and satirical in nature. Would you call that an example of plagiarism?"

"No, of course not. But you'll have noticed that wasn't one of the similarities I pointed out in my direct testimony."

"So noted. Now tell me, Mr. Glickman, to your knowledge is Mr. Elmo Gruntz himself a member of the Feline Cat Consortium?"

"Yes."

"Does he come to their conventions?"

"Never misses one."

"Was there some controversy over his membership?"

"To put it mildly. They didn't want to accept him for membership, thought he only wanted to join to make fun of them, make them uncomfortable. But he was able to point to cat characters in several of his books. According to their own rules, they had to let him in."

"Mr. Glickman, are you aware of the relative commercial success of Ms. Goodhew and Mr. Gruntz?"

"It's about a tossup. Goodhew and Whiskers have probably sold more copies overall, including paperback, but Gruntz makes the hardcover bestseller lists and they don't."

"Would you say that Iris Stapleton Goodhew has many reasons for personal rancor against my client that might explain this incredibly frivolous lawsuit?"

Andrea was on her feet. "Objection, your honor. Argumentative. Prejudicial. Calls for speculation." Why couldn't she have said "incompetent, irrelevant, and immaterial"? I always liked that objection. Anyway the damage was done.

There's no need to describe the rest of the proceedings in detail. Truthfully, it's too painful. Merv Glickman was undoubtedly the key witness, though both Iris (extremely impressive) and Elmo Gruntz (egregiously offensive) were called as witnesses. I'm not sure whether Elmo Gruntz was technically a plagiarist, but the jury let him off. Andrea explained to us afterwards how very difficult it was to bring a successful plagiarism action without copied passages you could compare side by side with the originals. Gruntz was far too clever to leave that kind of tracks. It bothered me that there was so little I could do to help, apart from providing the occasional encouraging nuzzle to the ankles of those I favored. Murder cases are my metier, not civil trials.

Yes, that was a depressing ending, but we're not quite done yet. As you know if you've ever read one, you never close the book on my stories at the end. You always are treated to a preview of what is to come, an abridged version of the first chapter or two of the next book in the series. Now, I know this isn't a book but a short story, but it's very important you get the teaser anyway. Call it crass commercialism if you must.

Now an advance look at the next Winona Fleming/ Whiskers McGuffin mystery, *Curio City Called the Cat* by Iris Stapleton Goodhew and Whiskers McGuffin, coming to your bookstores this spring.

Chapter One

Fred von Richtofen was in a bad mood. He had been interrupted at a crucial point in the creation of an unusually original and beautiful piece, one that would probably double his price at the gallery he regularly supplied with cat images in clay, bronze, papier mache, and other media. But it wasn't the art but the police work that paid his half of the bills, and unless he was prepared to live off Ingo's salary as CEO of the Purrfect Cat Food Company, he had to answer Brent Hooper's call.

"What took you so long?" Brent demanded, as his partner appeared at the front door of the large imposing mansion.

"It's the traffic headed for that damn antique show up the block at the fairgrounds." Fred had been out to his partner for years, but he still affected what he took to be a macho posture. In truth, he'd rather have been at the antique show than here.

As they stood over the body lying at the foot of a tall bookcase, Fred looked at a bloodstained trophy with the figure of a dog lying near a wound in the dead man's head. Shoddy work, his artist's eye told him, but he didn't think Brent would appreciate aesthetic observations at a murder scene.

Brent said, "This is a strange one, Fred."

"Murder, sarge?"

"Has to be. I climbed up the ladder to look at the top of the book shelf above where the victim is lying. There's a circle of dust where this big dog trophy stood up there. That's a heavy piece, Fred. It couldn't have fallen off by accident, unless there was a six-point-oh earthquake this morning we didn't feel or hear about. And I don't think the guy could have brained himself with it, do you?"

"But who could have swung it at him with sufficient force with him just standing there? It must have been pushed off, but how from that height? Who could have got up there to do it without him knowing and being suspicious? And what is the thing anyway? Some kind of award?"

Brent squinted at the part of the lettering that was visible. "I think it says basketball, but we better not move it till the scene of crime boys and girls have been here. Wasn't this guy kind of short for a basketball player?"

"Writer, wasn't he? Elmer Fudd, something like that."

Chapter Two
(from the memoirs of Whiskers McGuffin)

The massive antique tent show called Curio City must have covered two acres of the fairgrounds. I like to wander into various nooks and crannies where humans can't go and follow moving things people aren't interested in, so it was to be expected I would get separated from Winona for a while. She was working on a piece about antiques for Axel Maxwell's magazine. As she questioned a man selling art deco lamps, I reestablished contact, rubbing against her ankle and purring. She looked down at me with more love in her eyes than she ever directed toward Brent or Axel or even that Hugh-Grant-lookalike vet. I felt relaxed and secure. I knew if she was asked, she'd swear I'd been at her side all morning.

ABOUT THE EDITOR

JON L. BREEN, is the author of six mystery novels and over eighty short stories. Two of his books, *What About Murder?* (1981) and *Novel Verdicts: A Guide to Courtroom Fiction* (1984) have won Edgars, while *Synod of Sleuths: Essays on Judeo-Christian Detective Fiction* (1990), co-edited with Martin H. Greenberg, won an Anthony. He lives in Fountain Valley, California, with his wife and sometime collaborator, Rita.